P9-DYB-501

WITHDRAWN

THE
GHOST ROAD

THE GHOST ROAD

CHARIS COTTER

tundra

Tundra Books, an imprint of Penguin Random House Canada
Young Readers, a Penguin Random House Company

Library and Archives Canada Cataloguing in Publication

Cotter, Charis, author
The ghost road / Charis Cotter.

Issued in print and electronic formats.
ISBN 978-1-101-91889-0 (hardcover).—ISBN 978-1-101-91890-6 (EPUB)

I. Title.

PS8605.O8846G56 2018   jC813'.6   C2017-905847-9
C2017-905848-7

Published simultaneously in the United States of America by Tundra Books of Northern New York,
an imprint of Penguin Random House Canada Young Readers, a Penguin Random House Company

Library of Congress Control Number: 2017952670

Edited by Samantha Swenson
Designed by Terri Nimmo
The text was set in Harriet Text.

Printed and bound in the United States of America

www.penguinrandomhouse.ca

1 2 3 4 5   22 21 20 19 18

Penguin
Random House
tundra   TUNDRA BOOKS

For Zoe, who helped me break the curse

CHAPTER ONE

THE SHIPWRECK

The ship was going down. There was a tremendous crack and sails fell to the deck, a mass of canvas and ropes. A broken boom swung wildly in the wind and the deck tilted to an impossible angle. People were shouting and screaming, and I felt myself sliding toward the water, grabbing at anything I could to stop myself. Then I heard my name, and I felt a strong hand grasp mine, and I looked up into my mother's face.

"It's okay, Ruthie," she said, smiling in the midst of the rain and the wind and the chaotic, sinking ship. "I've got you."

I jerked awake and sat up, gasping for breath. I felt the

1

familiar pain in my chest that always came with this dream. My cheeks were wet with tears.

For some reason my room was pitch-black. Usually a sliver of light from the hall shows under my bedroom door, but Dad must have forgotten to turn on the hall light. I fumbled for my bedside lamp, but it wasn't where it was supposed to be.

Then I remembered. I wasn't in my bedroom in Toronto, surrounded by houses full of sleeping people, parked cars and streetlights. I couldn't call out to my father after a bad dream, because he and Gwen were in Greece. I was in Buckle, Newfoundland, at the end of the road, in the middle of nowhere. I was sleeping in the room my mother had slept in as a child, and my Aunt Doll was somewhere on the other side of the house. The side with electricity.

I lay back down in the bed, trying to get my breathing under control. I was still shaking from the dream, and I was afraid that if I closed my eyes, I'd be back on that sloping ship's deck, sliding toward the black water. If only I could turn on a light, I could chase the dream away. Why was there no electricity in this part of the house? It was 1978! Everyone in Toronto had electricity all through their houses, not just on one side. What kind of a place was Newfoundland anyway?

What had Aunt Doll said to me about the light in this room? Last night was a jumble of impressions: stumbling half-asleep from the car in the dark after the long drive from St. John's, climbing up the stairs, and walking along a hall, round a corner and down a couple of steps into this room. Aunt Doll had an oil lamp she put on the tall dresser. She said she'd show me how to use it tomorrow.

So no light. I took deep breaths, the way Dad taught me. In and out. "Everything can be controlled, Ruthie," he would say. "Just breathe."

I've had recurring nightmares ever since I was a little kid. The shipwreck dream was one of the worst. Dad would always be there, as soon as I cried out, talking quietly to me. Telling me to breathe. To wake up. To look around and see my room, that it was only a dream.

Except now he was on the other side of the Atlantic Ocean with Awful Gwen. And there was no light to turn on, and the dream was coming back: I could hear the creaking of the decks, the screams of the people drowning—no. I took another deep breath. I was safe in bed, and if I yelled loud enough, Aunt Doll would come. Or I could get up and find my way to her room and wake her up. I was fine. I breathed in and out.

But I could still hear the creaking of the ship. Wait—not the ship. Footsteps. Aunt Doll? Coming to check on me? But I remembered her firm footsteps from earlier in the night. These were quite different. Lighter. Quieter. Getting closer.

A faint glow appeared under the door, and then the door slowly opened.

I caught my breath. A girl in a long white nightgown tiptoed into the room, carrying a candle that skittled in the draft and

3

threw strange shadows across her face. She placed the candle carefully on the bedside table. Then she turned and climbed into the bed opposite mine. She leaned toward the light and her long blonde hair swung forward. She looked into my eyes for a second, smiled, then blew out the candle.

I closed my eyes. A delicious feeling of calm spread over me. I wasn't alone anymore. I could hear her breathing softly. In and out. In and out. I let my breath match hers. The shipwreck nightmare evaporated.

This must be my cousin Ruby. Aunt Doll said she was coming for the summer, but I didn't realize it would be tonight. Time enough to meet her properly in the morning. The darkness closed around us and we slept.

CHAPTER TWO

THE CANDLE

I woke up to a gray morning and a low roaring sound, as if I were near a busy expressway. I sat up. The bed opposite me was neatly made; Ruby must have gotten up early. I swung my feet out of bed and stood up. The floor was icy cold on my bare feet. I peered out the window. Gray clouds scuttered across a dirty-white sky and the sound of traffic ebbed and flowed.

Traffic? No. The ocean. Waves on a beach. I knew that sound well, but I had forgotten. The last time I had heard it was on a beach in Venezuela, last summer with Dad on one of our plant-hunting expeditions. And this summer he was doing it without me, with Awful Gwen instead. I pushed that thought away.

There was no beach in sight though—the ocean was on the other side of the house. Through the sheets of rain, I could see meadows stretching away to tall hills, with patches of dark green that were probably trees. The faint track of a road disappeared over the biggest hill. A crow squawked by.

As I turned back into the room, my arm caught something on the bedside table and knocked it to the floor. A picture in a silver frame lay on the floor in a spill of shattered glass. My mother's picture. I had wrapped it in my pajamas when I was packing my things in Toronto, and when I pulled them from the suitcase last night, it fell out. I dimly remembered putting it on the table beside my bed before Aunt Doll came in and kissed me good night and turned off the lamp.

The frame was okay but the glass was broken. I sat down on my bed and pulled my feet up and away from the splinters of glass, cradling the picture in my hands. My mother sat laughing in a deck chair, with me on her lap. I was about two. Dad said the picture was taken a week before she died. I couldn't really remember much about her. But I knew her face so well. From this picture, and from the recurring shipwreck dream. And from something I wasn't sure was a memory or a dream—the image of her face leaning over mine, laughing, eyes full of love.

I put the picture back on the table, beside a candle in a battered old brass candlestick. I could hear the muffled sound of a radio, and there was a faint smell of toast. Suddenly I was starving, and I wanted to meet Ruby. I climbed over the end of the iron bedstead to avoid the broken glass, dug some clothes out of my suitcase and pulled them on.

Aunt Doll was alone in the kitchen, putting breakfast on the table. She wore a red flowered housedress and a big blue apron, tied with a bow at the back.

"How do you like your eggs, dear?" she asked, holding a couple over a frying pan.

"Fried is good, over easy," I replied.

I sat down at the table, noticing there were only two places set.

"These are fresh laid this morning," said Aunt Doll, as she cracked the eggs into the pan.

"You have chickens?" I asked.

"Chickens? Oh my yes—hens, a few sheep and a cow. Nothing like the old days, of course, when this was a working farm, but we do alright."

"I never had fresh eggs before," I said, as I watched her slide two crackly-brown eggs onto my plate, then add some bacon.

"Fresh bread too," she said, passing me some thick slices of buttered toast. "I make that myself. And there's some of last year's partridgeberry jam. Daresay there are a lot of things you don't get up in Canada. I mean, Ontario." She sat down and started to tuck into her breakfast. Her cheeks were rosy from the heat of the stove.

"Isn't Ruby eating?" I asked, taking a bite of egg. It was delicious.

Aunt Doll looked up with a frown. "Ruby? What do you mean?"

"I saw her come in to bed late last night, but she was gone this morning. Where is she?"

"What are you talking about, child?"

"Ruby. I saw her last night. She came into my room with a candle and went to bed."

Aunt Doll laughed. "You were dreaming, my dear. Ruby's not here. She's not coming till later today."

"Oh," I said, feeling a little foolish. A dream.

It didn't seem like a dream. Not like the shipwreck. The girl in the night with her long blonde hair and her smile seemed as real as Aunt Doll this morning, sitting across from me at the table, spooning dark red jam onto her toast.

"And there won't be any candles in your room," she continued. "Too dangerous. I'll teach you how to use the lamp."

If candles weren't allowed, why was there one sitting beside my bed?

CHAPTER THREE

MAKING BREAD

After breakfast, I told Aunt Doll about breaking the glass. She clucked a bit but didn't make a big fuss. I borrowed her broom and some paper towels and went to clean it up. When all the slivers of glass were safely in the wastebasket, I sat on the bed and looked at the candle for a while. Then I took it and pushed it far under my bed.

Aunt Doll had told me to unpack, so I did. A large dresser stood against the far wall, with an old painting hung above it. The artist had painted a sailing ship in a fierce storm, balanced precariously at the top of a huge wave. It was night, and there was a full moon high above, half-hidden by dark clouds.

I shivered. As I pulled my shorts and sleeveless tops and a couple of sundresses out of my suitcase, I looked doubtfully out at the rain, which was still streaking down from the sky, almost sideways in the fierce wind. I had shrugged off Gwen's offers of help and packed for a Toronto summer. But here it felt more like April than July. I was already a bit cold without even venturing outside, and I was wearing all my warmest clothes.

I found the framed picture Dad had given me the day before I left, rolled in a cardigan at the bottom of my suitcase. Dad and Gwen on their wedding day, smiling blissfully into the camera. I pushed it to the back of the drawer, under my socks. Why did he think I would want to look at that all summer? I pulled out my diary. There was a better picture of Dad in there, of him and me in Venezuela last year, halfway up a mountain in our hiking gear, grinning our heads off. I looked at it for a minute, then snapped the diary shut as the familiar pain shot through me.

I felt the tears pricking into my eyes, and I felt like there was something in my throat preventing me from breathing. I shook my head angrily and clenched my fists, taking quick breaths.

"I can control it. I can control anything," I repeated to myself. Dad was in Greece, with Gwen. Dad and I wouldn't be going on any more botanical trips together, just the two of us. From now on, Gwen would always be there—in our house, in our kitchen, on our holidays. If I ever got to go with them, that is. This year Dad made it clear that it was their honeymoon and I was not wanted. So here I was in Newfoundland with an aunt I had never met before. I just had to get on with it. Breathe in and out. Control it.

After a couple of minutes, my breathing evened out and I flicked the tears away. I finished my unpacking and went downstairs.

Aunt Doll was up to her elbows in bread dough.

"There you are," she said, giving the lump of dough a vigorous shove, then a couple of punches. "All set?"

"Yes," I replied, sitting down at the table and watching her beat up on the dough. I'd never seen anyone make bread before. "I left half the drawers for Ruby."

"Mmfff," grunted Aunt Doll as she gave the dough a couple more slaps and then shaped it into smaller lumps.

"What's she like? Ruby I mean?" I asked.

My aunt gave me a sharp glance, "I told you last night in the car, don't you remember?"

She began to tuck the lumps of dough, three at a time, into a row of narrow baking pans.

"I . . . uh . . ." All I could remember about the drive was long low lines of hills stretching on forever in all directions, Aunt Doll talking a blue streak, white fog rising up and blanking everything out, and a slow rocking into sleep as Aunt Doll's voice went on and on. "I think I must have been asleep," I said lamely.

Aunt Doll burst out laughing. "And I'm after giving you the history of the family from Day One, and telling you all about Ruby and her three little brothers, and all the shenanigans your mother and Ruby's mother used to get up to when they were girls, and how I went dancing every night with the Yanks during the war, and you were sleeping the whole time?" She laughed again, and covered the bread pans with tea towels.

"Sorry," I mumbled. I wasn't sure how to take Aunt Doll.

"Never you mind," she said, reaching for the kettle. "Let's have a cup of tea and I'll tell you all over again. I guess I didn't notice how long you were asleep because I couldn't take my eyes off the road with all the fog."

"Who was Ruby's mother?" I asked, as Aunt Doll took some china cups down from the cupboard. She turned and looked at me, her mouth open.

"You don't know who Ruby's mother is? Didn't your father tell you anything?"

"I don't think he knows very much about my mother's family," I said. "He said my mother didn't talk about them."

Aunt Doll bit her lip. "Well for goodness' sake," she said, giving her head a shake and fiddling with the teacups. "What got into that girl when she left here I'll never know." Then she went quiet.

I watched as she cleared away the few dishes she'd used making the bread and finished making the tea. She put out a sugar bowl and a little jug of milk she filled from a tin with two holes poked in the top. Milk in a tin? Weird.

She saw me looking at it. Then she laughed. "Oh, you're probably not used to our milk. I do have fresh, if you prefer it.

But in Newfoundland you'll find most people like Carnation Evaporated Milk in their tea."

"I'll try it," I said, stirring in some of the yellowy milk and putting in a couple of lumps of sugar. I never drank much tea at home but I figured I might as well give it a shot. Dad and I were always big on trying different foods when we were traveling. And although Carnation milk wasn't as exotic as chili made with chocolate, which was a big favorite of ours in Venezuela last year, it was a new experience. I took a careful sip. Aunt Doll was watching me.

"It's . . . uh . . . good," I said. "Kind of sweet."

She smiled.

"So about my mother," I said.

"Your mother," echoed Aunt Doll sadly. "I still miss her. It was such a shock. Both of them on the same day. My girls." She shook her head again and drew a handkerchief out of her pocket and blew her nose.

"Both of who?" I asked.

"Meg and Molly," she said. "My nieces. Your mother and her twin sister, Ruby's mother. They both died on the same day."

"My mother had a twin?" I had no idea she even had a sister. "And they died on the same day?"

Aunt Doll took a long drink of her tea, her hand trembling slightly as she held the cup. "It was terrible, Ruthie. Your mother in Toronto and poor Molly here in St. John's. They both just dropped dead after supper. The exact same time."

CHAPTER FOUR

TWINS

I was dumbfounded. All I knew about my mother's death was that she died from a brain aneurysm. Dad told me, as soon as I was old enough to understand. She had a headache and went to bed early, and when he went in an hour later—she was dead. But I didn't know she had a twin sister. Who died the same day. At the same time.

"Twins," said Aunt Doll, shaking her head. "They were always joined at the hip. They did everything together: learned to walk, learned to talk, learned to read. They were inseparable."

"But . . . but . . . my dad never told me any of this! I didn't know Mom had a sister. I thought Ruby was a second cousin or something."

"No," said Aunt Doll. "You and Ruby were born just a few days apart. Up in Toronto. They were at nursing school together, Molly and Meg, and didn't they both get pregnant—" She stopped for a moment and looked at me, as if remembering I was only twelve. "Anyway, it was just one more thing they seemed to want to do at the same time. Have babies. Get married. Though not necessarily in that order," she finished with a short laugh.

"But then Molly came back here?" I asked. "They did separate?"

"Molly's sweetheart, George, was back here," said Aunt Doll. "He didn't want her to go, but she was set on it, and she stayed in Toronto till she finished her degree. When she got it, she came home and married George. And less than two years later, she was dead."

"At the same time? They died at the same time?" I couldn't get past that.

"I'm surprised your father didn't tell you. When I called to tell Meg that Molly was gone, your father told me that Meg had died the night before, about eight o'clock. And poor Molly died about half past six in the evening, so with the time difference—"

"Why *didn't* he tell me?" I couldn't believe he'd keep something like this from me. That Mom had a sister. That they both died at the same time.

"I don't know," said Aunt Doll, pouring another cup of tea. "Meg wasn't in touch with me much those last couple of years in Toronto. She seemed to be trying to put Newfoundland behind her. I don't know why. I always wondered if something happened here in Buckle before they went away to school." She shook her head.

"Like what?"

Aunt Doll gave me that I've-said-too-much look again. "Oh, I don't know. Someone or something she wanted to forget. Something like that. And Molly would never say. Those two would never give anything away about the other. Thick as thieves they were."

This was bothering me. A lot. I felt the pain in my chest again. I closed my eyes tight and tried to breathe in and out, slowly.

"Ruthie?" said Aunt Doll. "I've upset you. I'm sorry. Me going on and on. It was a long time ago. It's all water under the bridge now. Look, it's stopped raining. Why don't you go out and look around?"

"Uh . . . okay," I said, getting to my feet.

She looked askance at my cardigan. "Don't you have anything warmer than that?"

It was the beginning of July. "No—I—"

"Never mind. There's one of Ruby's jackets hanging by the front door. Red. She won't mind. And I think there's one of her green sweaters there too. That Toronto sweater won't keep out the damp."

I found the sweater and the red jacket. They fit just fine.

16

The first thing I noticed when I stepped outside was the smell of the air: sharp and sweet. The second thing was the ocean: it spread out in a wide arc around the headland, a shimmery silvery gray, sparkling in the sun that was just starting to break through the cloud cover. Across the bay were high cliffs, with birds swooping down to the sea. I took a deep breath. It was breathtakingly, heart-stoppingly beautiful.

I'd seen the ocean lots of times before. The Atlantic. The Pacific. But there was something about this view of the sea and the sky that brought tears to my eyes and made me catch my breath. Suddenly I wanted to run and jump.

I started down the driveway, walking sedately. I thought I'd better wait till there were no people around before I started acting like a little kid.

I really didn't know much about Newfoundland. Dad tried to get me to read some books about it, but I was so mad at him for sending me away that I didn't even look at them. All I knew before I got here was that it was a large island off the easternmost tip of North America, that it had only been part of Canada since 1949, almost thirty years ago. Before that, it was a British colony. I knew people did a lot of fishing, and I knew they talked with a lilting, almost Irish accent. I could hear that in Aunt Doll's voice, and some of the expressions she used I'd never heard before.

But no one had told me it was so wild and beautiful, that just looking out at the ocean would send a stab of joy right through me, like I'd just come home after years away.

CHAPTER FIVE

THE MEADOW

The road curved away from the house and then dipped down a hill. At the bottom, it divided into two—one road leading along the shore and the other heading up a hill toward the meadows I'd seen behind the house. I walked along that road, automatically taking note of the nodding wildflowers in the grass along the edge—the bright-yellow of creeping buttercup and fall dandelion, the pale lavender-blue of wild geranium, and one with a slight fuzz above clumps of tiny white flowers that I couldn't identify. I stooped to pick one of those, including the stem and the leaves, and put it carefully inside the outside pocket of my knapsack, so I could identify it later. When I got to the crest of the hill, I stopped.

A whole new landscape opened up before me—a wide, open valley with rocky meadows full of thick grasses striped by the wind and a brook running down the middle to the sea. Sheep were grazing on the far slope.

I had never been anywhere like it before. No people or houses for miles, just low hills climbing against the sky, the blue sea sparkling on my left, and fluffy clouds scudding across a bigger sky than I had ever seen. I looked back, down toward Buckle, and I could see Aunt Doll's house and the other houses scattered along the shoreline. A different world. A settled, cozy world. I turned my back on it and walked down the road into the wild, empty valley.

The road ended at the brook. I spotted the tiny purple flowers of blue marsh violets growing alongside the water, and stretching back along the brook and into a widening marsh were masses of the slender green iris leaves. In a couple of weeks it would be a sea of blue flags, when the flowers came out. There was a little cove off to the left, with a rocky beach and the brook tumbling down over a series of waterfalls to the ocean. On the other side of the brook, a narrow path led up toward the far hills.

I took off my shoes and socks, rolled up my jeans and waded through the icy water. The cold bit into my feet, but I was soon on the other side, hopping around to get them warm again, grinning like a jackass.

This was fun! I'd never been so alone in such a big place. Everywhere in Toronto were buildings, people and cars. Here there was nothing and nobody—only some seagulls calling over the water and the faraway sheep. I pulled my socks over my wet, cold feet and put my shoes on, then continued along the path. I was heading for the farthest-away hill, the one where I had seen the faint track of a road from my bedroom window. I wanted to see where that road went.

The sun warmed me and I took off my jacket and tied it around my waist. The path twisted and climbed. What had looked like one big sloping meadow from Aunt Doll's house was actually a series of little hills and dells, with piles of stones in odd corners and low, prickly Virginia rose bushes growing everywhere. The path grew fainter the farther I went and finally disappeared at the foot of a steep hill.

I clambered up, my feet sinking into spongy juniper. I couldn't tell where the ground was, and every so often one foot would sink down into a hole and I'd almost lose my balance. It was tough slogging, but I made it to the top.

I stood there panting, looking down at the next valley. It was different than the wide, sweeping one I'd just crossed. It was narrower, full of trees and deeper. Beyond the far side I could see hills disappearing into the distance. And on one of them I could still see a streak of silver climbing up over the top, the road.

A movement to my right made me spin in that direction. A man was standing about fifteen feet away, watching me.

I took a step back. All the big-city warnings about talking to strange men rushed into my head, and I was suddenly aware of how far I was from anyone who could hear me if I screamed.

CHAPTER SIX

ELDRED

He was tall and slim, dressed in an old brown jacket and work pants. As soon as our eyes met, he began to grin and move slowly toward me, spreading his arms wide, as if he expected a hug.

"Hello, Ruby" he said. "Welcome back!"

I took another step back. "I'm not Ruby," I said quickly. He dropped his arms and peered at me. His green eyes had a slow twinkle in them, like he found a lot to laugh at in the world.

"Well now," he said, smiling at me. "You are not. I see that now. But alike as two peas in a pod." His accent was much thicker than Aunt Doll's. I had to listen carefully to understand what he was saying.

"I'm wearing her jacket," I said stiffly.

"That must be it," he said, his eyes skittering away from mine. He turned and looked out over the ocean. "You must be the other one," he said softly, almost to himself.

"I'm her cousin Ruth."

"From Toronto?" He had a way of looking sideways at me, as though he was too shy to look at me directly.

I nodded.

"I knew you were coming. You do have the look of Ruby about you."

"Oh." I didn't know what else to say. I wasn't scared anymore, not since he first grinned at me.

"I'm Eldred Toope," he said, holding out a large, calloused hand to me.

I shook it and smiled at him.

"I'm a friend of Ruby's. I've known her ever since she was a toddler."

"Ruth Windsor," I said politely.

"And I know your Aunt Doll. I help her with her animals. Some of those sheep you see are hers. Some are mine."

I looked back into the valley, where I could still see the flock of sheep, grazing on the far hill.

"I come out here every day to count the sheep. Morning and night. Just to make sure there's none missing."

I wondered why he was way up on this hill. He could have counted the sheep from the other side of the valley.

"It's going to be a fine day," he said, looking up at the sky. "So how do you like Newfoundland so far, Ruth?"

"Oh, I love it," I said. "It's the most beautiful place I've ever seen!"

He glanced at me from under his eyelids. "Is it indeed? And have you seen a lot of beautiful places?"

I blushed. "Yes, I have. I've been to South America, and Ireland and Spain and all kinds of places with my dad. He's a botanist. We go hunting rare flowers every summer—" I broke off. "Except not this summer."

"Well, if it's rare flowers you're after, I can show you one or two," said Eldred. "I walk a lot and I see a lot. I know these hills better than anyone. Only you need to be careful, wandering out here by yourself. Did you happen to bring any bread for the fairies?"

"The what?"

He laughed at my expression. "You're from the mainland. You wouldn't know any better."

He reached in his pocket and pulled out a thick slice of bread.

"I'll share mine," he said, breaking off a piece. "Just put that in your pocket and you'll be fine. The fairies won't be bothered with you if you have a bit of bread in your pocket."

"Oh come on," I said. "I'm nearly thirteen. I don't believe in that stuff."

He took my hand and put the bread in it, and folded my fingers over it. Then he looked directly into my eyes. He wasn't smiling anymore.

"You're walking on a fairy path, my love, and just because you don't believe in them, doesn't mean they won't come after you."

CHAPTER SEVEN

THE FAIRY PATH

"A fairy path? What do you mean, a fairy path?"

He took me gently by the shoulders and turned me around so I was facing down into the next valley, the narrow one with the dark, twisted trees, deep shadows and winding track.

"The fairy path starts right here and goes down into the valley and through those trees and then up and over those hills and on to the barrens," he said, pointing off to the right. "That's been a fairy path for as long as anyone can remember. No good comes of it, I can tell you that. There's all kinds of stories. Mary Duck saw a bunch of little children all dressed in green out here one day, laughing and playing and calling after her. When she got closer, she realized they were fairies, but she had a bit of cake in her pocket so they never touched her."

"Children? Dressed in green?" I wasn't buying this.

He laughed softly, eyes twinkling again. "Oh, you don't have to believe me. I daresay you don't have any fairies up to Toronto. But they're still here, and they're dangerous. More than one person has gone missing down the fairy path and never been heard of again."

I shivered. The sun had gone behind a big dark cloud, turning everything gray again. A biting wind was blowing up off the ocean.

"You've got to respect them, you see, and stay clear of them. Then you'll be fine."

"You're kidding me, right?" I said. I was getting a little spooked in spite of myself. The valley did look a bit ominous: a tangle of trees and bushes and rocks.

He shook his head. "There's a lot of old things here, Ruth, old things from long ago. Maybe they've all died off in places where there are cities and highways and cars rushing back and forth. But out here in Newfoundland nothing much has changed for hundreds of years. There are still fairies. Spirits. Ghosts."

I thought uneasily of the girl with the candle last night.

"Where does that other road go, that one on the far hill?" I asked, just to change the subject.

"What road?"

I pointed to the faint silver track that led up over the far hill. "I could see it from my bedroom. Is it an old road?"

Eldred looked where I was pointing.

"You see a road there?"

"Yes. It starts just by that big rock."

He stared for a minute, then looked down at me. "You see it?" he asked again. "You really see it?"

"Yes. I was wondering if it was too far to walk. I'd like to see where it goes."

Eldred took off his cap and passed his hand over his thinning brown hair.

"Well, I'll be . . ." he murmured. "Never thought this would happen again."

"What?"

He looked at me then, his green eyes kind of sad and serious. "Not everyone can see that road, Ruth. It's a ghost road. I can't see it."

"But it's right there," I said, shading my eyes to see better. "It's a bit faint, but I can see it. It goes up over that hill." I pointed again.

Eldred stared at the far hill for a minute and then shook his head. "No. I can't see it, Ruth. I'll never see it."

"Maybe you just need glasses," I said. "It's a long way off."

He shook his head. "No. You don't understand. The Ghost Road goes to Slippers Cove, where no one has lived for a long, long time. It's a rough track over bog and rock, and over time it got overgrown and disappeared. No one has been able to find their way to Slippers Cove for years. No one except—" He broke off and looked at me sideways. "No one except a true Finn."

"A Finn? Someone from Finland?"

A small smile passed over his face. "No. From Ireland. The Finns used to live in Slippers Cove, long ago, and only people who have descended from them can see the road."

The sun had disappeared completely now and the dark clouds spread across the sky. The wind had picked up even more, and it was tearing at my hair and working its way under my jacket. I shivered. Beside me, Eldred was gazing at the far hill, frowning.

I started to wonder if there was something not quite right with Eldred. He really seemed to believe all this stuff. There was something about him that made me feel like maybe he wasn't all there, that part of him was off in his own world.

I became uncomfortably aware again that we were a long way from any other human beings. I turned and looked back the way I had come, then I caught my breath.

A small figure, all dressed in green, was running along the path from the sea, toward the hill we were standing on.

CHAPTER EIGHT

RUBY

I grabbed Eldred's arm. "Is that—is that a fairy?" I whispered. As soon as the words were out of my mouth, I cursed myself for being so silly. Yet I didn't let go of his arm.

He didn't answer right away, but stood stock-still, looking at the little green person. It had reached the bottom of the hill and was starting to scramble up the path. It had bright blonde hair and red shoes.

Eldred began to smile. "You could say it was a fairy," he said. "More like an imp."

I could see it better now. It was bigger than I thought. About my size.

It stopped and waved an arm at us.

"Hi, Eldred!" it called out. "Hi, Ruth!" Then it kept climbing.

It was a girl. I let go of Eldred and took a step away, feeling foolish. What was it about this guy that could get me so freaked out that I thought I saw fairies?

She scrambled up the last few yards and threw herself on Eldred in a big, long hug, laughing.

"I missed you so much, Eldred!" she said, pulling away.

"And I missed you, Ruby," he said, tousling her short blonde hair. "Life's some dull in Buckle when you're not here. But you'll be wanting to meet your cousin Ruth."

She turned to me, her eyes shining. "Ruth! Aunt Doll said I'd find you out here somewhere. I've been dying to—" Then she stopped, staring at me.

I stared back. She was just my size, wearing a bright-green sweater and green pants. Her cheeks were flushed pink with her climb. But her face . . . her face was my face. Blue eyes, small nose, high cheekbones, slightly crooked mouth, strong chin—it was like looking in a mirror. Even her hair was the same, except it was short and stuck out all over the place.

"Wow!" she breathed. "This must be what Aunt Doll meant. She said I'd be surprised when I met you." She spoke more like Aunt Doll than Eldred, but I could still hear that slight Irish lilt in her voice.

I swallowed. I felt off-kilter, like something in the world had kind of slipped, and things weren't quite right. I didn't know what to say.

"You're skinnier than me," I said finally.

Ruby laughed. "I guess. What do you think, Eldred? Isn't this weird?"

Eldred was watching us carefully, a tiny smile turning up the corners of his mouth.

"I was after thinking she was you, Ruby, when I first saw her climbing up this hill. Gave me quite a turn when she opened her mouth and told me she wasn't. Your hair's different. But otherwise you're a pair." He looked back and forth between us and shook his head, his smile widening.

I was still staring at Ruby. I couldn't help it. She was so like me—and yet not like me. Her features were the same, but she was more jumpy and it seemed like she couldn't stop moving. Whatever she was feeling went dancing across her face— surprise, delight, excitement—whereas I knew that I kept all of that pretty close. It was weird to watch someone else's emotions registering on a face that looked just like mine.

"Oh, we can have fun with this," said Ruby, grabbing my hands and pulling me into a little dance. "We can switch places, like in that movie, and play tricks on people."

"You won't fool me," said Eldred. "I know better. You may look alike, but you're very different." He smiled at me. It was as if he knew what I'd just been thinking.

"Ruth, now, she's a sensible girl who doesn't believe in fairies and keeps her two feet firmly on the ground. Not like you, Ruby, badgering me night and day to tell you stories about fairies and ghosts. You can learn from each other maybe." He walked over and picked up an old knapsack that was lying on the ground near where I first saw him. "I best be on my way. I'll see you both later."

Ruby gave him another hug and I nodded good-bye to him. He headed down the hill into the valley with the dark trees.

"Where's he going?" I asked.

"Oh, I don't know. He's always wandering. He has some rabbit snares along the fairy path. Probably he's going to check them."

"Rabbit snares?"

"Yeah, he catches them for food. Haven't you ever had rabbit?"

I shook my head. "No."

"It's yummy. Sooner or later he'll bring some round and you can try it."

We stood together in silence, watching Eldred as he followed the fairy path up the valley and disappeared into the trees. I felt suddenly shy and didn't know what to say to this new cousin who was both strange and familiar at the same time.

Ruby turned and looked at me, eyes wide and curious, like she was memorizing my face. Our eyes met and I looked away. It was just too weird.

I blurted out the first thing that came to my mind. "Eldred— is he . . . umm . . . I mean, is he—all right?"

Ruby laughed. "You mean is he crazy? No. He's a sweetie pie. He's just a little . . . different." She started hopping around in a circle. "Aunt Doll says he was stolen by the fairies when he was little and that's why he's so odd. But he tells the best stories."

She stopped hopping and came back to me, looking eagerly into my face again. "Wait till you hear them. His mother was a storyteller. And so was her mother, and hers before that. It runs in the family. He's got all the stories, from way back."

I felt uncomfortable with her staring at me like that. I looked off toward the far hill, and the Ghost Road. I looked back at her. "Do you—do you believe the stories he tells? About the fairies and all that stuff?"

She reached in her pocket and pulled out a crumbly piece of bread.

"What do you think?"

I reached into mine and pulled out the bread that Eldred had given me.

Our eyes met. We both began to laugh.

CHAPTER NINE

GANNETS

"**A**unt Doll is the best baker," said Ruby through a mouthful of blueberry muffin. "Wendy's baking is never as good as hers."

"Who's Wendy?"

Ruby took another enormous bite. "My stepmother."

"You call her Wendy? Not Mom?"

Ruby made a face. "She's not my mother."

We were sitting in a little rocky basin, high over the ocean. Ruby had brought me there because it was sheltered. The rocks were on three sides of us, with the fourth side open to the water. We could see for miles, up and down the coast. The stiff wind had whipped the sea into whitecaps and the sun played hide-and-seek with the dark clouds. Ruth had pulled out a little "lunch" from her pocket that Aunt Doll had provided her with for the walk: fresh blueberry muffins smothered in butter.

"Aunt Doll wasn't expecting me so early, but I was up at the crack of dawn and I just kept tormenting Dad till he finally gave in and drove me here. They're all having a longer visit with Wendy's mom in Clarenville, but I couldn't wait to get here. I wanted to meet you so bad, ever since Aunt Doll said you were coming. Aunt Doll told me about you a long time ago, but I never thought you'd come." She licked the butter off her thumb and grinned at me.

"Well, I always spent summers with my dad," I said. "Till this year. And I never knew much about Newfoundland. I didn't even know I had a cousin, or that our mothers were twins."

"I guess that's why we look so much alike," said Ruby. "Look, there's gannets!" She pointed out over the water.

A seabird was swooping low over the ocean. It hung in the air for a moment, then plunged straight down into the water.

Another one swooped down and dived. Then another.

"I love the gannets," said Ruby. "You don't always see them."

"I've never seen a bird dive like that."

"You can always tell a gannet because of the way it dives. And if you're close enough, you can see they have black wing tips."

We watched the birds for a while.

"So, your dad got married again? That's why you're not with him this summer?"

I nodded.

"So you've got a stepmother now, just like me."

I sighed. "Yes. What's yours like?"

Ruby made a face. "She's a pain. She's always bugging me about something. Dishes. Cleaning my room. Homework. The boys take up all her time. And Dad's. I can't wait to get out here to Buckle every summer."

She frowned and looked out over the wide sweep of the sea. In profile, her face still looked like mine, but from an angle I wasn't used to. Then she turned back to me and I had that tilting feeling again, like I was looking at myself. This was going to take some getting used to.

"What about your stepmother? What's she like?"

I wrinkled up my nose. "She's really nice and sweet, and kind—and I can't stand her! I call her Awful Gwen. She's always there. I never see my dad alone anymore. She's so interested in everything I do. Too interested. Asking me all kinds of questions all the time and trying to be my friend. And cooking all these fancy meals where we have to sit and make polite conversation. Before, Dad and I used to read books while we ate. I miss that."

Ruby grinned. "Awful Gwen. I like it! Dad tried to get me to call Wendy 'Mom' when they first got married, when I was five. But I couldn't. I always knew she wasn't my real mother."

A shadow of sadness seemed to pass over her face, like a cloud over the sun.

"Do you remember her?" I said softly. "Your real mom?"

She kept watching the gannets. "Sometimes. I can see her laughing and hugging me, and telling me she loves me. But she looks just like she does in this picture I have of her holding me on her lap, and I'm not sure if I'm making it up or if I really remember her."

"That's exactly the same with me," I said. "I have a picture just like that, of my mom with me on her lap. And then I have a memory of her laughing and talking to me, but I don't know if it's because of the picture or if I really remember it. I just hang on to it because it's all I have."

"Wow," whispered Ruby, staring into my eyes. "Ruth. It's almost as if we have the same memory."

The mirror effect came back and I almost felt dizzy with it. The back of my neck tingled and a shiver ran down my back.

"I didn't know . . ." I began shakily. "I didn't know till today that our mothers died at exactly the same time. Did you?"

She nodded, never taking her eyes off mine. "Yup. I always thought that was so weird. Aunt Doll says they did everything together. Even dying. Because they were twins."

I felt my eyes filling with tears even as I saw Ruby's spilling over. We both reached out at the same time and grasped hands. The sound of the seabirds and the beat of the ocean waves on the rocks below faded away and we were held together in a moment of sadness that felt like it would never end, there on that high hill with the clouds and the wind and the big wide world stretching out in all directions.

"Twins," I repeated softly, staring out over the water. "Just because they were twins."

CHAPTER TEN

THE SHEEP

"This way," said Ruby, leading me down a path that led off down a hill from the main path.

"But aren't we going back to Buckle?" I asked.

"Yup. This is a shortcut." The path wound around a couple of low hills, steadily going downhill.

Ruby stopped suddenly and I banged into her from behind.

"Hey!" I said.

Ruby was looking down at an expanse of water that flooded the path. It was about eight yards across, too wide to jump and it looked deep. A brook, cascading down the hillside, had pooled there on the path and widened as it seeped into a marsh.

"The other way was dry," I said.

Ruby grinned. "I know. I came that way. But I needed to check this out. Come on." And she started to climb up the rocks at the side of the waterfall. Then she ducked behind a big rock and I lost sight of her.

Scrambling up behind her, I found my cousin standing looking down at a makeshift bridge over the brook: an old piece of broken board balanced precariously between two rocks—one on the edge of the brook, and the other in the middle.

"They did it again!" said Ruby happily, stepping carefully out onto the board, which wobbled dangerously. She made it to the rock in the middle, then took a giant step to another rock and then a last jump took her to the far shore.

"Who did what?" I asked, eyeing the board. It looked like it could tip over and tumble down the waterfall any minute.

"The fairies!" cried Ruby, laughing. "Every year they make a fairy bridge here. It gets washed away a couple of times every summer, but they find another board somewhere and lay it down."

"Why would it be fairies?" I said. "Why couldn't it be a human being who makes the bridge?"

"Because nobody ever comes this way, that's why. Only me."

"What about Eldred?"

"No. I asked him once. He sticks to the main path, where he can count his sheep. No, it's the fairies, and I always thank them."

She did a gracious curtsy and called out, "Thank you, fairies!"

I rolled my eyes. Honestly. Ruby was nuts.

"Come *on*!" called my cousin. "This saves us about ten minutes."

"I don't know . . ." I said.

"Don't be a chicken," said Ruby.

I took a deep breath. I'd taken some rough hikes with my dad in the jungles of Costa Rica, the mountains of Spain, the Amazon wetlands . . . this was just a tiny brook. I put one foot on the board and it quivered.

I put my other foot down. More quivering.

I took another step. And another. Just as I made it to the rock, the board shuddered and tipped, then went clattering down the waterfall. I took a big jump to the rock Ruby had used, and then one more jump to the shore.

I turned and watched as the board caught in some rocks and stuck.

"Don't worry," said Ruby. "The fairies will fix it. Next time we come, it will be all set up again for us. Thank you, fairies," she called out again, giving me a nudge. "You say it," she said. "And curtsy. They like that."

I called out a squeaky "Thank you, fairies," and did a little dipping curtsy, feeling like an idiot.

"Come on," said Ruby, grabbing me by the hand. We hurried along the path, which led us up another hill, around a corner and smack dab into a flock of sheep.

The sheep all looked up in alarm and went running off down the hill, panicked.

"What's wrong with them?" I asked.

"They're scared of humans," said Ruby. "Only Eldred can get them to come to him. They always run when they see me, no matter how gentle I am with them."

"That's too bad," I said, watching the sheep. They'd stopped a good way off and were looking back suspiciously at us, as if they expected us to come after them any minute. They were fluffy and silly-looking, with their mouths hanging open.

"Come back, sheep!" I called, holding out my hand. "Come back you silly sheep! We don't want to hurt you."

"It's no use," said Ruby. "I've tried. They never come."

"Hey you sillies," I called. "I won't hurt you."

The nearest sheep took a step toward me. And then another.

"Come," I called softly. "Don't be shy."

The sheep walked slowly toward me. The others watched.

I started walking toward the sheep, murmuring softly, and the sheep kept coming.

"Well I never," said Ruby behind me.

The sheep came right up to me and sniffed my hand. Its warm breath tickled. The others started edging closer. I laughed softly and patted the sheep on its head. I turned back to look at Ruby, who hadn't moved.

"It's a miracle!" said Ruby. "Honestly, they won't come to any-one else. Not Aunt Doll. Not anyone from Buckle. Only Eldred. And now you."

I patted a couple of sheep, and then turned back to Ruby. The sheep stopped and watched me go.

"Animals always come to me," I said. "Cats, dogs, cows. Dad says I have 'animal magnetism.' It's almost funny sometimes. They just make a beeline for me."

Ruby was staring at me. "I wonder," she said.

"Wonder what?"

"Nothing. Come on, I'll race you home." She took off up the path with me at her heels.

CHAPTER ELEVEN

SPITTING IMAGE

Ruby and I tumbled into the kitchen, out of breath and laughing.

"You cheated!" I gasped. "You tripped me!"

"I could have beaten you by a mile," said Ruby. "I was going slow just to give you a chance. Boy, are you out of shape, Toronto Girl!"

"Ha!" I said, grabbing her by the sweater and shaking her, "I was beating you fair and square until you tripped me at the gate." Ruby stumbled into me and we both fell backward, into a pair of strong arms.

"Hey!" said a man's voice as he steadied us. "Looks like you two have made friends."

I spun around and looked up into the grinning face of a big man with curly brown hair and blue eyes. I took a step back and looked at the floor, embarrassed. I hadn't been aware of anyone in the kitchen besides Aunt Doll standing at the sink with a tea towel in her hands.

"You're still here!" said Ruby, stepping by me and throwing her arms around the man. "I thought you'd be gone by now. Aren't you going to visit Nan?"

"Yes," said the man, tousling her hair. "I wanted a chat with your Aunt Doll first." He looked over Ruby's head at me. "I'm Ruby's dad. Your Uncle George. Nice to meet you, Ruth."

"You too," I said politely. I still felt awkward. I watched as he bent toward his daughter, listening to her chatter away about Eldred and the sheep. He was so different from my father. I couldn't imagine hugging Dad in public. Or even hugging him at all. My dad wasn't very demonstrative: he gave me polite cheek kisses and occasionally patted my shoulder. Still—I missed him. Seeing Ruby laughing and hanging on her dad's arm sent a little sharp pain through me, like someone poking me with a needle.

"And she looks just like me, doesn't she, Dad?" said Ruby. "I nearly fell down the hill when I first saw her."

Uncle George skittered his eyes in my direction and then looked back into his daughter's glowing, upturned face. "Definitely a strong resemblance."

"Resemblance?" scoffed Ruby. "She looks just like me, Dad! If her hair was short and she had more of a tan, you wouldn't be able to tell us apart."

Aunt Doll laughed. "I told you you were in for a surprise, Ruby. I nearly fell over backward myself when I saw her at the airport, looking out at me with your blue eyes!"

"You never said anything to me," I said, going over to the sink to get a glass of water.

"No, I thought I'd let the two of you discover it for yourselves."

"But isn't it just uncanny, Dad? Isn't it weird?"

He cleared his throat. "I don't know. Cousins often look alike. Why everyone said my cousin Terry and I looked like brothers when we were twelve. Not so much now. You might grow out of it."

"Grow out of it?" squeaked Ruby, incredulous. "No way. We're practically identical."

Aunt Doll was looking very closely at us.

"Go on, stand together, here by the window," she said. "Let's have a look at you in the light."

Obediently, Ruby and I stood together.

I was watching Uncle George. He looked from my face to Ruby's, then back again. He bit his lip and then turned away. I wasn't sure, but I thought I'd seen tears start in his eyes.

Aunt Doll wasn't so guarded. She started to shake her head and fumbled in an apron pocket for a handkerchief.

"Jesus, Mary and Joseph," she said, wiping her eyes. "You're as alike as two peas in a pod. But somehow when I see you together I can see something else. You're the spitting image of your mothers at your age. Aren't they, George?"

"Stands to reason," said Uncle George gruffly. "Look, Rubylove, I need to go and visit your Nan. Will you come along, just to say hello?"

Ruby made a face. "Do I have to? She hates me."

"She doesn't hate you," said her father, looking pained. "She's just—just—" He faltered, not able to find the right word.

"She just hates me," said Ruby. "She's an old witch."

"Ruby!" said Aunt Doll sharply. "Don't talk about your grandmother like that."

"You called her a witch yourself, last summer!"

"I never did!"

"I heard you, talking to Eldred. You said that old witch was pure poison and how she had a son like Dad you'd never know."

Aunt Doll blushed and Uncle George laughed.

"You shouldn't eavesdrop," she said faintly to Ruby.

"Never mind, Doll," said Uncle George. "No offense. I know she's difficult. But she's still my mother, and I need to go and see her. And you might as well come with me now, Ruby, and get your first visit over with. You know she'll want to see you once a week while you're here."

"I don't know why," grumbled Ruby. "She only sits me down and tells me everything that's wrong with me, and how I come from bad stock, and how Mom was a Finn, and nothing good ever came from Finns, and you broke her heart the day you married Mom."

"She's never going to let it go, George," said Aunt Doll. "She's kept that feud alive in her bitter old heart all these years. You'd think that when Molly died she'd leave it in the past, but—"

"There's nothing I can do about that, Doll," said Uncle George. "Don't you think I've tried? I've told her again and again to put it to rest, and not to burden Ruby with it. But she pays me no mind. She never did. But with Dad gone, she's all that's left of my family, and Ruby needs to see her. Come, Ruby."

He headed toward the door. Just before he left he remembered me and turned back. "It's a pleasure to meet you, Ruth," he said, and smiled. "Have a great summer. If you're anything like Ruby, you'll never want to go home."

Ruby followed him out, making a face at me as she went.

CHAPTER TWELVE

THE FEUD

"You'll be ready for your lunch," said Aunt Doll, opening the fridge. "I'll make some egg-salad sandwiches. By the time they're on the table, Ruby will be back. She won't stay long with the old—" She glanced over at me and laughed. "With her grandmother," she finished.

"Why is she so mean?" I asked.

"Where to begin?" said Aunt Doll, taking out a glass bowl full of eggs. She put a pan of water on the stove to boil. "There was never any love lost between our family, the Duggans, and the Barretts as long as I can remember. And Mildred was a Barrett before she was a Peddle."

"What's a Peddle?"

"Oh for goodness' sake, what you don't know about your own family! Ruby is a Peddle, and George is a Peddle. I'm a Duggan, and so was my sister Daphne, Meg and Molly's mother. And Daphne married a Duggan, a distant cousin, so Meg and Molly were Duggans too, from both sides."

"Wait!" I said. All these names were whirling around in my head. It was just like when Dad got excited about plant classification of some obscure wildflower subspecies and started tracing its connections and I got lost after the first two names. "I need a piece of paper."

Aunt Doll laughed and shook her head. "You wouldn't need to write it down if you grew up with it the way you should have. But look in the drawer in the kitchen table. There should be something you can write on there."

I pulled out a scratch pad and a pen from the drawer.

"Okay, so Ruby is Ruby Peddle, and her dad is George Peddle. What came after that?"

Aunt Doll laughed again. "I'm a Duggan, Dorothy Duggan, Doll for short. My sister Daphne was also a Duggan, of course, and she married a Duggan, so her daughters, Meg and Molly, were also Duggans."

I wrote that down. "She married her cousin, you said?"

"A distant cousin, at least a fourth or a fifth, one of the Duggans from Bonavista, no near relation to my father, who was a Duggan from Fossil's Cove, who was no near relation to

51

the Duggans of Buckle—" She broke off, seeing my face, which was scrunched up in a frown. "Well, never mind about all those Duggans for now."

Phew. That was a relief. My head had started whirling again.

"So, you said Ruby's grandmother was a—what?"

"A Barrett. Mildred Barrett."

I wrote that down. Aunt Doll kept talking.

"And the Duggans and the Barretts never got along. We never had any trouble with the Peddles until the day Mildred Barrett married John Peddle—"

I scribbled that down.

"—who was a poor wisp of a man who never could stand up against Mildred—and she wouldn't have a Duggan in their house and John was forbidden to associate with my uncle Patrick, my mother's brother—"

I wrote down "Uncle Patrick."

"—although they'd been quite good friends before." She stopped to take a breath. "But the Barretts—why if a Barrett saw a Duggan coming down the road, they'd cross over and look the other way to avoid speaking to them. And Mildred did her best to keep her son George away from all of our lot, for all the good it did her. He went to school with Molly and Meg, and they all became fast friends, despite everything his mother did to try and stop it."

By this time Aunt Doll was deftly chopping celery and green onions into tiny bits and the eggs were boiling on the stove. I put down the pen. There was something very peaceful about watching her work. I'd never seen anyone so comfortable and quick in a kitchen.

"But how did it start?" I asked. "What did the Barretts have against the Duggans?"

Aunt Doll shrugged. "Who knows? The Barretts always thought they were better than the rest of us, that's for sure. Not that they had any reason. They were fishermen, like everyone else in Buckle. No more education than any of us, no more money. But the two families were always at odds. In a small place like this, it's not easy to ignore your neighbors. From what my father told me, the feud went way back, maybe all the way to Ireland."

Now Aunt Doll was slicing and buttering a loaf of raisin bread. "I made this for you yesterday," she said. "Never met a child who didn't like raisin bread. Ruby gobbles it down." She smiled at me and handed me a piece of raisin bread thick with butter. "It's good to have someone to cook for again. It gets a little quiet here in the winter."

I took a big bite out of the bread. It was divine. "What do you mean, Ireland?" I asked once I could speak again.

"Ireland! Where we all came from in the 1800s! Oh my. I can see you're in need of some education, my dear. Don't you know you're Irish?"

"Noooo . . . Dad only told me Mom was from Newfoundland. That's as far as we ever got."

"Obviously!" said Aunt Doll with a snort, and began draining the eggs. "It's a sin the way you've grown up, way off there in Ontario with nobody to tell you about your family. Well, we'll see what we can do to fix that this summer, starting right now."

She was running cold water over the eggs, then peeling away the shells. I helped myself to another piece of raisin bread and butter.

"Buckle was first settled by the Irish in the 1820s. People came on ships from Ireland. Our family, the Duggans, came out in 1832 from Waterford on a ship named *Cathleen*. Everyone who could muster up the fare got on that boat to Newfoundland, where they thought they could make a living with the fishery. But they nearly didn't make it. They were heading toward St. John's, farther along the coast, when a bad storm blew up and they were blown way off course, and the ship went aground and broke up just off the shore here. People had to swim for their lives."

"There was a shipwreck?" I asked, remembering my dream. I suddenly wished I hadn't had that second piece of raisin bread. It was forming a hard lump in my stomach.

"Yes, terrible thing," said Aunt Doll, mashing the eggs and not noticing anything strange about me. "There were Barretts and Duggans aboard that ship, along with the Finns, Dunphys and Keegans—many of the families you still see here in Buckle. Luckily they were nearly all of them saved. The crew got most people into the boats and to shore. But a few poor souls didn't make it."

I closed my eyes. I could see the slope of the deck, and the lifeboats swinging out over the water and my mother leaning over to grasp my hand. I could hear the screaming of the wind and the crashing waves and the breaking of wood against rock.

A cold little shiver traveled up my spine. I'd been having the nightmare about the shipwreck as long as I could remember. Was this where it came from? An old family story? But no one had ever told me that story before now.

"Ruth. Ruth!" said Aunt Doll, concerned. "Are you okay? You've gone white as a sheet."

I opened my eyes. "I'm fine," I said faintly. "Just . . . just thinking about how awful it must have been. The shipwreck."

"You're a sensitive creature," said Aunt Doll. "Just like your mother. She never liked me talking about the shipwreck either. Molly didn't mind, but Meg would go white, just the way you did, and make me stop. Too much imagination, that was her problem."

She sighed and shook her head. "Never mind all that now." She put an egg-salad sandwich on a pretty blue plate on the table in front of me.

"Nothing like a bit of lunch to cure a bad attack of imagination," she said with a laugh.

I couldn't help it. I laughed too and took a bite.

CHAPTER THIRTEEN

THE FINNS

"The witch wants you to come next time," said Ruby, taking a pile of sweaters from her suitcase and stuffing them into one of the dresser drawers I'd left free for her.

I was sitting on my bed watching her unpack. She didn't seem to have any shorts. I shivered. It had clouded over again and started to rain a bit.

"Why does she want to see me?" I asked. "She's not my grandmother."

Ruby shrugged. "She's nosy. She wants to see what kind of a child Meg had. And she probably wants to torture you the way she does me about how the Finns are no good and never will be."

"I don't get it. Who are the Finns? Eldred told me they were people who lived in some little cove that disappeared long ago. What have we got to do with the Finns?"

Ruby slammed down the top of her suitcase, fastened the buckles, then shoved it under her bed. She'd unpacked everything and put it away in five minutes flat. She glanced out the window.

"Ooo, there's Eldred going into the barn. Let's go talk to him. He's the one who should tell you the story of the Finns. No one can tell a story like Eldred." And she was out the door and clattering down the stairs. I scrambled up off the bed to follow her, grabbing the rain jacket from the hook in the hall where I'd left it.

The barn was dim and had a pungent, earthy smell: a mix of sweet hay and old cow manure. There were no animals in it now, but there was a loft piled high with hay. Off to one side I could just make out a figure standing in the shadows. There were tools hanging all over the wall and a long, high counter crowded with more tools, scraps of wood and bits of old iron.

The figure turned as we came in.

"Eldred!" said Ruby. "Ruth needs to hear about the Finns. Can you tell us?"

"I'm supposed to be fixing your aunt's toaster," said Eldred, stepping into the light. He had a frayed piece of wire in his hand. He had that same air I'd noticed earlier, of being half here and half somewhere else. He looked at us with a slow, wondrous smile, as if he had never seen two girls before. Almost as if we were two unicorns that walked into his barn.

"Oh come on," said Ruby, darting behind him and pulling out a low, three-legged stool from under the counter. "Her toaster can wait. It's my first day, Eldred. I haven't had one of your stories since last fall."

Eldred laughed and sat down in a chair with a broken arm that was leaning against the wall. Ruby sat down on the stool and turned her face up to him, alight with anticipation. I had a sudden impression of her sitting listening to him tell stories back through the years, right on that stool, here in this barn. I looked around and saw an old wooden crate in the corner. I pulled it up and sat down on it.

"Well now, the Finns," began Eldred, smiling a little and glancing at me shyly from under his bushy eyebrows. "The Finns came over from Ireland, years ago. With the Duggans and the Barretts and the Keegans, and a lot of the other families that settled in Buckle."

"On board the ship *Cathleen,*" said Ruby in singsong voice. "And there was a shipwreck, and then the Finns went to live in Slippers Cove and the rest of them settled here in Buckle."

"Who's telling the story, Ruby?" said Eldred, but he wasn't mad.

"You are, but it always starts the same," said Ruby.

"Yes, well, it starts with the shipwreck. Then the Finns and the Keegans went to live in Slippers Cove, and there they stayed. As the years went by, once in a while a boy or a girl from Buckle would marry a boy or a girl from Slippers Cove, and go there to live, and soon there was a small community there, just five or six houses."

"Then the storm came," said Ruby.

"The storm came. It was a hurricane, late September in the year 1879. There was heavy rain and strong winds. All the brooks overflowed their banks and the fields were awash. Full of water. There was a lot of damage in Buckle: the barn that used to stand here had its roof blown clean off."

"But Slippers Cove was hit worst of all," said Ruby.

"Yes. Slippers Cove was hit worst of all," went on Eldred. "The day after the storm blew on out into the Atlantic, the people in Buckle were busy trying to repair the damage to their homes and outbuildings, so they didn't give much thought to the Finns. But by the next day, when they would expect that someone would come by from Slippers Cove, either by boat or walking over the downs, and nobody came, they started to worry."

"Vince Duggan had a brother married a Finn," said Ruby.

"Yes, Vince Duggan had a brother Boyd in Slippers Cover, who was married to a Finn," said Eldred, "so Vince was concerned about his brother and his brother's young family. Boyd had two little girls, twins they were, just two years old. So Vince took his friend Ernie Doyle, and they walked over the downs, along the road to Slippers Cove. It was a four-hour walk. There were parts of the road that were washed out, and they had to

59

wade through water up to their knees in spots. But when they finally got to the top of the hill that looks over Slippers Cove, they beheld a dreadful sight."

"Slippers Cove was a tight little cove," intoned Ruby.

"You need to know that Slippers Cove was a tight little cove, well-protected by high cliffs, with a rattling little brook running down a steep hill from the downs. The houses stood on a bit of flat land by the water, with the brook running in between, down over the rocks to the sea.

"When young Vince and Ernie stood at the top of the hill, two days after the storm, all the houses were gone. There was nothing there but a wide pool of water, and beyond that the cove: empty. There wasn't any sign of the houses: no wreckage, no debris. But the little brook that used to clatter down the rocks was now a powerful waterfall, fifteen feet wide."

"They'd been washed out to sea in the storm," said Ruby. "All the houses, all the people. Gone."

"Gone," echoed Eldred. "All gone. Vince and Ernie could hardly believe their eyes. Vince fell to his knees with a cry as it came home to him that his brother and his brother's wife and their sweet babies were gone. Ernie put his hand on his friend's shoulder and wiped the tears from his own eyes."

"But then he heard a noise," said Ruby.

"A noise of someone crying," went on Eldred. "But it wasn't his friend Vince. Ernie turned toward the noise and saw the root cellar."

"The root cellar had been built on top of the hill," said Ruby.

"Because there was no room for it down by the houses. And it was an old-fashioned cellar, built the way they did in those days, no cement. Just flat rock all around, with a flat rock ceiling, all laid careful like it was the roof of a cathedral."

"A cathedral," said Ruby.

"And that's where the crying was coming from," said Eldred. "Ernie left his friend and walked over. The root cellar had been built just below the crest of the hill, where it had some shelter from the ocean winds. The crying had stopped by now and all was silent. Ernie stooped to go in. It was dark. Ernie took a box of matches from his pocket and lit one."

"And that's when he saw them," said Ruby.

"And that's when he saw them," said Eldred. "Two little girls with bright blonde hair and blue eyes, sitting in the middle of the root cellar, with crates of potatoes and carrots and turnips all piled up around them."

"Twins," said Ruby.

"Yes," said Eldred, glancing over at Ruth again, a strange light in his eye. "They were twins."

CHAPTER FOURTEEN

THE SIGHT

"Twins," I echoed. I felt half-hypnotized by the story. I could see the hillside, and the root cellar, and the man with the matches. And the two little girls, faces grimy with tears and terror.

"Well, as you probably guessed, these were Vince's brother's children, Fiona and Fenella, all that was left of the thirty-two inhabitants of Slippers Cove. Why they were in that root cellar, no one could ever figure out. But they were safe. Everyone else drowned, swept out to sea by the flooding brook."

"Or a tidal wave," put in Ruby.

"Or a tidal wave," agreed Eldred. "There was no way to be

sure, but the fact that the houses were swept out to sea suggested a rogue wave. In the weeks to come, people found wreckage way down the shore, as far as Lost Harbour. Meanwhile, Vince took the two girls, Fiona and Fenella, home to his wife, Shelagh, who had three little boys of her own already. But she welcomed them with open arms, and they grew up with all the love as if they'd been born to Vince and Shelagh."

"And ever since that day—" said Ruby.

"Ever since that day, there's always been twins in the Duggans' family. Once a generation, twin girls—blonde hair, blue eyes—true descendants of the Finns of Slippers Cove."

"Oh," I said. "So our mothers—"

"Our mothers were the last of them," said Ruby. "They were true Finns. But there were no more twins after them. Each of them gave birth to only one baby."

"Me and you," I said.

"Me and you," she repeated. Her eyes were shining. "When's your birthday, Ruth?"

"December fifth. Why?"

"Just wondering. Mine's December tenth."

I looked at her for a moment. Eldred was silent, watching us. I squirmed a little on the hard wooden crate. He was a little strange, the way he looked at me like he could read my mind. And his slow way of talking with a half-smile on his lips as if he was sharing a secret joke with me. And that dreamy, faraway look in his eyes.

63

"Aunt Doll says our mothers did everything together," said Ruby. "Even having kids. They were inseparable, she said, until my mother married my dad and brought me back here, and your mother stayed in Toronto and married your dad. She never came back to Newfoundland."

"But then they died on the same day," I said.

"Twins are curious creatures," said Eldred. "Your mothers now, they were identical on the outside: no one could tell them apart. But on the inside, they were different. Molly was always laughing, playing tricks, running wild. Meg was the quiet one, always had her head in a book. And, of course, Meg had the Sight."

"Oh yes, tell her about the Sight," said Ruby.

"The funny thing about the Finn twins," began Eldred, "was that one of them was always born with the Sight."

"What's the Sight?" I asked.

"Second Sight," said Ruby impatiently. "Don't you know anything?"

"Well, I've heard of Second Sight, of course I have." I said stiffly. I was getting tired of everyone in Newfoundland treating me like I was stupid. "I just don't believe in it. I think it's a lot of nonsense."

Ruby bristled. "What do you know? You're from Ontario. If you were from here, you would know that it is true. People with the Sight can see things, see things that are going to happen, see things from the past. And ghosts. And fairies."

"It's just pretend," I said. "All that stuff. You don't really believe it, do you, Eldred? Isn't it just a game you play with Ruby?"

"Game?" Ruby almost shouted, jumping to her feet.

Eldred put out a hand to her. "Calm down, Ruby," he said. "Sit down and let me explain it to Ruth."

Ruby sat down, glaring at me.

"The gift of Second Sight goes way back, as far as anyone can remember. Even in ancient Greece there were oracles and such who could see the future. Irish people tend to be more gifted with it than other folk, not sure why. Maybe because they believe in it so strongly."

"Just because you believe in something doesn't make it true," I objected.

Eldred smiled a slow smile at me. "Doesn't it? I'm not sure I agree with that. But anyway, it seems to run in families with the Irish. Some people have it . . . some don't. The Finns always had it, one of the twins. The Barretts had it too, once in a while. In fact, Ruby, I wouldn't be at all surprised if your Nan, Mildred Peddle, didn't have the Sight. She was a Barrett before she married John Peddle. But I'm not sure you'd ever get her to admit it."

"She's a witch," said Ruby automatically.

Eldred smiled again. "That's as may be. In the old days, witches were not unknown in Newfoundland. And often they were the ones with the Sight."

"It's all fairy tales," I said. "I don't believe in fairy tales. My dad's a scientist. He always told me, ever since I was little, that all that stuff is just pretend. Not real. Science is real. Science explains things. Things you can see and touch. There is absolutely no proof that ghosts, fairies, predicting the future or any of that stuff is real."

Ruby started to sputter. Eldred held up his hand again.

"There are places where people still believe in those things," he said. "Places in Ireland, places in Newfoundland. Other places in countries all over the world where people see spirits and can divine the future. Maybe there are no ghosts in Toronto; I don't know, never been there. But there surely are ghosts here in Buckle."

"Have you seen them?" I felt I had to keep pushing my argument, now that I'd started it, but I wasn't quite as convinced as I made out. Ever since I got here, I'd had this strange, disoriented feeling, like everything was slightly skewed. My dreams last night of the shipwreck and the girl with the candle, meeting Eldred on the fairy path, looking into Ruby's shining eyes as she talked about the fairies building the bridge. I felt I had to fight back or be swallowed up by it.

Eldred didn't answer right away. He seemed to be listening to some faraway voices. Finally he stirred and looked at me. "Maybe," he said. "Maybe I have. Felt them, more like. But my mother saw them."

"Have you seen them?" I asked Ruby. "Or fairies? I mean, really seen them?"

Ruby shook her head. "No. I've wanted to forever but I never have. But I know they're there. I can feel them, like Eldred says."

"Some people see them. Some people don't. People with the Sight see them for sure. Your mother, Meg. Now she had the Sight. And she saw ghosts. I don't know if she ever saw fairies. But there's no doubt she could see things the rest of us couldn't. I believe she could see into the past. And perhaps into the future. But she didn't talk about it." He looked troubled and shook his head as if to chase some unpleasant thoughts away. He stood up abruptly. "I need to get to work now. That's enough stories for today."

CHAPTER FIFTEEN

WILDFLOWERS

Ruby jumped up and announced that she was going to help Eldred fix the toaster. I stood a little awkwardly at the doorway to the workshop, watching them. Eldred lit a kerosene lamp that cast a dim light over the workbench. Ruby started to dig through a box of wires. Neither of them paid any attention to me. Again, I felt like they had been together like this many times before. They were easy with each other, finishing each other's sentences. Ruby stood up triumphantly with a long wire and held it out to Eldred.

I might as well have been invisible, a ghost myself. I backed away and stepped out into the rain, pulling up the hood on the jacket. Rather than go in the back door and into the hall that led past the kitchen, I circled around the house to the front door. I didn't want to talk to Aunt Doll just then. I didn't want to talk to anyone. I stopped for a moment on the porch and looked out over the bay. Sheets of rain streaked over the water, and I could barely see the far shore. A few seabirds swooped and called, impervious to the cold water pouring out of the sky.

I went in, shaking the rain off my coat and hanging it on the hook. I could hear the radio in the kitchen and Aunt Doll humming along to some music that was playing. I went quietly up the stairs. I wondered if Ruby was mad at me because I said I didn't believe in the Second Sight. That was just silly. But the way I had suddenly become invisible to her was disconcerting. She'd been so friendly before, and I'd felt so relaxed with her, like I'd known her forever.

I went down the corridor to our room and sat on my bed for a while, listening to the rain drumming on the roof. I thought of Dad and Gwen, who had probably arrived in Greece by now. It would be hot there, and sunny.

I stood up suddenly, went over to the dresser and pulled out the book Dad had pressed into my hands at the airport: *Wildflowers of Newfoundland.* I fumbled in my knapsack pocket and found the fuzzy white flower I had put there earlier. The flower head was wilted and drooping now, but I wanted to identify it.

As I flipped through the pages, the delicate watercolors and the careful descriptions began to work a gentle enchantment upon me, the way wildflower books always did, and soon I was lost in the book.

My father had taught me to identify wildflowers almost as soon as I could talk, and my interest in them grew as I did. It wasn't just their intricate beauty that drew me to them: it was the study of botany itself. Everything about wildflowers could be explained and categorized. Sometimes they were hard to identify, but if you just went through the checklists, sooner or later you would get it. Leaves, flowers, stems. And the names were so evocative in English: crackerberry, leather-leaf, smaller enchanter's nightshade; and so poetic in Latin: *Cornus canadensis, Chamaedaphne calyculata, Circaea alpina.*

I found myself rethinking the idea Dad had proposed to me at the airport when he handed me the gift, which included the book and a brand-new box of artist's colored pencils.

He and Gwen were leaving on a later flight, so they walked me to my departure gate. Surrounded by people and luggage, Dad had shuffled his feet a bit, cleared his throat and then suggested that maybe I would like to do a study of Newfoundland wildflowers over the summer, and we could go over it together in September.

I just wanted to get away from him. The gift was making it worse. As if a stupid little project of Newfoundland wildflowers could make up for being left behind and not going to Greece. I shrugged, and looked away, only to have my eyes alight on

Awful Gwen, who was standing in the background, watching us with a fond smile. I shifted my position again, so Dad blocked her from my view.

My dad was doing more throat-clearing and looking off into the distance, fumbling for some way to say good-bye to me. Even though I was so angry with him, I felt a stab of pity for him. He was never good with expressing any kind of emotion. Finally he leaned over and kissed my cheek.

"Good-bye, Rue," he said, using his old nickname for me, which is a bit of a botanist's joke, since rue is a kind of herb. I had a whiff of his familiar smell, a mix of laundry detergent and aftershave, and then he turned back to Gwen, and the two of them walked down the hall toward their gate.

I was left alone with the helpful flight attendant who had been charged with looking after me till she handed me over to Aunt Doll in St. John's. She started expressing interest in the book and my pencils, but I shoved it all into my bag and asked her where the washrooms were.

After crying silently in one of the stalls for a few minutes, I came out and washed my face. Looking at my reflection in the mirror, with women swishing by me to wash their hands or reach for the paper towels, I tried to find some courage to go on with. Tears were still brimming in my eyes and I looked bereft. I felt bereft. This would be the longest I had even been away from my dad, two months. With people I didn't know. In a place I had never been.

I must have been there for a while because the flight attendant came in to look for me. She came up behind me and put a hand on my shoulder. I could see her looking at my face in the mirror.

"Come on, honey," she said. "You'll be all right. Was that your stepmother?"

I nodded, unable to speak.

"Thought so. I had one too. Look, let's go get you a Coke and a magazine, and then it will be time to board."

When I tried to pay with my money for my treats (she threw in a bag of chips and a Jersey Milk chocolate bar), she shook her head.

"Your dad gave me five dollars and told me to buy you something to cheer you up," she said. "He seems like a nice guy."

The memory of the airport, the kind flight attendant and the treats faded away, and I was once more in the back bedroom at Aunt Doll's house with the rain streaking down outside. I focused on the book in my hands. Maybe I *could* do the little study of Newfoundland wildflowers. I didn't have to do it for him. I could do it for me. It would be comforting to do something so familiar in this unfamiliar place.

I turned a page and there it was, a picture of the wildflower I had found on the road, with bunches of tiny white flowers atop each stem and the fuzzy effect made by tiny stamens reaching past the flowers. Labrador tea, the book said. You could actually make tea from the leaves if you dried them out.

I pulled out my sketchbook and colored pencils. Maybe I could start the wildflower project tomorrow. If it stopped raining. Or right now. I could at least do a quick sketch of the Labrador tea specimen.

I opened up the sketchbook and sat there for a moment with my Staedtler 2B pencil, fully intending to draw the flower.

I stared at the blank page for a moment. The paper was thick and white—Dad had bought me the most expensive sketchbook he could find. Probably because he was feeling guilty about leaving me. He usually bought cheaper ones for our expeditions.

Pushing that thought away, I turned the sketchpad sideways, so the longer side of the page was at the top and I had a good wide surface to work on. Then I wrote two words along the top of the page: FAMILY TREE.

CHAPTER SIXTEEN

FAMILY TREE

I knew a little about family trees. The winter before, a girl in my history class, Stephanie Sutherland, created a family tree for a project. When she presented it to the class, she boasted about how she could trace her family back to a small village in England in the 1750s. It was very complicated, with lots of little rectangular boxes joined by lines. She got A+ on it and the teacher put it up on one of the bulletin boards in our history classroom, right beside my desk. It was there for weeks and I spent a lot of time looking at it instead of listening to Mrs. Metcalfe droning on about Canadian history.

I was fascinated by all the connections Stephanie had

made—the aunts, cousins, great-grandmothers and great-great-grandfathers. And jealous. Not so much of her mark (even though I only got B+ on my project about the French-Canadian voyageurs), but mostly of her family. If I had made a family tree then, I would have only been able to fill in four boxes: me, my mother, my father and Aunt Doll.

But now I could fill in a lot more boxes, and maybe it would help me sort out what Aunt Doll and Ruby and Eldred were telling me about the Finns and the Duggans and the Peddles. They were all swirling around in my mind, all these new relatives I didn't know I had until today.

I dug into my pocket and found the crumpled piece of paper I'd used to write down the family names while Aunt Doll was explaining it to me. I unfolded it and laid it on the bed beside me.

Now. Where to begin? I decided to start with Ruby and me and work my way back into the past.

"Ruth Windsor," I wrote at the top on the left, and made a little box around it. Under that, I wrote "Meg Duggan," and made a box around that. Then I added "Bill Windsor." I joined my box to theirs with straight lines.

Then I wrote "Ruby Peddle" on the top on the right, inside a box, and under that, "Molly Duggan, George Peddle," in boxes, and joined them together. I added everyone else I'd heard of so far—Aunt Doll, Daphne, Meg and Molly's parents, Ruby's grandparents.

I sat back and looked at my efforts. My family tree now had eleven boxes, seven more than it would have had yesterday.

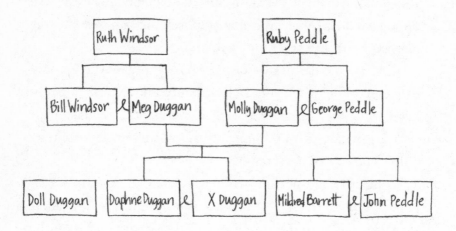

But what about the Finns?

I turned the page and wrote "Ireland" across the top. Underneath that I put "The ship *Cathleen,* 1832," then made three boxes: one for the Finns, one for the Duggans, and one for the Barretts. Then I wrote in all the names I could remember from Eldred's story.

Phew. That's all I knew. It was a lot less confusing now that it was down on paper. It reminded me of when I drew up the plant classifications for wildflowers to sort out what Dad was telling me.

That was what I liked. Facts. Order. Connections. This

family tree had nothing to do with ghosts or fairies or the Sight. And if Ruby ever spoke to me again, maybe she could help me make some more boxes and fill in some of the blanks between the two of us in Buckle in 1978 and our ancestors who came from Ireland on board the ship *Cathleen* in 1832.

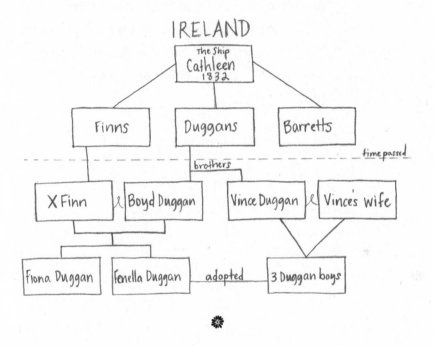

Ruby stayed out in the barn all afternoon, and I huddled under a blanket on my bed, poring over my family tree and reading about Newfoundland wildflowers. At supper, she chattered away, half-ignoring me. Aunt Doll didn't seem to notice. By the time we went to bed, Ruby was treating me politely, as if

I were a little old lady visitor she had to be kind to, but didn't need to engage with. I found it supremely annoying.

Childish. That's what she was, with her talk of fairies and ghosts and her conviction that she knew better than me just because I was from Ontario. I turned my back to her and closed my eyes. I'd like to plop her down at the corner of Yonge and Bloor streets with a subway ticket and see how she managed then, with no fairy bridges to get her across the street and no Eldred with his enigmatic smiles and stories to back her up. I finally fell asleep, fuming.

CHAPTER SEVENTEEN

THE GHOST

I don't know what woke me up. The room was very dark. As I lay there, aware this time that I was in Aunt Doll's house in Newfoundland, and not in my room in Toronto, I heard a noise in the hall, just as I had the night before. A soft footfall, coming down the hall toward our room. Then the door creaked open and a golden, flickering light illuminated the room.

It was the girl again, just as she'd been the night before, wearing a long white nightgown and carrying a candle. She approached my bed and stood smiling down at me. Then she sat on Ruby's bed and held the candle up so she could see Ruby's face. The girl reached out and gently touched Ruby's hair, smoothing it back from her forehead. Ruby stirred. A sad, tender expression flitted over the girl's face and then she looked over at me.

She held up the candle in front of her face so I could see her face clearly. She looked so familiar. A lot like Ruby. But not quite Ruby. A little older, a little different. She smiled at me slowly, with a mischievous gleam in her eye. I felt sure that I knew that smile from somewhere.

"The window," she whispered, and then pursed her lips and blew the candle out.

"Wait!" I cried, reaching out toward her, but there was nobody there. Something clattered to the floor and I felt the air move as if someone had walked away from me toward the dresser.

Ruby woke up. "What's wrong?" she said sleepily.

I felt around on the floor till I found what had fallen. A candle.

"Ruth!" said Ruby. "What's happening?"

It was too dark to see her. I stumbled over to the dresser and found the matches and the lamp.

"Can you light this thing?" I asked.

Ruby jumped out of bed and banged into me.

"Give me the matches," she said, and soon the lamp was glowing. She put it on the table between our beds.

"Now tell me what's wrong," she said.

I looked down at the floor. The brass candleholder was there, the one I'd shoved way under the bed the day before. In my hand was a candle, half-burnt.

"I don't know," I said. "I must have been dreaming. There was a girl, and she came in with a candle, and then she dropped it and—"

"If it was a dream, why are you holding the candle?" asked Ruby. She was looking at me intently.

"I don't know, I—oh dear," I said, sitting down suddenly on the bed. "I don't feel so good."

Ruby came and sat beside me and started rubbing my hands. "You're cold as ice," she said. "And you're white as a sheet."

"It must have been a dream," I said. "I had the same dream last night, only I thought it was you. I thought you had come and were going to bed; she looked like you, and she got into bed and blew out the candle, and it was there in the morning and—"

"Whoa," said Ruby. "Hang on. You dreamed about a girl with a candle, and then the candle was there in the morning?"

"Yup," I said, nodding my head. I stared at her, drinking her in. She was real and warm and solid.

"And then you dreamed of her again tonight and this candle was on the floor?" She pointed to the candle, which I'd put on the table.

"Go on!" she breathed. "You've seen a ghost, Ruth!"

"No," I said, shaking my head. "Not a ghost. I don't believe in ghosts." I was starting to shiver.

"Here, get back in bed," said Ruby, pushing me under the covers and climbing in beside me.

I was freezing, and I couldn't stop the shivers. Ruby lay back on the pillow and pulled the covers up to our chins.

"Take a deep breath," she said. "In and out."

I tried that. In and out. The way I did with all my nightmares. In and out. The way I had the night before, when the shipwreck dream woke me up. In and out. The shipwreck. The one my mother saved me from, every time I had that dream.

"Oh no!" I cried and grabbed Ruby by the arm. I was colder than ever and I felt all the breath whoosh out of me.

"What?" she said, trying to shake her arm loose. "Let go. You're pinching!"

I clung to her. "It was my mother!" I said. "I know that smile. It was my mother, but she looked different because she was younger, not grown up."

"Your mother?" breathed Ruby. "The ghost was your mother?"

"Not a ghost," I said, my teeth chattering. "A dream."

Clickety-clackety footsteps came briskly down the hall and the door opened. Aunt Doll stood there. She was still dressed, so I guess it wasn't as late as I had thought.

"What on earth?" she asked, looking at the two of us.

"Ruth had a bad dream," said Ruby quickly before I could speak. "So I lit the lamp. She's cold."

Aunt Doll bustled over and put her hand against my forehead.

"Oh for goodness' sake," she said, pulling some quilts off Ruby's bed and laying them across us. "It's like an icebox in here. I'll get you a hot water bottle and something warm to drink. Are you all right, child?" she said, peering at me.

"Just c-c-c-c-old," I said.

"Ruby, rub her hands. I'll be back in a jiffy." And she clickety-clacked down the hall and down the stairs.

"You said it was a dream," I said, as Ruby started jiggling my hands to warm them.

"Just to keep her off the scent," said Ruby. "Now tell me everything."

CHAPTER EIGHTEEN

COCOA AND COOKIES

"I have this dream about a shipwreck," I began. Ruby was still rubbing my hands. I pulled away. "It's okay," I said. "I'm starting to warm up a bit." Just sitting beside her was making me feel warmer. She was humming with energy.

"A shipwreck," she repeated, her eyebrows going up.

"Yes. I've had it ever since I was a little girl. I'm on a ship and it's going down in a storm, and my mother is there, and she saves me. It's always the same."

Ruby's eyes were big. "Wow," she breathed.

"Yes," I said, trying to ignore her. I knew she was going to make a big deal out of the shipwreck. "And then I wake up and

I'm usually scared. So I had the dream last night and at first I didn't know where I was. But then I remembered I was here, and I couldn't turn on a light, like I usually do when I have a bad dream, because there's no electricity on this side of the house."

"Yes," said Ruby, nodding her head. "Go on."

"But then I heard some footsteps in the hall and I thought it was Aunt Doll, but it was this girl in a long nightgown, with a candle, and I thought it was you."

"Why me?" she said. "Did she look like me?"

"I didn't even know what you looked like! I just thought, hey, a girl, coming to bed, it must be you and you got here early."

"Okay. So then what happened?"

"The girl came in, put the candle on the bedside table, got into your bed, smiled at me and blew out the candle. Then I went to sleep. I could hear her breathing and . . . and . . ."

"And what?"

"And I felt safe. Like things were going to be okay."

"Wow," said Ruby again. "So then what happened tonight?"

"I woke up like before, and I heard footsteps, and again I thought it was Aunt Doll, but then the door opened and this kind of golden light came into the room—"

"Golden light?" Ruby looked like she was ready to burst.

"Yes," I snapped. "The light from the candle. She was carrying a candle again. But the funny thing was, Ruby, yesterday I took that candle, which I found on my bedside table, and I shoved it way under my bed. So I don't know how she had it again—"

Ruby was out of bed in a flash and crawling under my bed, rooting around. She emerged with her hair all standing on end and a triumphant look on her face.

"No candle there. It has to be the same one," she said.

"Where is it?" I said, looking around. The last place I'd seen it was on the bedside table, and the holder was on my bed.

"I whisked it under the covers when I heard Aunt Doll coming," said Ruby. "We're not allowed to have candles in here. Because of fire."

She scrambled under the covers and fished around till she came up with the candle and the holder.

"That was quick thinking," I said. She grinned.

"Go on," she said. "What happened next?"

"Well, the girl smiled at me and then went over and sat down on your bed."

"My bed?" she yelped.

"Yes. And she touched your hair and kind of smoothed it back—" Ruby's hand went up to her hair and, if possible, her eyes got even bigger and rounder.

"And then she looked sort of sad, but she turned to me and held up the candle and smiled and looked all mischievous and said, 'Window,' and blew the candle out."

"Window?" repeated Ruby. "She said 'window'? Are you sure?"

"Yes, I'm sure. She said window, blew out the candle, and then when I reached out to her, the candle dropped on the floor and you woke up and she was gone."

"Wow!" said Ruby, getting up on her knees and bouncing on the bed. "Wow! Wow! Wow! Ruth! You saw a ghost! And you said you think it was your mother?"

"I kept thinking that she looked familiar. I thought tonight maybe it was because she looked like you, but even last night, before I ever saw you, she looked familiar to me. And then I realized: it was the smile. It was my mother's smile, the one I remember when I was sitting on her lap. The one in the picture."

Ruby turned to the picture of my mother and me, which was still sitting on the table.

"This one?" she said.

I picked up the picture and looked at it. My mother was smiling out at the camera.

"Yes," I gulped. "It was my mother, only younger."

"I saw this yesterday," said Ruby softly, leaning over my shoulder and touching my mother's face with her finger. "She looks exactly like my mother. Exactly."

We heard Aunt Doll coming down the hall, and Ruby snatched the picture from me and put it back on the table. When Aunt Doll came in, we were sitting together in bed, our hands neatly folded on top of the covers.

Aunt Doll looked at us and narrowed her eyes.

"Too good to be true, the two of you," she said, putting a tray with cookies and two steaming mugs down on the table. She handed me a warm bundle: the hot water bottle, wrapped in a towel. "Put that down near your feet. Now, you're not to be up half the night. Get this down you and then back to sleep. Are you warmer now, Ruth?" she said, laying her hand against my forehead. Her hand was warm. It felt good. My father never did that to me when I was sick. He just went looking for the thermometer.

"Yes," I said, smiling up at her. The hot water bottle was deliciously warm on my bare feet. She bent over and kissed my forehead, and then bestowed another kiss on Ruby.

"Monkeys," she said. "You're a couple of monkeys. If that light isn't out in ten minutes, I'll be back, do you hear me?"

"Yes, Aunt Doll," we said in chorus and then began to laugh. She shook her head and left the room.

As we devoured the oatmeal cookies and steaming cocoa, Ruby started to quiz me again.

"Could you see through her? Did she kind of float above the floor? Did she have a light around her head, like an aura?"

"Honestly, Ruby! She looked like a regular person. I thought she was you when I first saw her."

"But you see now she was a ghost, right?" asked Ruby, brushing away the cookie crumbs that were sprinkled all over the quilts.

I was quiet for a moment, remembering the girl and the way she looked at me, the twinkle in her eyes.

"A dream—" I said weakly.

"No, you were awake. Admit it, Ruth. You were awake both times."

Reluctantly I nodded my head. "I certainly felt like I was awake."

"Oh, Ruth," said Ruby, clutching my hand and nearly spilling what was left of my cocoa. "You see what this means, don't you?"

"Well, if it really was a ghost—"

"It was, it was," sang Ruby happily.

"Well, then, if I really saw my mother's ghost, here in this room, then it means that maybe my dad was wrong. And I was wrong. And there really are such things as ghosts." I hated to admit it, but what other explanation was there?

"And? And?"

"And maybe this house is haunted," I went on.

"And?"

"And what?" I had no idea what she was getting at.

"Oh don't you see, Ruth?" she said, bouncing up and down a little. "Don't you see? It means you can see ghosts. It means you have the Sight."

CHAPTER NINETEEN

THE SECRET PASSAGE

When I opened my eyes the next morning, our bedroom looked very ordinary and dreary, with rain pouring down outside the window. I found it hard to believe that I'd seen a ghost there the night before. Ruby had managed to steal most of the covers in the night and I was freezing.

I sat up and surveyed the room. It was just big enough for the two double beds and the dresser on the opposite wall. Aunt Doll had said something to me that first night, something about how when she grew up she'd shared it with her three sisters. "Two to a bed," she said. "And the three boys next door. Those were the days of big families. We only had seven, but it

was nothing to have ten or twelve children. Those poor wor, she went on, shaking her head.

Then I thought about my mother and her sister, sharing room all those years ago. Just like Ruby and me. I wonder they fought. And if my mother saw ghosts . . .

I carefully crawled out of bed, so as not to disturb Ruby, stood between the two beds where the ghost had been stand the night before. I'd felt the air move after I grabbed the can as if she were walking away from me toward the door.

But the door hadn't opened again. Where did she go?

"What are you doing?" asked Ruby sleepily.

I looked at her. One eye was open.

"I'm trying to figure out where the ghost went last night."

Ruby sat up. "What do you mean? She disappeared. She a ghost. She didn't have to go anywhere."

I shook my head. "It didn't feel like that. It felt like she was moving away from me, across the room, but she didn't go out the door."

"You be the ghost; I'll be you," she said.

I picked up the candle in its holder, from the table where Ruby had placed it the night before. Then I stood holding the candle in front of my face. I made as if to blow it out.

"Now sit up and grab for me," I said, and Ruby obligingly sat up and swiped at me. I put the candle on the floor and then took a couple of steps away from her. The door was on my right. Straight ahead of me was the closet door.

"The closet!" breathed Ruby, coming to the idea at the same time I did. I grinned at her. She leaped out of bed and came to stand beside me.

I opened the door. I hadn't investigated it before, because I had no clothes to hang up. Ruby pushed past me.

"Wait till you see this," she said, burrowing into the dresses and coats that were hanging there, encased in long plastic bags. It was a tight fit, but she squeezed through.

"Wait for me," I said and followed her. It took a little pushing for me to get through, but I made it, only to be confronted by another row of hanging clothes. Beyond it I could hear Ruby urging me on.

"Come on, Rue," she sang out. "Just push through."

Funny. She'd called me Rue, just like Dad. I pushed against the clothes and suddenly I was out in the daylight again, in a room with two double beds neatly made up with quilts. I could see the ocean through the window on the opposite wall.

"It's a secret passage," said Ruby, throwing herself on one of the beds and bouncing up and down. "Isn't it cool? I discovered it years ago."

I turned back to the closet. It just looked like an ordinary closet. I parted a couple of shirts and there was the row of clothes we could see from our room.

"They just didn't bother putting up a wall at the back," said Ruby.

"Have you asked Aunt Doll about it?"

"She says it was always like that, and they used to have fun playing hide-and-seek and sneaking back and forth when they were supposed to be asleep."

I went and sat on the other bed. If anything, this room was even colder than ours. "Did our mothers have brothers?"

Ruby stared at me. "How can you not know that?"

I shrugged, embarrassed. "I don't think my mom told my dad much about her family. He's never told me anything. I didn't even know she had a twin."

"That's a sin, not knowing anything about your family," said Ruby, sounding just like Aunt Doll, who had said more or less the same thing the day before. "My mom and your mom had one brother, Uncle Jack, who was two years older than them. He went away to school on the mainland when he was sixteen and became an engineer. He lives in British Columbia. Every once in a while he visits. His kids are nearly grown up, so I don't really know them."

"Oh," I said, looking out the window. It was odd that my mother hadn't told my father anything. Wasn't he interested? Why wouldn't she talk about her family?

"Why wouldn't your mother tell your dad about her brother and sister?" said Ruby, again, as if her thoughts were following along exactly the same path as my own. "Do you think something happened here she wanted to forget about?"

"I don't know," I said, shaking my head. "We should ask Aunt Doll."

"It could be some family secret," said Ruby, her eyes big. "Some deep dark family secret."

"Like what?" I asked, trying not to roll my eyes. Ruby was so dramatic.

"I don't know, but Aunt Doll always said it was strange that Meg never brought her baby or her husband home to meet the family. Aunt Doll's feelings were hurt. She was sort of like their mother, you know, because she came back from St. John's to look after them when their mother died."

"Their mother died?"

"Yes, when they were twelve."

"Wow . . ." I said.

"What?" Ruby came and sat down on the bed beside me. "Why are you looking so funny?"

"I didn't know they'd lost their mother too. I mean, they grew up without a mother, just like us."

Ruby looked out the window, screwing up her face.

"Yeah. I never really thought about it."

"It's sad," I said.

There was a silence. Ruby sighed.

"It's not really fair," I said softly. "I'd give anything to have a mother. A real mother."

"Me too," said Ruby, and slipped her hand into mine.

CHAPTER TWENTY

PARTRIDGEBERRIES

Ruby gave herself a little shake and stood up. "But what about the ghost?" she asked, not looking at me. She started prowling around the room. "Do you think it came in here?"

I frowned. "I don't know why. But I did have the impression that she came this way."

Ruby started opening the dresser drawers. "Nothing in here," she said. "This is where my brothers sleep when they come, so I guess Aunt Doll leaves the dresser empty for their clothes." She looked around. "There's not much else in here." She fell to her knees and lifted up the quilts to peer first under one bed, then under the other.

"No ghosts," she reported with a grin, getting to her feet and dusting off her jeans.

"Ruby! Ruth!" It was Aunt Doll, calling from what seemed like a long way away. Ruby went to the door and yelled, "What?"

"Breakfast! Sleepyheads . . ."

"We'll be right down," hollered Ruby. She had a very loud voice.

We went back into our room through the hall, got some clothes on and went down to breakfast.

"Another rainy day," said Aunt Doll cheerfully, dishing up some scrambled eggs for each of us. "You'll be thinking badly of Newfoundland, Ruth. But it's always like this in early July. I always tell visitors, don't come till after July fifteenth if you want any chance of good weather. Try my partridgeberry muffins, Ruth. Last year's berries, but they're just fine frozen."

"What's a partridgeberry?" I asked dubiously, turning the muffin around and around. It was speckled with reddish berries.

"Ha ha ha—*oomph*," choked Ruby, whose mouth was full of scrambled eggs. When she could talk, she gave a hoot. "You look so funny, Ruth. I can't believe you don't know what a partridgeberry is."

"Leave her be, Ruby," said Aunt Doll. "They don't have partridgeberries in Ontario. It's something like a cranberry," she said to me. "Except smaller and more sour."

"Oh," I said, still eyeing the muffin uncertainly.

"Put some butter on it and give it a try," said Aunt Doll.

I did. Ruby kept on laughing as she scarfed down her eggs. The muffin was delicious, with a sharp little squirt of flavor from the partridgeberries.

"How come Meg never told Ruth's father anything about her family?" asked Ruby, jumping right into the subject. "She doesn't know anything about us. She didn't know her mom had a twin sister, or a brother, and she didn't know that their mother died when they were kids, and she doesn't know what a partridgeberry is—"

I poked her in the arm. "Come on, leave the partridgeberries out of it."

"But it's all part of it," insisted Ruby. "She doesn't know anything about Newfoundland, and she's grown up in Ontario like she has no family out here. How come?"

Aunt Doll shook her head and sighed. "I don't know. It was all very mysterious. I've had my theories over the years, but I've never found out for sure. Meg said she wanted to make a life there, and for the first couple of years, she said the baby was too small to travel and her husband was too busy, but those were just excuses. I knew that. But I couldn't force her to come home, and I couldn't get her to tell me what was really going on. And Molly was no better. Those two were always thick as thieves, and if they wanted to keep a secret, you had no hope of wringing it out of them. They were like that as children and just the same when they were grown."

She stood up. "Now go away and play. I want to do my numbers." She plopped herself down in a big stuffed chair by the window and pulled a pink newspaper out of the magazine rack.

"What numbers?" I asked, curious.

Aunt Doll settled her glasses on her nose and opened the newspaper. "My stocks. I follow the market. I have quite a few investments, and I like to keep up. I get the papers from London and New York."

"Oh," I said. It didn't seem to fit, Aunt Doll and the stock market.

She laughed at my expression. "And you thought I was just a pretty face! If you'd been listening instead of sleeping in the car the other day when I was telling you the story of my life, you would have heard all about my career in St. John's."

"She worked for a hotshot lawyer," said Ruby, tipping her chair back on two legs. "She had the best clothes, didn't you, Aunt Doll?"

"I did. I still have some of them up in your closet. It was the 1950s and I had big skirts, fancy suits, little sweaters . . ." She sighed. "And I learned everything there was to know about the stock market from Mr. Pigeon, who was the sharpest lawyer in St. John's. And a businessman. He had investments all over the world . . ." Her voice trailed away and she had a faraway look in her eye.

"She was in love with him," sang out Ruby, and then her chair tipped over backward and she fell in a heap.

"How many times have I told you not to do that?" said Aunt Doll. "And I wasn't in love with him, you wretched child. I admired him. He taught me a lot. I knew almost as much as he did by the time I left. I had big plans." She sighed again.

"But you came back here to look after Meg and Molly, right? After their mother died?"

Aunt Doll nodded. "Yes, after my poor sister Daphne died. It was so sudden. The children were orphans, because Bob had died when they were little, and then Daphne—they said it was a stroke, but she was only thirty-one and never sick a day in her life. So my father was here on his own with the two girls and Jack, who was fourteen . . . I had to come back. They all needed looking after. My other sisters and brothers had families of their own, off to St. John's or Ontario. So I came. There was no one else."

"That must have been hard," I said. "To leave St. John's, and your job and your life there."

Aunt Doll gave a sniff. "I didn't have time to miss anything. Jack was no trouble, but those two girls were a handful, and my father wasn't much better. Couldn't even cook an egg. But I never had children of my own, so in a way it was a blessing for me to have my sister's girls to bring up. Poor Daphne," she said with a shake of her head. She gave the newspaper a shake. "Now go on with you! Find something to do and leave me in peace."

I followed Ruby out of the room. She was hopping on one foot. She hopped across the hall, opened the door to the living room, and hopped through. I hadn't even been in there yet.

"Poor Aunt Doll," I said, going in after Ruby. "She must have really missed her sister."

"Yup," said Ruby, hopping over to a large stuffed sofa covered in big pink-and-green flowers and plopping down on it. "Bad enough to lose a sister, but on top of that they were twins. That must have made it worse."

CHAPTER TWENTY-ONE

THE PHOTOGRAPH

"Twins?" I said, stopped in my tracks. "Aunt Doll and Daphne were twins?"

Ruby nodded. "They weren't identical, like Meg and Molly. Daphne was blonde, like the Finns, and Aunt Doll was dark, like the Duggans. But they were really close. Aunt Doll told me once it broke her heart in two when Daphne died."

I walked across to join her on the sofa.

"There sure are a lot of twins in our family," I said, looking around the room. It was big, with windows on two sides and floor-length curtains of the same flowery material as the sofa. There were two chairs to match the sofa, a rocking chair, a piano, two bookcases, and a round table in front of the window facing the road. A woodstove sat in the middle of the wall at the far end, with a doorway to one side.

"Yes. Only girls though. And it's usually been the Finn twins, blonde hair and blue eyes. Aunt Doll is the only one that didn't fit."

"I like this room," I said, getting up and walking over to the bookcase. "It's pretty. Old-fashioned, but pretty."

"I do too," said Ruby, coming and looking over my shoulder at the books. "Aunt Doll hardly ever comes in here. She spends all her time in the kitchen. She says her mother decorated this room to look like an English country house, and people in Buckle used to make fun of them, because I guess her mother was a bit of a snob. She was another twin. And she died young too. And her sister."

"What?" I said, turning to Ruby. "What's with all these twins dying young? Didn't any of them live to be old ladies?"

Ruby shrugged her shoulders. "Well, Aunt Doll's pretty old. At least fifty. But she's not a Finn, like the rest of them were. I guess a lot of them did die . . ." Her voice trailed off as she looked at me.

I counted on my fingers. "Our mothers. Their mother. Their grandmother and great-aunt. All twins. All died young."

"People died younger in the old days," said Ruby. "They didn't have good medical care back then."

"Aunt Doll said her sister died of a stroke. Good medical care wouldn't help that. And our mothers died suddenly too."

"I never thought of it before," said Ruby, frowning. "It was all a long time ago."

"We should ask Eldred about it," I said, and pulled out a book with a familiar title. "Did you ever read this, Ruby?"

"What is it?" said Ruby, bending over it.

"*The Princess and the Goblin*," I said. "It's a really good fairy tale."

"I thought you didn't like fairy tales," said Ruby, pulling the book out of my hands to look at it.

I made a face. "I don't believe in them. But that doesn't mean I don't like them."

Ruby laughed. "You're a fake, Ruth Windsor. I bet you're probably just as big a believer as I am in ghosts and fairies. You just pretend to be all scientific and reasonable about everything. Hey, look! This was your mother's book." She put her finger on the signature on the flyleaf.

I took the book back. *Meg Duggan* was written in neat schoolgirl handwriting along the top.

"Wow," I breathed, taking the book back to the couch and sitting down with it. I turned the pages slowly. They were soft and worn, as if the book had been read many times. "My mother must have loved this book as much as I do. I've never . . . never held anything that was hers before," I said in a shaky voice. I could feel tears pricking behind my eyes.

Ruby came and sat close beside me, laying her hand on my arm. I could feel the warmth from her body. "You were meant to find that book, Ruth. I think it was waiting for you. I've never picked it up, and I've been through a lot of these books. Some of them have my mother's name in them too."

I turned another page. There was a photograph there, almost as if it were used as a bookmark. I picked it up.

It was old and faded, a black-and-white picture of a big house. Ruby peered at it.

"Hey!" she said. "That's this house! It's taken right outside here." She pointed at the windows on the first floor. "Those are the living-room windows." Then she pointed at the ones above. "And those are the bedrooms. That's our room," she said, pointing to the one on the right. "And that's the boys' room, where we were this morning," she said, pointing to the one on the left.

"What's that one?" I said, pointing to a small round window in the middle. It almost looked like a porthole.

Ruby leaned in closer. "Gee, I don't know. I've never seen that before." Then she turned to me, her eyes big.

"The window!" we both said at the same time. I felt a shiver go up my back.

"What the ghost said," breathed Ruby. "Come on!"

And she tore out of the room.

CHAPTER TWENTY-TWO

MEASURING

Ruby was in the hall stuffing her feet into rubber boots and hauling on a jacket. I grabbed the coat I'd been wearing the day before. There was another pair of rubber boots about my size so I slipped my feet into them and followed Ruby outside.

I gasped as the icy rain and wind hit me in the face. It was driving in from the ocean and felt more like winter than summer. Ruby was disappearing around the corner of the house. Once I got behind the shelter of the house the wind was cut, but there were still sheets of rain. I peered up at the house, but I was too close to see it properly.

Ruby grabbed my arm and pulled me across the lawn, to the edge of the property where an old rail fence separated the neatly cut lawn from a meadow.

We looked back at the house. It looked more or less the same as it had in the photograph, with two windows on the first floor and two on the second. But there was no round window in the middle.

The wind was stronger here, away from the house, and it cut through my jacket like a knife. I started to shiver.

Ruby walked slowly toward the house, staring at it. I looked for any signs of a boarded-up window, but the clapboard went straight across. Ruby stood still for a moment, frowning. Then she said, "Tape measure," and headed toward the barn.

The barn was dark and full of shadows, with the patter of the rain loud on the roof. Ruby didn't seem to need a light to find what she was looking for. She picked something up and came back to where I was standing, blinking in the doorway.

"Tape measure," she said again. "We need to measure those rooms. That window must be behind one of the walls."

We clattered in the back door and past the kitchen, where Aunt Doll didn't even look up from behind the pink newspaper. We dumped our jackets and boots in the front hall, then headed up the stairs, along the hall and down the passage to our room. Ruby went into the boys' room and looked carefully along the outside wall. It was smooth, with just the one rectangular window. Then we went into our room and examined the wall in there, but there was only the one window on that wall too:

a rectangular one that matched the window in the b

There was no sign of the little round window in the ph

"Right," said Ruby. "Let's measure the hall first."

My job was to hold the end of the measuring tape w
paced out the length of the hall. She stopped at the w
the far end.

"Thirty-two feet," she called out. "Let go."

I did and the tape zipped along the hall and snap
into its container. Ruby grinned.

"Pretty cool, huh? I helped Eldred build a new chic
last summer. This tape is his pride and joy." She duc
the boys' room.

I held the tape again, this time in the corner of t
behind the door, while she walked slowly toward the c
the opposite wall.

"Twelve," she said, and snapped the tape back.

In our room I stood in front of the closet and she hau
tape up over her bed to the other wall.

"Twelve," she said again, a slow smile lighting up he

"But that's only twenty-four," I said. "Where's the
eight feet?"

"Precisely, my dear Watson," she crowed. "Let's me
the depth of the closet. From the inside."

This proved more difficult. I had to hold the end of th
on our side of the closet while she pushed through the
of clothes.

Her voice from the other side was muffled, but triumphant. "Eight! Come on!"

I scrambled through and she gave me the end to hold again while she first measured the length of the closet, then from the edge of the closet to the outer wall, climbing over one of the beds to get there.

Her eyes were shining. "The closet is only three feet long inside, but it's nine feet from there to the wall. So . . .?"

I stared at her. "So, there's space missing," I said. "I need a piece of paper."

We went back to the bedroom and I tore out a page from my sketchbook. We sat on my bed and I quickly drew a rough floor plan of the second floor.

"The closet is three by eight," I said, drawing it in. "So that leaves a space six by eight, behind—"

"Behind that wall," breathed Ruby, looking at the wall opposite our bed, where the big dresser stood.

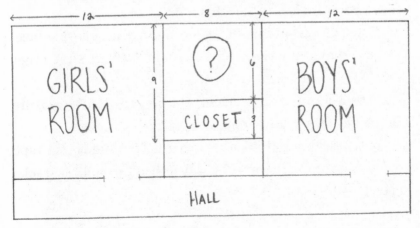

It was all very well to discover that there was a hidden room behind our bedroom wall, but there was no way to get into it. We managed to move the dresser out far enough to examine the wall behind it, but there was nothing. No secret doors. We moved the beds in the boys' room and went over that wall too, but to no avail.

The closet was a little more difficult to access. There were too many clothes in there, as well as a couple of cardboard boxes. We finally started hauling stuff out into the boys' room, closing the door first so Aunt Doll wouldn't notice if she happened to walk by. Soon the beds were piled with several long plastic clothes bags.

"What is all this stuff?" I asked.

"Aunt Doll's clothes from when she worked in St. John's," said Ruby. "She let me go through them last summer. Great outfits. She never threw anything out."

"And the boxes?" I said, hauling one out and putting it on the floor between the beds.

"Shoes," said Ruby. "Purses, hats."

"Oh," I said wistfully, laying my hand on the top of the box.

"Don't even think about it," said Ruby. "We've got to find our way into this room."

She came up with a flashlight, also from the barn, and once the closet was empty we ran its beam along the walls, ceiling and floor. There were narrow fitted boards halfway up the walls, like we had in our bathroom back home. Wainscoting, that's what Gwen told me it was called. We went over it all and there was no door.

Ruby sat back on her heels, frowning. "It's got to be here somewhere. It just doesn't make sense."

"Unless whoever boarded up the room didn't want anyone to get in. Otherwise, why hide it?"

"Ruby! Ruth!" called Aunt Doll.

We jumped. Ruby scrambled to her feet and slipped out into the hall.

"Yes?" she called out.

"It's stopped raining. I need you to do an errand for me."

"We'll be right there," hollered Ruby.

"It's okay," she said in a lower voice to me. "She hardly ever comes to this side of the house. We'll just shut the door and look again later."

CHAPTER TWENTY-THREE

THE WITCH

"But I just saw her yesterday!" wailed Ruby. "I don't want to see her again!"

"She called and told me she wants her tin back," said Aunt Doll, tucking some muffins into a cookie tin that was covered with painted red cherries. "She sent me over some date squares last week and now she wants it back. And you never send back an empty tin, Ruth," she said, smiling at me. "That's considered very bad manners. Of course," she said, turning back to Ruby, "what she really wants is to get a good look at Ruth."

"So why do I have to go if Ruth's the one she wants to see?"

"You know very well," said Aunt Doll, closing the lid with a snap. "Ruth doesn't know the house, and anyway, your Nan will never let on that she's just plain curious about Ruthie. Take this and stop your complaining."

Ruby snatched the tin from Aunt Doll and headed to the front door.

"Boots!" called Aunt Doll. "The grass is soaking wet."

We booted up and took along our rain jackets, because even though the rain had stopped for the moment, the clouds still hung heavy and dark over the far shore of the bay. Ruby stormed out the door and I scrambled to keep up.

"It's not a big deal," I said. "We don't have to stay long."

"It's the principle of the thing," said Ruby, kicking along the gravel road. "Usually all I have to do is visit once a week, and this is twice in two days. She gives me the creeps. You'll see," she continued darkly. "She's a witch."

I half-walked, half-trotted beside Ruby, trying to look in every direction at once. This was the first time I'd come this way and there was lots to see. The road curved along the shore, with a rocky drop of about fifteen feet to the water. It was a rough gravel road, with plenty of potholes filled with water from the rain. Ruby began a kind of a skipping hop, leaping over the potholes (and sometimes splashing down into the edge of one), with me trying to follow suit.

There were seagulls calling and swooping down over the water. The sides of the road were speckled with wildflowers:

the tiny white stars of three-toothed cinquefoil, the purplish brushes of red clover, and the slightly fuzzy flowers of what I now knew was Labrador tea. A few spruce trees that were smaller than me struggled to grow against the wind from the ocean. To our left was a meadow that rose gently up to a slope about a hundred yards away. On the right, I could see a rocky beach and a cement wharf a bit farther along that stretched about thirty feet out into the bay, with a few boats tied up on either side.

We walked and hopped for about ten minutes till we got to the other houses. There were six or seven of them clustered around another road that ran up the hill toward the highway. Past the crossroads were other houses along the cliff above the beach, and more along the road curving away from the far side of the bay. Ruby led me along to a dark-brown, two-story house that stood glowering over the far end of the beach. It had a dark-red door with a big knocker in the shape of a lion's head.

Ruby picked it up and rapped on the door three times, making a face as she did so.

"Everyone just walks in and out of each other's back doors," she said. "But Nan insists we knock at the front door. Like we were in town . . ." She broke off as the door creaked open.

It was very dark in the hall beyond the door. All I could see were two eyes glittering in a pale face that seemed suspended in the darkness. As the door opened farther, a figure seemed to coalesce from shadows: a tall woman all dressed in black with a white face and dark eyes that drilled into mine. A delicious smell of fresh baking wafted out of the house.

"Hi, Nan," said Ruby, bouncing through the doorway and breaking the spell. I realized I'd been holding my breath.

The woman's eyebrows rose slightly in disapproval as she looked down her nose at Ruby.

"Aren't you going to introduce me to your . . . cousin?" she said in a dry, creaking voice that sounded like it wasn't used very often.

Ruby turned.

"Ruth, this is my Nan, Mrs. Peddle," said Ruby, winking at me.

I stuck out my hand and it was grasped tightly by a cold, bony hand.

"How do you do?" I said politely.

The witch (yes, she was definitely a witch!) hung on tight to my hand and gazed deep into my eyes. I wanted to pull away but I didn't want to be rude. It felt like she was looking right inside to the back of my head where I kept all my secrets.

"As I thought," she murmured, finally letting go of my hand and standing back to usher me into the house. "Just as I thought. *Humph*."

When she closed the door, the hall was completely engulfed in darkness again, and I stumbled along, following Ruby's voice.

"I'll just bring these into the kitchen, Nan," she called, and a door opened, letting a shaft of light into the hall.

I headed toward the light as fast as I could go, not liking the idea of the witch at my heels.

The kitchen was very old-fashioned, with a big wood-burning stove with a steaming kettle on it against the far wall, a set of ancient yellow-and-brown cupboards, and a scrubbed wooden table and stiff chairs. A smallish window behind the sink looked out over the water and the back door was firmly bolted.

Ruby plopped the tin on the table. "Aunt Doll sent you some muffins," she said.

The witch sniffed. "Now what did she do that for? What am I going to do with a tin full of muffins on my baking day?"

She bent over, using a towel to take a hot tray of gingerbread men out of the oven. She laid them on the counter and gave me a sly glance.

My breath had deserted me again. She reminded me so much of the witch in "Hansel and Gretel." And why was she cooking . . . gingerbread men?

"I thought you and Ruby would like these," she said, as if she had read my mind. "George was always partial to them when he was a boy. Children always like my gingerbread."

I peered over the cookies: they had raisin eyes and chocolate-chip buttons.

"Yummy," said Ruby, reaching for them.

"Too hot!" said the witch, slapping at her hand. "Sit down and have a glass of milk. And let me take a look at you two."

The kitchen chairs were as uncomfortable as they looked. The witch gave us each a glass of frothy milk and filled a plate with the still-warm gingerbread men.

"There now," she said, settling into a chair. "Eat up."

She was smiling a crooked little smile and looking from Ruby to me and then back again. She actually had a rather long nose and a sharp, well-defined chin, just like a witch. I shuddered. But the gingerbread man was delicious. Gingery, sweet and crisp. I wondered idly if it might be enchanted and put some kind of spell on us, then I shook my head to chase the fancy away. She laughed, watching me as though she knew exactly what I was thinking.

"Well, look at you two," she said with another laugh, which was dangerously close to a cackle. "A pair of true Finns, the two of you. Alike as two peas in a pod. Just like your mothers. You could be twins."

CHAPTER TWENTY-FOUR

WYNKEN, BLYNKEN AND NOD

"T wins," repeated the witch. "So many twins in your family. Strange." Her eyes narrowed and her lips twitched in the ghost of a wicked grin.

Ruby glugged down the last of her milk and glared at her grandmother. "So what's wrong with twins?"

"It's unnatural," replied the old woman. "Uncanny. Nobody trusts a twin."

Ruby started to sputter, but I put my hand on her arm to quiet her.

"Why not?" I asked. "Why can't you trust a twin?"

"Because they're the devil's work," hissed the witch. "It's

always the two of them against everyone else. I told George," she said, her mouth tightening into a sneer. "I told him, time and time again, that those two girls were playing tricks on him, toying with him, but he wouldn't listen. Oh no. He was in their thrall. He went through every day with nothing but them on his mind, and I knew no good would come of it."

"You're talking about our mothers," said Ruby angrily, rubbing her sleeve across her mouth, which was smeared with milk and gingerbread crumbs. "You've got no right—"

"I've got every right," spat Mrs. Peddle. "They stole my boy from me and laughed at him behind his back and had him turned every which way till he didn't know if he was coming or going. The day they left to go to the mainland was the best day of my life. I thought they were gone for good and George was finally free."

Ruby jumped to her feet. Her face was red and her eyes were brimming with tears.

"I won't sit here and listen to this again," she said. "You hated my mother, and you were glad when she died. Every time I come here, all you can talk about is how awful she was, and how much I look like her, and you have no right! My father loved my mother; she was a good person, he told me so, and—"

A sob bubbled up and caught her words in her throat. She stumbled toward the door. "Come on, Ruth, let's get out of here."

I stood up to follow her. A slow smile of satisfaction spread over the old woman's face as she looked into my eyes.

"You're not afraid of the truth, now are you, me duckie? I can see that. And I know who you are. You're the one who got it. I see it in your eyes. Just like the other one. The one who stayed away. Come back by yourself sometime, without Ruby, and I'll tell you what you need to know about your mother. And about everything else. Some of it you'll want to hear—" Her smile widened. "And some of it you won't."

Her words sent chills up and down my spine, yet there was something so compelling about her eyes. I felt like she looked deep into me and understood me in some way that no one ever had. That she knew things about me that I hadn't discovered yet.

And despite her cruelty to Ruby, and the nasty things she said about our mothers, I was surprised to find that there was something that I liked about this fierce old lady in her big, empty house. Maybe it was the spark of mischief in her eyes. Or the feeling that I knew her just as well as she seemed to know me.

I left her smiling to herself in her kitchen and headed out the front door. The bright light blinded me for a minute. At first, I didn't see Ruby. The road back the way we had come was empty. But when I turned, I saw her, running in the opposite direction, her green jacket bobbing against the gray road. She was already a hundred yards away, following the road around the harbor, up the hill.

I set off after her. It didn't take me long to run out of breath. Half-running, half-walking, I made my way along the road.

There were only a couple more houses, then some sheds by the water, and then nothing. Just the road and the meadows, and an ever-increasing view of Buckle Bay spreading out to my right. The road changed from gravel to dirt, from dirt to grass, and then Ruby ducked to the left and out of sight.

When I got to where she left the road, I could see that there was a path winding off to the left, up and down over the uneven ground. I followed it for about ten minutes. It ended at a cemetery, bordered by trees. I caught a glimpse of Ruby's green jacket and there she was, hunched beside a gravestone.

I walked through the gate and approached her slowly. The cemetery was a mix of old and newer stones. Some of the older ones were dark gray, with the words barely legible. A few were broken off halfway, or leaning over at an impossible angle. And then there was one or two old stones made from bright white marble, and these shone out like beacons in the shadows. The grass wasn't very high, and it was studded with orange hawkweed, dark-purple columbine and buttercups.

Ruby half-sat, half-knelt before a light-gray granite stone. Her face was hidden, but I could see her shoulders shaking. She was crying.

I didn't know what to do. I wasn't used to people crying. Dad never cried. When I cried I did it in my room, under the covers, or in the bathroom at school, where no one could see me.

I stood there watching her for a moment and then without thinking about it, I knelt down beside her and laid my hand

on her back. She turned to look at me, her face red, eyes swollen.

"Ruth," she said in a ragged voice. "Ruth, she's so mean."

"Yes, she is," I said softly. I kept my hand on her back, patting her gently while she cried some more. The wind had died down—the graveyard was in a sheltered spot, in a kind of dip between two hills. The sun was struggling to come out.

Gradually, Ruby grew quieter, and finally stopped crying. She rummaged in her pocket and came up with a grimy handkerchief. She pulled away from me, blew her nose and then gave one last, shuddering sigh.

"Sorry," she said, a little embarrassed. "I just got so mad. And it's the same every time I see her. She never stops criticizing Mom. And me. And Aunt Doll. And Dad's no use. He just tells me I have to visit her, and she's an old lady and I should be polite. I hate that."

She got up and started striding around.

"You don't know, Ruth, you just don't know what it's like for me. It's awful. I hate living with Wynken, Blynken and Nod all year and only coming out here in the summer. Wendy just puts up with me; I know she doesn't want me there. And Dad just wants to keep the peace, so he usually goes along with her and doesn't stick up for me. And then when I get out here, where I want to be, where I belong, I have to visit that horrible old witch and hear her tell me what a wicked girl my mother was and how she never should have married Dad."

She started kicking at the grass. "I hate her!" Kick. "I wish she'd die." Kick. "I wish they'd all die! Wendy." Kick. "Wynken." Kick. "Blynken." Kick. "And Nod." Kick. "Ow!"

She had kicked a broken old gravestone instead of the grass.

I couldn't hold it in any longer and a big laugh came sputtering out.

"What are you laughing at?" She looked so outraged, holding her sore foot and glaring at me, that I laughed some more, and then she started to smile just a little.

I caught my breath and managed to speak. "I'm sorry, Ruby, I shouldn't have laughed, but you looked so funny hopping around. And you gotta tell me," I said, laughter still bubbling up. "You gotta tell me, who on earth are Wynken, Blynken and Nod?"

CHAPTER TWENTY-FIVE

BUCKLE GRAVEYARD

R uby grinned and suddenly she looked like her usual, happy self again. "Oh. I never told you. That's what I call my little brothers. They're Wayne, Brian and Ned, but it drives them crazy when I call them Wynken, Blynken and Nod."

"Why?" I asked.

She sat down beside me on the grass. "It started a while ago. Wendy had this book she would read to them when Ned was a baby, about Wynken, Blynken and Nod, these three little fishermen who went to sea in a shoe, and she started calling them that, and it was so cutesy and they were so pleased with themselves that . . . uh . . . well, I started calling them that too, but told them they were little babies and made fun of them, and . . . and . . . well, it started to make them really mad. Every time I called them Wynken or Blynken or Nod, they'd start hollering and screaming at me." She grinned again, remembering.

"Oh," I said.

Ruby looked at me. "Okay, so I was mean to them. Don't say it. I know I was. Dad told me, and Wendy told me, again and again, but what would you do, Ruth? What would you do if you had to live in St. John's with these three little kids and listen to their mother reading to them every night, and you were just lying in your bed next door listening to their stories night after night, and you didn't have a mother to read to you, and your father was always away or busy, and when he was home, the boys were all over him and he never had time for you?"

She was getting all worked up again, and the tears weren't quite dried enough not to spill over again.

"It's okay, Ruby," I said. "I understand. I don't blame you."

She gave a big sigh. "Well, Dad and Wendy do. But those little rats suit their names. Every time Wayne and Brian do something bad and try to blame me for something, they stand there all innocent blinking their eyes, and Ned just agrees with everything, nodding his head up and down. He's only three so he just goes along with his brothers with everything."

She stood up quickly, like she couldn't bear to sit still for another minute, and started balancing along the top of a fallen gravestone, and then hopping from one to another, trying not to touch down on the grass.

I stood up and went over to look at the gravestone, the one she'd been crouching in front of. Then my breath caught in my throat and I just stared.

MARGARET ANN (DUGGAN) WINDSOR "MEG"

BORN SEPTEMBER 5, 1946

DIED DECEMBER 10, 1967

———

MOLLY SUSAN (DUGGAN) PEDDLE

BORN SEPTEMBER 5, 1946

DIED DECEMBER 10, 1967

———

LOVELY AND PLEASANT IN THEIR LIVES,

AND IN THEIR DEATH THEY WERE NOT DIVIDED

2 SAMUEL 1:23

Ruby hopped back and saw what I was staring at.

I opened my mouth, but no sound came out.

"Ruth," she said, grabbing my arm and giving me a little shake. "Ruth, are you okay? What is it?"

I kept shaking my head. It was the oddest feeling, having the words in my throat but not being able to make them come out.

Finally I managed a kind of croak. "My mom—my mom—"

Ruby glanced at the gravestone, then back at me, then the light dawned.

"You didn't know?" she whispered. "You didn't know she was buried here?"

I shook my head.

"Sit down," she said, hauling me down to the grass. "Take a deep breath."

I obeyed.

"And another," she said.

I continued to breathe, in and out.

"Your dad never told you?"

I shook my head.

"What's wrong with him?" she said. "He never told you anything about your mom, about her family, about Newfoundland, not even that her ashes were sent back here to bury?"

I tried my voice. It was shaky, but I had the connection now.

"He doesn't like to talk about it. It makes him sad, I think, so I stopped asking about her. A long time ago."

"It's not fair," said Ruby, pulling angrily at a tuft of grass. "You have a right to know about your own mother."

"Why is she here? I don't understand."

"Aunt Doll told me Meg and Molly both made wills before they went off to school, saying that no matter where they died, their ashes were to be sent back here and buried in the Buckle graveyard, side by side. Aunt Doll said they were worried about leaving Buckle, both of them, and thinking they might not ever come back. So then when Meg died, your dad sent the ashes back. And since Molly died the same day, they buried them together."

"Oh," I said, and stared at the gravestone. "It's so sad," I whispered. "Almost like they knew something was going to happen."

"I know," said Ruby. "I've always wondered about that. If they had some premonition. Or if Meg did, that is. She was the one with the Sight."

I stood up and started walking toward the back of the cemetery, pretending to look at the gravestones.

"Ruth?" called out Ruby. "What are you doing?"

I turned. "Nothing. Just—nothing."

She jumped up and came after me. "What's wrong? And don't say 'nothing.' We were in the middle of an important conversation, so why—Oh. I get it. You didn't like it when I mentioned the Sight."

"It's not that," I protested. "I'm interested in these old gravestones." I glanced at the one beside me. "Like this one." I bent over to read it.

"You are not!" said Ruby. "You just don't want to talk about it because you're scared. You do have the Sight, Ruth. You saw the ghost, twice, the sheep came to you, and Eldred told me that animals recognize people who have the Sight and you said animals always love you and—what?"

I just pointed at the stone.

FIONA MARY (DUGGAN) WHALEN

BORN JUNE 7, 1877

DIED JANUARY 1, 1910

———

FENELLA MARGARET (DUGGAN) BRENNAN

BORN JUNE 7, 1877

DIED JANUARY 1, 1910

IN THEIR DEATH THEY WERE NOT DIVIDED

"Isn't that cool?" said Ruby. "Those are the twins they found in the root cellar, the first Finns who were adopted by the Duggans. Our great-great-great-great-something grandmother and aunt."

"But they died so young," I said. "Just thirty-two. And on the same day, just like Meg and Molly."

"They did?" asked Ruby, squinting at the inscription. "I never noticed. I knew this was here, because Aunt Doll pointed it out to me once, but when I come here I always go to my mother's stone. Hmmm, 1910. Both of them." She frowned.

"Isn't that . . . isn't that quite a bit of a coincidence?" I said uncertainly.

"According to Eldred, there's no such thing as coincidence," said Ruby, going over to another gravestone, reading it quickly and then moving to another. "Everything happens for a reason."

"Well, scientifically," I began, quoting something my father always said, "coincidences are part of a random pattern of causality and—"

"Here, look!" cried Ruby, waving me over to a stone that stood a few yards away.

I went over and peered at it.

LUCY ALICE (WHALEN) DUNPHY

BORN OCTOBER 3, 1900

DIED MAY 10, 1935

———

LILY MARY (WHALEN) DUGGAN

BORN OCTOBER 3, 1900

DIED MAY 10, 1935

AND IN THEIR DEATH THEY WERE NOT DIVIDED

"They were thirty-four when they died," she said grimly. "That's—" She counted on her fingers. "Meg and Molly, Lily and Lucy, Fiona and Fenella—that's three sets of twins. All of them Finns, all of them dying young, all of them dying on the same day as their twin. That's not a coincidence. That's a curse."

CHAPTER TWENTY-SIX

THE CURSE

"A curse," I echoed. "But . . . but there's no such thing as a curse. Not really. It's just a superstition."

"Then you tell me," said Ruby, her eyes glinting. "You tell me why every set of twins in our family has died young, and always on the same day."

"It can't be every set of twins," I protested. "Just these three . . . wait a minute, wasn't Aunt Doll a twin? She didn't die on the same day as her sister. Where's Daphne's grave?"

It wasn't far away.

DAPHNE ELIZABETH DUGGAN
BORN APRIL 15, 1926
DIED MARCH 3,1958

"See?" I said to Ruby, who was frowning. "It doesn't hold up."

"Oh, it holds up all right," said Ruby. "Daphne was thirty-one when she died, so she died young too. Aunt Doll didn't die because she isn't a Finn."

"What do you mean?"

"Aunt Doll and Daphne weren't identical, like the others. Aunt Doll is dark and Daphne was blonde. I've seen photographs of her. Daphne was a Finn, but Aunt Doll isn't."

I shivered. The sun had disappeared again and a cruel little wind whispered in the trees at the edge of the cemetery. It sounded almost like a human voice, muttering and sighing. Ever since Ruby had brought up the subject of the curse, I'd felt this growing sense of dread, like a shadow was creeping up all around us, swallowing up the light and making it hard for me to breathe.

"No, Ruby. It doesn't hang together. It's not true. There's no such thing as curses and ghosts and fairies and all the rest of this crap you're trying to put over on me all the time. I don't believe in it. We live in 1978 and this a modern world where we understand why things happen. All those twins died because of some illness or some accident, and I'm not gonna listen to any more of your fairy tales. Nobody is cursed."

I stopped. I realized I was yelling. Ruby just stood there, looking at me, not saying a word. My hands were shaking.

"There's something else I need to show you," she said finally, and turned and started walking toward the darkest part of the graveyard, in the corner, under the trees.

I hesitated for a moment. I wanted to get out of there fast. Go back to Aunt Doll and get her to teach me about stocks and bonds and baking bread. Anything that was brightly lit and ordinary, with no shadows.

"Come on," called Ruby.

I went.

She was standing beside another old stone, this one larger than a regular gravestone. It had a lot of writing on it.

It began, "In memory of the thirty inhabitants of Slippers Cove, who lost their lives in the hurricane of 1879, when their houses were swept into the sea." Then listed all the people who had lived and died there, including "Caitlin Bridget (Keegan) Parsons" and "Catriona Irene (Keegan) Duggan, born 1850, dear mother of Fiona and Fenella."

"Twenty-nine," whispered Ruby, and I felt her warm hand slip into mine. "They were twenty-nine when they died, Ruth. On the same day."

The chill that went through me had nothing to do with the breeze. I felt like the world was tipping and everything that was sure and certain was slipping away, and I was sliding into something dark and cloying that was going to swallow me up. I could hear that voice again, murmuring in the wind. It sounded so human. I could almost, but not quite, make out the words.

"It can't be a curse," I said weakly. "I don't believe it."

Ruby gave my hand a tight squeeze. "Eldred will know," she said. "Let's go find him."

❋

We found Eldred in the chicken house with tiny black chicks running around his feet. He looked up with a grin.

"They're full of mischief today."

Ruby gave a little squeal of delight and ran forward, chasing one till she could corner it and pick it up. She held it gently, encased in her two hands like a little cage. Then she laughed.

"It tickles. Try it, Ruth. It feels so funny."

I started a little reluctantly after one of the chicks, but he was too fast for me. Ruby laughed, and Eldred leaned down and scooped it up, then placed it in my hands. I closed my fingers the way Ruby did.

It was like nothing I'd ever felt before. I could feel its little heart beating steadily and wings fluttering against my fingers. I felt like I held a little ball of light.

Ruby laughed again, watching my face. "Isn't it the best feeling? Newborn chicks," she said, and then placed her little captive down carefully on the straw. I followed suit.

Eldred murmured something to the hens, and they clucked around him as he produced some seed and filled their feeders. When he had done, he looked up at Ruby.

"You didn't just come here to see the chicks, now, did you? What do you want from me?"

Ruby laughed and grabbed his arm, swinging on it a bit.

"A story," she said. "I always want a story, you know that, Eldred."

"That you do," he responded. "Let's go into the barn where we can sit down."

Once we were settled in the barn, Ruby and Eldred on their old chairs and me on the crate I'd sat on before, Eldred said, "Right. Out with it, Ruby. What's on your mind?"

Ruby glanced at me, a glint of mischief in her eyes.

"Tell us about the curse, Eldred. The curse on the twins."

A look of alarm passed over his face. He tried to hide it by looking away and saying slowly, "Now what curse would that be?"

"You know," said Ruby. "You must know. We've just been up to the cemetery and we saw all the graves. Every set of twins since the ones that died in the flood, every single set of twins has died young. And both of them on the same day."

"Except Aunt Doll," I put in firmly. "Her twin died and she

didn't. I think it's all just coincidence, or some health issue all these twins had, some weakness . . ." I stopped. Eldred was looking at me like he could see right through me and it was no use pretending.

"I wish that was true, Ruth," he said. "I really do. It's not something we ever talk about, and your Aunt Doll would have me for dinner if she knew I was talking to you about it. But . . . you have a right to know, just like your mothers before you."

"I knew it!" breathed Ruby. "There *is* a curse."

"Yes," said Eldred. "And as far as I know, it goes back even further than those two little Finns in the root cellar. Right back to Ireland, or so the story goes."

The shadows in the barn seemed to deepen around me, and I felt that smothering feeling I'd had in the cemetery. I closed my eyes, and suddenly I was in the shipwreck dream for just an instant, the storm raging, the decks tilting, my mother calling my name, "Moira! Moira!" There were people screaming all around me, or was it the wind? It sounded like the wind in the cemetery, a wind with a human voice.

Suddenly I understood the words: "By water! By water! By water!"

I opened my eyes and the barn was gone. I was on the ship, drenched with rain, and my mother was reaching for my hand.

"Ruth!" called a sharp voice, and the ship blinked away, and I was back in the barn, lying on the ground, with Ruby looking frightened above me, and Eldred just behind her.

I started to sit up, but my head was spinning. A gentle hand stroked my hair. For a moment I thought it was my mother, but when I could focus, I saw that it was Ruby.

"Just lie still," she said.

Eldred's face swam into view. "You'll be okay in a minute, Ruth. Ruby, get her some water."

Ruby ran off. I lay on the floor, with the sweet smell of dried hay around me, and Eldred sitting quietly a little way off.

Ruby was soon back with the water and she helped me sit up a bit so I could drink it. It tasted so delicious, like the best drink I'd ever had. Eldred and Ruby just sat there, watching me as I took little sips and slowly came back to myself.

"What happened to me?" I asked, looking at Eldred.

"You tell me," he said.

I hesitated. "I felt it before, in the cemetery, when Ruby started talking about the curse. Like I couldn't breathe, and everything was closing in on me, and there was a voice muttering in the wind. Only this time, when I closed my eyes . . ." I faltered.

Ruby reached for my hand and gave it a squeeze.

"It's okay, Ruth," she said softly. "You can tell us."

"My dream . . . the one I always have," I said. "The one about my mother and the shipwreck, where she saves me, only this time I wasn't asleep, and I couldn't reach her, and the voice in the wind was screaming, 'By water, by water!' over and over again. And my mother was calling my name, only it wasn't my name, but it was my name, I don't know . . ."

"What name was it, Ruth?" asked Eldred.

"Moira. She called me Moira. And the wind was scream-ing. And then when I opened my eyes, I was still in the dream. And . . . this time I was going to die, in the shipwreck . . ." I was starting to cry.

Ruby put her arms around me and hugged me hard. "You're not going to die," she said. She was warm and solid and real.

"No," said Eldred. "You're not. It's the Sight, Ruth. You have the Sight. You're a true Finn. It was the past you were seeing, back when the curse was new."

CHAPTER TWENTY-SEVEN

DUSTING

"But I don't believe in the Sight," I said. I didn't sound convincing. Not even to myself.

"It doesn't really matter if you believe in it or not," said Eldred. "You've got it. Every generation, one of the Finns has the Sight. Your mother, Meg, had it. And her mother, Daphne, your grandmother, she had it too. And her mother, Lily, your great-grandmother. And her mother, Fiona, your great-great-grandmother, the one who was found with her sister in the root cellar, she had it too. Before that . . ." he went on, a faraway look in his eye. "Before that I don't know. But I can guarantee that there was one in each generation. That's how it works."

I gave it one more try. "But it's not scientific. It's super-stition. There's no such—"

"No, it's not scientific," said Eldred. "Not as far as they've discovered so far. But it's real just the same."

"You saw the ghost," said Ruby. "Twice. And now you've had a vision. Right, Eldred?"

"What ghost?" he asked, frowning.

"Her mother," said Ruby. "In our room."

He looked at me. I nodded my head.

"I thought maybe I was dreaming . . ." I said. "But it didn't feel like a dream."

"Listen to me, Ruth," he said, leaning forward and fixing me with his strange green eyes. "The Sight is a gift. It's not always comfortable. Well, maybe never comfortable. But it's a gift nonetheless and there's no use denying it. You need to learn how to use it, and it will help you, and help the people around you. If you keep trying to deny it, you'll just make your-self sick and scared and you'll only be half what you could be."

"But I'm scared *now*," I whispered.

"You need some protection," he said.

"Ruby! Ruth!" Aunt Doll's voice wavered on the sound of the wind. "Lunch!"

"Better go," said Eldred. "Ruby, tell her about the candle. And mind," he said, with a faint smile, "not a word about any of this to Doll or we'll all be sorry." Then he winked at me.

Aunt Doll kept us busy most of the afternoon helping her with cleaning, baking and preparing the vegetables for supper.

"By the time you go back to Ontario, you'll know how to run a house yourself," she promised me. "Everyone helps out here, don't they, Ruby?" Ruby groaned, and went back to sweeping the kitchen floor.

"Now I want you to turn out your room," said Aunt Doll when Ruby finished sweeping. "Do a good dusting and sweep under the beds and then you can have some free time before supper."

Ruby rolled her eyes, grabbed a couple of rags and headed upstairs with the broom. I followed.

First we went quietly into the boys' room next door through the secret passage and returned all the clothes bags that we'd left on the beds back to the closet. Ruby was right: Aunt Doll hadn't been up there all day, or we would have heard about leaving such a mess.

Then we did as Aunt Doll had asked. I swept under the beds, making sure the candle in its holder was pushed way back against the wall under my bed. Ruby dusted around the dresser and the bedside table.

"What's this for?" she said, picking up my sketchbook and Newfoundland wildflowers book.

"Oh, just a little project my dad asked me to do while I'm here," I answered. "He thought it would be fun for me to do

some sketches and identification of Newfoundland wildflowers . . .”

Ruby opened up the sketchbook.

“Doesn’t look like wildflowers to me,” she said, looking at
the drawing I’d made of the family tree. She flipped over the
page and looked at the one I’d made starting with Ireland and
the shipwreck, then went back to the first page.

“Hey, this isn’t bad,” she said, sitting down on my bed to
look at it more closely. “But you’ve left a few people out.”

I went over and sat down beside her.

“I just put in all the people I could remember that Aunt Doll
mentioned.”

“We can add more now,” said Ruby, picking up my pencil
and knotting her eyebrows for a moment.

“My brothers, for a start,” she said, “and Wendy.” She joined
a box to her dad’s and put Wendy’s name in it, then added three
little boxes coming out from theirs and wrote “Wynken,
Blynken and Nod,” inside them, with a little snort of laughter.

“I guess if you add Wendy, I’ll have to add Awful Gwen,” I
said, taking the pencil from her and adding a box joined up to
my dad’s for Gwen.

“And Aunt Doll has two other sisters, besides Daphne, and
three brothers,” said Ruby, taking the pencil back and adding
them to the diagram. “Effie, Jane, Ernie, Tom and Samuel,” she
murmured. “But there’s not room for all their names.”

“You remember them all?” I asked.

She nodded. "Aunt Doll is always talking about them, telling stories about when they were little. And I've met them. Ernie and Jane live in St. John's, but the others are on the mainland. They all came back for the Buckle Come Home Year two summers ago." She peered at the sketchbook again. "Daphne's husband's name was Bob Duggan." She wrote that in. "Now who else can we add?"

"Daphne and Doll's mother and father," I said, taking the pencil back. "Lily and—"

"Clarence," supplied Ruby.

"And Lily's twin sister, Lucy was it?"

"Yup," said Ruby. "And we should put in my Uncle Jack, Meg and Molly's brother."

I made a box for him, and then added Fiona and Fenella to the first page and joined Lucy's and Lily's boxes to Fiona, their mother.

"What were the names of the twins that died in the flood?" I asked. "The ones on the tombstone?"

Ruby thought a minute. "Caitlin and Catriona. Catriona was a Duggan, so she was the one who married Boyd Duggan and she was Fenella and Fiona's mother."

I wrote them down under Fenella and Fiona, joining Catriona's. Then I sat back and looked at it for a moment.

"Oh, one more thing," I said, and then darkened all the borders around the boxes who were twins and drew a little *T* above them. "Twins."

We sat there, looking at it.

"Five sets of twins," said Ruby softly. "Four of them died young. Plus Daphne."

I turned and looked at her.

"The curse," we both whispered together.

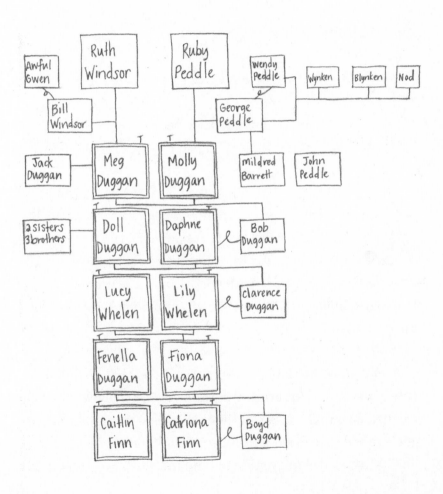

CHAPTER TWENTY-EIGHT

THE FLAME

Aunt Doll called us down to supper just after we finished the family tree, and we didn't get another chance to talk alone until we went up to bed. We got into our pajamas in the lamplight, and then Ruby got down on the floor and crawled under my bed.

"What—?"

I could hear her rummaging around and then she made a little "aha" of satisfaction and came back, the candle in the candleholder in hand. She lit the candle, blew out the lamp, and got into bed with me, holding the candle carefully.

"Eldred said to tell you about the candle. It's for protection, so you don't get all freaked out about the Sight and ghosts and stuff."

"Okay," I said, swallowing. The room suddenly seemed full of shadows.

"This is something Eldred showed me a long time ago, when I used to get scared about all the ghost stories he told me. It really works. Don't worry!" she said, grinning. I guess she could see how scared I was just by looking at me.

"Just look into the flame," she said.

I did so. It was a bright gold triangle, with a shadow of black at its base. It kept changing shape, just a little, first narrowing and then widening. Beside me I could hear Ruby breathing softly.

"Feel anything?" she whispered.

At first I didn't think I did. But the more I looked at it, the more I wanted to. The gentle movement of the flame was hypnotic. I blinked and looked at Ruby. "What's happening?"

"It's okay," she said, touching my arm. "Just keep looking at it."

I turned back to the candle flame. I felt my breath slowing down, and I felt sleepy.

"Now imagine," said Ruby. "Imagine you're inside that flame. It doesn't hurt. It's just warm, golden light all around you. Feel it from the top of your head to the tips of your toes."

It felt a little silly. But I tried. And soon my breath seemed to be going in and out in rhythm with the wavering flame, and a delicious feeling of warmth started to spread through me.

"Nothing can hurt you," said Ruby in a low voice. "You are the flame and the flame is you. You are filled with light, and you are protected."

My eyes started to close.

"Just go to sleep, Ruthie," said Ruby, and the last thing I remembered was the sound of a quick breath blowing out the candle.

❀

A long time later I woke up. The candle was lit again, but for some reason it was up in the air. I blinked. I could see Ruby with her head on the pillow beside me, fast asleep. The candle was hovering above us. Then I became aware, all at once, that someone was standing there, holding the candle. I heard a soft laugh, and the person moved the candle closer to their face, and I saw who it was.

The ghost. My mother, but as a teenager. Meg. Her long blonde hair gleamed in the candlelight. Her eyes were alight with mischief.

"Shhhh," she said, a finger to her lips, motioning toward Ruby. Then she beckoned me to follow her and moved slowly toward the closet.

I wasn't scared. I knew she was a ghost, but I wasn't scared. Maybe it was the golden flame she carried and how safe it made me feel just to see it, or maybe it was her conspiratorial grin.

I knew I wasn't dreaming, but nonetheless I felt like I was in some golden bubble with this girl who would become my mother, and nothing bad could happen.

I climbed carefully out of bed. Ruby murmured and stirred, but then was still. The floor was freezing on my bare feet.

The candle flickered ahead, and I could see the girl's long white nightgown, almost touching the floor, and her hair that reached down her back. She parted the hanging clothes and went into the middle of the closet. I was so close behind her I could have touched her, but I didn't want to. She felt more like light than substance, and I didn't want to see my hand pass through her.

She turned to the wainscoting and pushed something, then leaned over and pushed something at the bottom, then part of the wall wasn't there anymore and she bent over to go through. I didn't hesitate, but went through after her.

She turned, then, and looked at me. She was right in front of me. Her blue eyes were filling with tears, and she looked happy and sad at the same time. She opened her mouth to speak.

"Break it," she said softly. Then she kissed her fingertips and blew me a little kiss, her eyes shining. And then the candle went out.

I was alone. And completely in the dark.

CHAPTER TWENTY-NINE

THE DARK

"Break it"? What did she mean, "Break it"?

"Mom?" I whispered. "Meg?"

But there was no answer. She was gone.

The dark closed in around me. When I breathed in, I felt it pouring into me. Pressing down on me. Black. Thick. There was a bitter, burnt smell in the air.

I had to get out. I tried to calm the panic. All I had to do was find the door. I tried to focus on that one thought. Find the door.

I turned to feel my way back to the opening in the wall, and tripped over something on the floor. I bent down and groped around. My fingers closed on something hard, made of metal with a curved handle—the candleholder, without the candle. I picked it up so I wouldn't trip over it again in the dark, and took tiny steps till I touched the wall. It was solid. No doorway.

I put the candleholder on the floor and then felt along with both my hands till I hit another wall, at right angles to the first. I thought I must have missed the opening, so I went slowly back, each step tentative, but there was no opening. The dark pressed closer.

Then I hit another wall.

I stopped and took a deep, raggedy breath. There was no door. I couldn't get out.

I took another breath and squeezed my eyes shut. "You are in control," I said, trying to concentrate on my breathing. "You are in control."

But I wasn't. I was afraid to move, unsure of what might be in the room with me. Something else on the floor that I could trip over? Or something, something . . . the memory of the breathless, cloying feeling when they talked about the curse came back, and the horrible whispering voice on the wind, and I felt a scream starting deep inside . . .

And then suddenly I remembered the candle flame, and Ruby, warm and sleepy in the bed beside me, her voice rising and falling, the flame flickering gently, and I tried to see it. I tried to imagine it, golden and bright, filling me up, lighting up the room. And then I remembered my mother's eyes, blue and steady, looking at me with love.

My breathing slowed, and the urge to scream died away.

I had to be logical about this. I came in through a door, so I could get out through a door. I just had to find it. Yes, it was dark, but that was just the absence of light. Nothing bad was there. My mother wouldn't have brought me into a place where there was danger.

I knew the door had to be somewhere on that wall. I moved back the way I had come, my hands running slowly over the surface. This time I took time to try to understand what my hands were feeling.

I felt rough wood boards, each about ten inches wide, fitted closely together. I pushed in different places along the wall, but it was solid.

When the ghost had led me in, she'd pushed something at the top of the wainscoting in the closet, about the height of my waist, and then she'd leaned lower down, near the floor. Unfastening something?

Starting at the corner, I felt carefully along the board that was about the right height, trying to *see* it with my fingertips. Trying to find something that was different.

About halfway along, something snagged my finger. A sliver? I ran my fingers slowly by it. It felt like a narrow crack.

I moved my fingers straight down, but nothing felt different until just a few inches above the floor. Another crack, a little wider this time.

I tried to pry it open, using my fingernails, but it didn't budge.

I sat back on my heels and tried to think. When the ghost had led me in, the door seemed to disappear. It must have swung inside the room. So it didn't open into the closet, but into this room.

Maybe . . . maybe you could only get in from the closet. And once you were in, you couldn't get out.

The fear came again, and this time it hit me full on. I was trapped. I couldn't get out. I'd seen a movie once where a man had been holed up in the wall of a castle and left to die, and the image had haunted me ever since. Nobody could hear him, nobody could let him out. He died there, in a small, airless space, just like this one—

Suddenly feeling like I couldn't breathe, I took a shuddering breath. The air that came into my lungs was cold. Cold and stale. It had the faint, musty smell of a place that hadn't had any fresh air for a long, long time, overlaid with a lingering whiff of burned wood, like there had been a fire here a long time ago.

I had to get a hold of myself. I wasn't in a castle. Ruby lay asleep in the next room, a few feet away. If I yelled loud enough, I'd wake her up and she could come and get me out. But chances were I'd wake up Aunt Doll as well, and I didn't want that.

I had to figure out another way to get out that didn't involve loud noises. Maybe there was another opening into our room? I had to explore this space. This dark space.

I stood up. I followed the closet wall to the wall adjoining our bedroom and slowly started making my way along it, my left hand running along the wall and my right held out in front to detect if there were any obstacles. I shuffled my feet along the floor, hoping not to stub my toes on anything that lay in my way.

This wall had the same rough boards. Partway along my fingers dipped into nothing. A hole. About three fingers wide. A whisper of fresher air trickled in. I wiggled my fingers and felt something hard on the other side. The wall of our bedroom? I pushed and something gave way. There was a loud crash as something fell to the floor on the other side.

"Where's the fire?" said Ruby, and I could hear her jumping out of bed. "Ruth! What? Where are you?" Her voice had a frantic but sleepy edge, like she wasn't properly awake.

"Over here," I said softly. "In the wall."

"In the—what?"

"The wall where the dresser is. Come over."

I heard her stumbling across the room. Then she tripped over something.

"OW!"

"Sshhh!" I said. "We don't want to wake Aunt Doll."

"What's this picture doing on the floor?" she said groggily. "I can't see you, Ruth. Why are you in the wall?"

I stifled a giggle. "Wake up! Listen to me. I got into the secret room and I can't get out."

"Ruby? Ruth?" called Aunt Doll from the hallway. "Are you okay?"

"Stop her!" I whispered. "She can't find me in here!"

Ruby stumbled from the room and then called out, "It's okay, Aunt Doll, the picture just fell off the wall and woke us up. We're fine." I could hear her footsteps going down the hall to meet Aunt Doll.

"Well, for goodness' sake," said Aunt Doll. "It woke me from a deep sleep. Are you sure you're okay? What about Ruth?"

"She's fine."

"I should come and take a look at it. That's very strange. It's never happened before. They say when a picture falls off the wall it means . . ." She faltered. "Oh never mind."

"Look at it in the morning," said Ruby with a huge yawn. "I just want to go back to sleep."

Aunt Doll yawned in response. "Well, if you're sure. Good night, dear." And her footsteps retreated into the other part of the house.

Ruby was back to me in a flash, giggling.

"That was close," she said.

"You're quite the actress," I said.

"You mean I'm a good liar," she said. "Lots of practice. Now how on earth did you get in there?" she asked.

"More important, how on earth am I going to get out?"

CHAPTER THIRTY

THE HIDDEN ROOM

"Well, how did you get in?" asked Ruby.

"The ghost. My mother. She led me in through the closet."

"You saw the ghost?" squeaked Ruby. "Again?"

"Yes. And she brought me in here and disappeared. And then I couldn't get out. But I found this little hole in the wall. It must have been hidden behind the picture."

"Ooo," breathed Ruby. "That's so weird. Someone must have put the picture up to hide the hole so the room would stay secret."

"Can we talk about that later? Help me get out of here! There's some kind of door in the wainscoting. Meg unlocked something at the top and at the bottom. Come into the closet and I'll try to guide you."

I followed the wall over to the place where I had found the tiny crack. It took me a while to find it, because I was so disoriented in the dark. I could hear Ruby's muffled voice coming from the other side and her fingers running along the wood.

"I can't feel anything," said Ruby.

"Wait a minute . . . There!" I found it. I tapped on the wall. "Try to put your hand where I'm tapping. On the ridge that runs along the top of the paneling. There has to be something there, something that unlatches the door."

I tapped softly and I could hear her fingers on the other side.

"Nothing," she said. "It's smooth."

"Keep looking," I urged. "It's got to be there somewhere."

More scrabbling against the wall. Then, "Oh! Here's something," she said. "A tiny crack, oh, and here's another a little way along."

"Try pushing it or pulling it or sliding it," I said.

"I can't budge it," she said, and then as something clicked, "Hey, Ruth, something happened."

"Okay, now go straight down to the floor and try along the baseboard. There's got to be another latch down there."

"I found it!" she said, and then there was more pushing and pulling, and then another click and I felt the wall give way and a beam of white light from the flashlight poured into the room.

Above the light I could see Ruby's grinning face. I threw my arms around her.

"I am so glad to see you, Ruby, you have no idea."

"I guess you are," she said, hugging me back. "Stuck in here in the dark? How scary is that?"

"Scary," I said.

She shone the flashlight into the room.

"Wow," she whispered. She took a step, and then I grabbed for the door, which had started to close behind her. We stared at each other, realizing what had nearly happened.

"There doesn't seem to be a way out, once you're in," I said shakily. "We need something to prop it open."

Ruby shone the flashlight around the room. It seemed to be empty, except for a small trunk on the far wall.

"I'll get a book," she said, and bending her head, went back through the door and into the closet.

As her steps faded away into our bedroom, the darkness swallowed me up, and I had that panicky feeling again, like the walls were going to close in on me. I swallowed, and tried to breathe deeply, but then Ruby was back with the light. She propped a book between the door and the wall so it couldn't close.

Then we took a closer look at the hidden room. The walls were unfinished wood. Above the trunk was a round window, the one we had seen from the other side in the picture. But on the other side of the glass was the back of the clapboard on the outside of the house.

The trunk was dark red, about two feet wide, one foot deep and one foot high. We went and knelt beside it. The hasp was tied shut with a silky green ribbon, tied in a bow.

Ruby pulled one end of the ribbon and it fell away. She opened the trunk.

A strange scent drifted up from inside. Some kind of sweet flowers, dried grass and salt wind. I drew a deep breath, and for a moment I saw a hillside, high above the sea, with a blue sky above and grasses dotted with flowers. Then the scent faded, and the picture was gone.

Ruby was rummaging around in the trunk.

"Nothing here," she said. "Just a bunch of dried grass and flowers and a book."

She pulled it out and shone the flashlight on it.

"*The Secret Garden*?" she said, and opened it.

"Oh, I loved that book," I said, and peered over her shoulder.

Inside the front cover was written in flowing script, "Molly Duggan."

"Oh," said Ruby in a funny voice. "Mom." She began to turn the pages slowly.

Something fell out. Ruby bent to pick it up. It was a pale-blue envelope. She brought it into the light. Then we gasped, both together, like we were one person.

The envelope was addressed in that same flowing handwriting to Ruby Peddle.

CHAPTER THIRTY-ONE

THE LETTER

There were several sheets of thin, pale-blue paper folded inside, filled with handwriting. Ruby held the flashlight so we could both read it.

December 9, 1967

My darling Ruby,
I am writing this letter for you on the night before your second
birthday. Maybe you will read it, maybe you won't. It's hard
to imagine you grown up enough to read a letter. You're such
a funny girl, always running, always into something. And so

curious and sweet! But I must write it. I will leave this letter in the nursery, and put my trust in fate. After Mother died, Meg and I found this room, and it became our secret. If you're anything like we were as girls, I have no doubt you will find out about this room and its sad history. I think we were meant to find it and discover its secrets, and perhaps you are too.

Meg and I have thought long and hard about how much you should know, and we have disagreed about it, and debated it for many sleepless nights while I was still in Toronto. And since I've been home, we've written back and forth and talked on the phone about it, weighing the dangers with the benefits, and we are now finally in agreement.

We will leave it to the Fates. If you find this letter, then you were meant to, and it all begins again. If you find it, Ruby, and I am still with you, come to me and I will tell you the whole long, sad story. But if I am gone, you must try to contact Ruth, and the two of you must work together.

Work together to break the curse. As Meg and I did. Or tried to do. If we are both dead, dying on the same day, then you know we were unsuccessful.

The Finns are cursed. It goes way back to Ireland. Every generation has twin girls, and none of them live to see their children grow up. They all die young, and they both die on the same day.

We found out about the curse at the age of twelve, when our mother died. She and Doll were the exceptions, because

Doll was never a Finn, but a Duggan through and through. So Doll lived, but our mother died. And we heard Doll one night, in the week after the funeral, talking to Eldred. She was crying and saying she thought they would be okay, because they weren't identical twins, and all the others who were cursed were identical. And Eldred said he didn't know how it worked, but it was a terrible thing, the curse.

And then Doll got really mad and said, "Well, I won't have it. I won't have Meg and Molly growing up believing in it. It's believing in it that makes it happen, it's superstition. People can talk themselves into anything," and then she started crying again. But she made Eldred promise never to tell us about the curse.

So that's when we started searching. We went through the cemetery, looking at the dates, and we realized that every set of twins had died young, on the same day. Except for Doll and our mother.

We knew better than to ask Doll about it. We asked Eldred, but he wouldn't break his promise to Doll. But he told us that maybe if we went to Slippers Cove, we might find out more. And he told us about the Sight.

Of course, we already knew the story of the flood, and how the twins Fiona and Fenella Finn had been found in the root cellar. But Eldred told us that one of the twins always had the Sight, come down through the generations from Ireland, and that the twin with the Sight could see the Ghost Road and find

Slippers Cove, where no one had been since 1902, because it was lost, lost by sea and lost by road and no one could find the way there.

Well, we already knew that Meg had the Sight. She'd had strange experiences, seeing and hearing things I couldn't, and knowing sometimes when things were going to happen. We kept quiet about it, the way we did about a lot of things. Grown-ups, except for Eldred, would just laugh at us if we talked about ghosts or premonitions, so we didn't tell anyone. When Eldred said there was always one twin with the Sight, it came as no surprise to us. Or to him.

But he wouldn't talk about the curse and said it was best left alone. Then he closed up like a clamshell and we couldn't get anything else out of him. When we told him what we knew about the curse, he just shook his head and said the damage was done. And he said he didn't know anything more himself.

All we could think of to do was to find Slippers Cove, and see if there was anything there that could help us.

The funny thing was that Meg had seen the Ghost Road for years. She was always saying things like, "I wonder where that road goes," and then I'd look and I wouldn't see anything, and I'd think she was imagining it. But that summer, after our mother died, we set out to find it and follow it to Slippers Cove.

It's getting late now so I can't write any more. I'm going to put this in the nursery tonight, and hope to write more tomorrow.

In case I don't get the chance to write more, Meg and I agreed that if you found your way this far, you will probably go farther, the way we did, and you need to know something: you and Ruth aren't cousins; you're twins. In the end we thought all we could do to stop the curse was to keep you and Ruth apart, so you'd never know. We hoped that would keep you safe.

I found out I was pregnant after Meg and I moved to Toronto to go to nursing school. I didn't tell George. We had broken up when I left Newfoundland because he didn't want me to go to Ontario with Meg. I didn't know what to do, but for a while I thought I could bring up the baby myself with Meg's help. I was so mad at George. But then when we found out I was going to have twins, Meg and I started planning.

We thought that if you never knew about the curse and you never knew you were twins, you might be protected from it. And I did want to be with George, because I've always loved him, ever since I was a teenager. So after you were about two months old, I told him that I'd had his baby and I wanted to go home to Newfoundland and get married.

It was one of the hardest things I've ever done, leaving Ruth behind with Meg. But we thought it might break the curse. If you've found this letter, Ruby, and Meg and I are both gone, then our plans have come to nothing. This letter is a backup plan. Because if you know about the curse, then you must fight it. You must break it. You must find a way. To save your lives, and the lives of your future children.

I will write more tomorrow about what we found in Slippers Cove, and maybe that will help you. Know that I love you and Ruth more than I can ever say, and all that Meg and I have done was the best we could think of to try and save you two from this awful thing that has haunted our family for so many years.

Till tomorrow, my sweet girl.
Mommy

CHAPTER THIRTY-TWO

THE SECRET

The world seemed to tilt. Ruby and I knelt beside that dusty old trunk clutching the letter as if we were on the edge of a cliff about to slide off.

We stared at each other.

"Twins," we both whispered at the same time, and then the world lurched upright again. A look of wonder and delight flooded Ruby's face, and I knew she was seeing the same look on my face.

"Twins," we both said again at exactly the same time, and began to laugh. Tears started to my eyes and I could see the same in hers.

"I knew there was something," said Ruby, flicking away her tears. "I knew there was something uncanny about it. The way you look just like me and how we say things at the same time and think things and—"

"We're sisters!" I said, grinning. "You're my sister. I can't believe it. This is so amazing!" And I hugged her. She hugged me back and I felt happier than I ever had before. More than Christmas. More than holidays with Dad. I felt like I was home.

She pulled away and there was more wiping of tears and laughing. And all the time we just kept staring at each other in the dim light from the flashlight, which Ruby had dropped into the trunk. I was looking at her face again, my face, and seeing me in her, looking back. And yet she wasn't me, not inside. She was different; she was Ruby, but so much connected to me, more than anyone, more than my dad—

"My dad!" I said. "I don't understand. He's not my father?"

I pictured him, with his glasses slipping down his nose, peering at some flower, touching it delicately with one finger, turning to talk to me with his eyes alight with enthusiasm. He *was* my father. He had always been my father. He always would be. But Uncle George? He was also my father?

Ruby had picked up the flashlight and was searching through the box.

"Where's the other letter? She said she was going to finish telling us the next day."

The box was empty. Just a small bunch of dried flowers and grasses, tied with a green silk ribbon. I untied it and looked more closely at the flowers. Yellow lady slippers, perfectly preserved—the flowers, not the leaves, which could give you a rash. And tiny, delicate flowers in sets of two on one stem—twinflowers.

I smiled. How perfect. Molly must have loved wildflowers, like I did. Molly. My mother.

I thought of the girl with the blonde hair who had shown me this room, and the smiling face in my photograph. No. Meg was my mother, just like Dad was my father. Molly was my . . . birth mother. And Uncle George was my birth father. It was like I suddenly had four parents instead of two.

Ruby was looking at the letter again.

"She said she was going to write another letter," said Ruby. "I don't understand. Where is it?"

I was carefully gathering the dried flowers and grasses. I put them to my nose and sniffed. They held the same faint, sweet scent that I'd noticed when we opened the trunk.

Lady slippers and twinflowers. I hadn't seen any on our walk yesterday. Lady slippers need a sheltered spot, some woods or a gully. Twinflowers? I wasn't so sure about where they grew. I needed to look them up in the book.

"Oh no," said Ruby, her voice breaking.

I looked up. She was staring at the letter.

"It's dated December ninth. She said it was my second birthday the next day. That's when she died, Ruth, December tenth. My birthday."

Of course. I should have seen that. My mother had died on December 10 too. But not on my birthday. My birthday was December 5. I wondered which date was the true one.

"She never wrote another letter. She died the next day." Ruby's eyes were filling with tears again. "We'll never know what she was going to tell us."

I put my arm around her.

"Oh yes we will, Ruby. We're going to figure it out. One way or another, we're going find the answers."

"It's just that . . . I wanted to hear more from her," said Ruby. "Getting this letter . . . she's talking to me. I want her to keep talking. I don't want it to stop."

I hugged her. I knew exactly how she felt. All my life I had wanted something of my mother's. Something to hold on to. Something more than a picture in a frame and a wisp of a memory. Seeing her ghost was like having her brush up against me for just a moment. This letter was all either of us had of Molly. We needed more.

"I have to go and talk to the witch," I said suddenly. "She knows. She told me she knows what really happened and she said she would tell me."

"Nan?" said Ruby, horrified. "Nan knows?"

"Yes. When you ran out the other day, she said I should come back. I think . . . I think she knows I have the Sight. I think she has it too."

"But she hates me," said Ruby. "She won't tell me anything."

"I have to go alone," I said. "She'll tell me. I know she will."

"If you say so," said Ruby doubtfully. Her eyes strayed back to the letter.

"The curse," she whispered. "Mom said the curse was real. And that they were trying to break it—"

"But they didn't," I finished. A shiver went down my spine. "And they died." Ruby looked back at me and the full horror of what the letter had said finally sunk in.

"We're next," said Ruby.

"Yes," I replied. "Because we're identical twins, we're cursed too. If we don't break it, we'll die young too."

"On the same day," said Ruby. "At the same time. Just like Meg and Molly."

"And all the others."

We stared at each other. It was impossible, incredible.

And true.

And with that light of understanding dawning between us, a creeping cold came into the room, that same breathless feeling I'd had before, only this time it was so much stronger, and I saw the fear I felt reflected in Ruby's eyes.

And then the flashlight went out.

CHAPTER THIRTY-THREE

WHISPERING

Ruby made a little squeak and I felt her hand on my arm. I gripped it tightly.

"It's just the flashlight," I began. "The batteries must have given out—" but even as I said it, that breathless, smothering feeling was growing, filling the room. Fear seemed to pour into me from the heavy darkness.

"What's happening?" whispered Ruby, gasping. "I can't breathe."

"We gotta get out of here," I said, pulling Ruby to her feet. "Come on."

We stumbled in the direction of the secret door, but we must have got turned around, because all we could find was solid walls.

"It's this way," said Ruby, yanking on my arm. But there was only wall.

"Did it close again?" said Ruby. "Are we trapped in here?"

A whispering, like a thin breeze, began in the walls around us. A murmuring. Like the voices in the wind in the cemetery and on the ship. I could almost make out the words, but not quite.

"Ruth?" said Ruby. "Did you hear me? I said, did the door close?"

I tried to focus. "No, we would have heard it if it closed," I said, and pulled her in the direction where I thought the door was. The whispering grew, but this time I felt the opening and we ducked through it and back into our room. Everything was pitch-black.

Ruby let go of my hand. It sounded like she was heading toward the bedside table.

"I'll just light the candle," she said.

The whispering followed us.

"What is that?" I said.

A match flared and illuminated Ruby's white face. She looked terrified.

"What?" she said, lighting the candle. The flame flickered, then steadied.

"That whispering. It started in the secret room."

Ruby stood very still, listening.

"I don't hear anything," she said.

It was getting louder.

"Ruth, Ruth!" she cried, coming toward me with the candle. "What's wrong? You look all funny—"

I could hear the words now. Someone was hissing in a horrible voice: "By fire! By fire! By fire!"

The candle flame was growing, spreading through the room, and then suddenly everything was on fire, an orange blaze shot up, and around me furniture crackled in a roaring fire. It wasn't our bedroom anymore. The walls were dark, there were no windows, and a big fireplace filled one side of the room. A table and chairs were overturned on the floor, burning, and a man lay on the floor. I could see his eyes staring. He was dead. The flames engulfed the room, and then it all blinked out.

I was standing in our bedroom and Ruby's hands were on my shoulders. The candle burned gently behind her on our bedside table. There was no fire.

"Ruth, Ruth, are you okay?"

"I—I don't know . . ." I said slowly, and then coughed. My mouth tasted of bitter wood smoke.

"Sit down," she said, and brought me over to my bed. I obeyed, and sat staring at the candle. She pushed a glass of water into my hands.

"Drink," she said.

The water was sweet.

"What happened? Your eyes went all funny, like in the barn before. Like you weren't here anymore. Like you were somewhere else."

"I was somewhere else." In a shaky voice, I told her what I had seen and heard.

"Oh, Ruth," she whispered, when I finished. "It's the Sight. You're seeing something that happened."

"Didn't you hear the whispering? It was all around us in the secret room. And then it followed us in here, and when you lit the flame . . . Ruby, am I going crazy?" I gripped her arm. "I feel so weird . . ." And I started to shake. "I don't know what's real anymore or when I'm dreaming or awake . . . I don't understand what's happening to me."

"Get under the covers," she said. "You're freezing." She tucked me up and got in beside me. I could feel her cold feet on mine under the covers.

"You're not crazy, Ruth," she said. "It's the Sight. People have visions sometimes. Visions of the past. Or visions of the future. Eldred told me."

"But I don't want to have visions. They're horrible," I said.

Ruby sighed. "I wish you could give them to me," she said. "I've always wanted to have the Sight, to see ghosts and fairies, to have visions. To see into that other world that's so close, but so hard to get into."

I was warming up. "What other world?" I said sleepily.

"The bigger world," said Ruby. "The world where spirits live. Where past and future and present are all mixed up. The world where there's magic and wishes and fairies. Where dead people are alive and live people are dead."

I shivered. "It's too scary, Ruby. You don't know. You wouldn't want this."

"Oh, but I do," said Ruby fervently. "But only one twin has the Sight. And that twin is you."

I smiled. "Twins," I said. And there, inside the warm bubble of light from the candle, I felt that same feeling I'd had my first night here, when the ghost got into the other bed and smiled at me: safe and warm and happy.

"Twins," said Ruby, blowing out the candle.

And then we both fell asleep.

CHAPTER THIRTY-FOUR

POLISHING

"So tell me about this feeling again," said Ruby.

She was dusting the piano in the living room with a feather duster. I was applying furniture spray to the coffee table, then rubbing it up into a shine. Ruby had to show me how because I'd never polished furniture before. We had a cleaner at home who came every week, and she wouldn't dream of asking me to help her.

Aunt Doll had sent us in here after breakfast, instructing us to dust and polish everything. She woke us up at eight when we didn't appear for breakfast. We both had slept in, worn out by all the excitement the night before.

"You mean what happened in the secret room?"

"The nursery," said Ruby. "That's what my mother called it in the letter."

"Yes, the nursery," I said. "I wonder why they called it that?"

"I guess it was a baby's room," said Ruby.

"Well, duh," I said, flicking my dust cloth in her direction. It fell short.

"Where did you learn to throw?" she asked, picking it up and hurling it back at me. It hit me in the face.

"I didn't," I said, and went back to polishing the table. Aunt Doll had told me to keep at it till I could see my face in it. I peered at it. I could see a kind of blur that was probably my face.

"Tell me about the feeling," repeated Ruby.

"You said you felt it too," I replied, moving to a table beside the couch and spraying some furniture polish onto it. "In the nursery. When the flashlight went out."

Funny thing about that flashlight. When we had retrieved it from the nursery that morning before breakfast, it was working just fine. So it wasn't the batteries.

"Oh, right. I couldn't breathe. It got really stuffy all of a sudden."

"Well, that's what I keep feeling. I felt it in the cemetery, when we found all those graves, and then I felt it in the barn when we were talking to Eldred about the curse, then I felt it in the room. And then the whispering started."

"Tell me what they were saying again? The whisperers," said Ruby. "In the barn and last night."

"I think . . . I think there was only one. When I was on the ship I heard screaming in the wind, and then there was just this one voice saying, 'By water! By water!' in a kind of hiss. And last night it was saying, 'By fire! By fire!'"

I shuddered. I didn't want to think about what I'd seen the night before. It had seemed so real: the dark room, the smell of smoke, the man's eyes staring. I shook my head, as if that would get rid of the pictures in my mind, and tried to concentrate on polishing the small table under the window.

"It's something to do with the curse," said Ruby thoughtfully. "'By fire, by water.' There was a fire in your vision last night, and when we were in the barn, it was the shipwreck, so there had to be water. A lot of water, if you think about it."

"Brilliant, Ruby," I said, rolling my eyes. "I guess there is a lot of water in the ocean."

"Well, yeah. There is," she said, grinning. She had given up on the dusting and was sitting on the piano stool, twirling gently.

"But how are we going to figure it all out, Ruby?"

"If only Eldred was here," she said. We'd gone looking for him after breakfast, but he was nowhere to be found. Finally Aunt Doll told us he'd gone to see a man down the shore about some medicine for one of his sheep and he'd be gone all day.

"I wonder how much he knows," I said, rubbing at the table. "Wasn't there something in the letter from Molly about him not knowing that much about the curse?"

Ruby put down her duster and dug in her jeans pocket and pulled out the letter.

I went and looked over her shoulder at it.

"Here," said Ruby, pointing. "'And Eldred said he didn't know how it worked, but it was a terrible thing, the curse.'" She ran her finger down a little farther. "And here, 'he told us that maybe if we went to Slippers Cove, we might find out more.'" She read on. "And here, 'he didn't know anything more himself.'"

She looked up at me.

"Maybe that's it. Maybe we have to go to Slippers Cove."

I didn't want to. I didn't want to do anything. I didn't want to see the fire again, or the dead man, or the shipwreck. I didn't want to see any more visions, or hear that whispering and chanting again, or feel the walls closing in on me.

Ruby was reading the letter again, going back up the page a bit. "Listen," she said. "This is what she said about it: 'the twin with the Sight could see the Ghost Road and find Slippers Cove, where no one had been since 1902, because it was lost, lost by sea and lost by road and no one could find the way there.'"

She looked up at me. "That's you, Ruth. You've seen it already. You can find the way."

"Maybe," I said reluctantly. But there was something I had to do first.

"How far is it?" I asked, looking out the window. It was another gray day, and although it wasn't exactly raining, it looked like it might start any minute.

"I'm not sure. Eldred thought it took about four hours to get there, according to the old stories," she replied, following my gaze. "We need to go on a clear day, start early, take a lunch. Tell Aunt Doll we're going on a long hike. She won't mind." Ruby folded the letter carefully and slid it back into her pocket. Then she picked up her duster and turned back to the piano, running it along the keys. "Let's get this finished and then we can make our plans. Maybe we can go tomorrow."

"Okay," I said. "But first I need to talk to someone."

"Who? Eldred?"

"No. The witch. I told you last night. She knows something."

"Oh, come on, Ruth, you don't want to talk to her. Believe me, she's nothing but poison."

"She has something to tell me. About my mother, she said. And other stuff. She said some of it I'd want to hear and some of it I wouldn't."

Our eyes met. "I wonder what that could be," said Ruby softly. "What you don't want to hear."

I swallowed.

"I don't know. Something awful I guess. But isn't it better to know than just to keep on wondering and being scared?"

"Chances are we'll still be scared, once we know," she said gloomily.

"I have to go, Ruby. She definitely knows something. I got the strangest feeling while I was there with her, after you left, like she could see right into my head . . ."

Ruby shivered. "She's done that to me before. It's like she knows what you're thinking."

"Didn't Eldred say something about her having the Sight? If she does, maybe she can help me."

Ruby shook her head. "No, you don't get it, Ruth. She's nasty. She doesn't want to help anyone. She's like a spider, sitting there in that dark house, spinning her webs, trying to catch people in them. Dad hates visiting her too; he's never happy after. She's the only person I've ever met who can make Wynken, Blynken and Nod sit down and be quiet. They're terrified of her. And Wendy will hardly even put a foot inside the house."

"So everybody's scared of her," I said thoughtfully.

"Yup. Pretty much. She's a witch."

CHAPTER THIRTY-FIVE

THE SPIDER

I knocked at the witch's door. I could feel Ruby's eyes boring into me. She was high on the hill behind Buckle, watching me through an old pair of binoculars we found on the bookshelf in the living room.

I told her she didn't need to, but she had insisted.

"What if she pushes you into the oven?" she said. "Or locks you into a cage to fatten you up?" She grinned at me.

"Come off it, Ruby," I said. I knew she was just kidding around, but it wasn't helping my nerves.

"I'll just stay up on the hill till you come out. And if you're not out in about an hour, I'll come and knock on the door. Will you need that long?"

"I don't know. Maybe."

"If she turns you into a toad, I'll take care of you," said Ruby. "I'll keep you in a little box and feed you flies—"

I gave her a push and she nearly fell over, laughing.

"Okay," said Ruby. "You're on your own. But I'll be watching the door every minute. If you get really scared, just get out of there. Or scream or something."

"I'll be okay," I said, but it was hard to watch her walk away. She turned and waved, a big grin on her face. I waved back, then walked along the road to the witch's house.

The knock seemed to echo through the old house. Nothing happened. There were no footsteps, no sounds behind the door. I knocked again.

It was chilly on the doorstep. It wasn't really raining, but there were teeny tiny drops of water in the air, like rain only finer. I lifted my hand to knock again, but before I made contact with the door, it swung open.

I peered inside. "Mrs. Peddle?" I called uncertainly. I couldn't see anything.

She glided out from the shadows behind the door. Dressed as before, in a long, faded black dress, her hair up in a bun, her eyes sharp and dark. A sweet, delicious smell of baking wafted out from behind her.

She smiled at me. A twisted, mean little smile.

"Well, well," she said in her creaky, high voice. "Look what the wind blew in." She looked past me into the street.

"No shadow today?" she said. "Where's the other one?"

"She . . . uh . . . she's at h-home," I stuttered.

"Ha!" laughed the witch. "You're not as good a liar as your sister," and then stood back to let me in.

As I walked into the gloom, it hit me like a smack to the back of my head. The witch had called Ruby my sister, not my cousin. She knew.

I walked down the hall into the dim kitchen, the witch gliding silently behind me. On the table, cooling on a wire rack, was a freshly baked batch of crisp oatmeal cookies. Mrs. Peddle motioned to a chair, watching me like a cat at a mouse hole. A tall glass of milk sat on the table beside an empty plate.

"You knew I was coming," I said.

She cackled. Really cackled. There is no other way to describe the creaky laughter that bubbled out of her.

"Sit down," she said. "And help yourself to cookies. I think you'll like them. The other one does."

I sat down. At first I thought maybe I could hold my dignity and not have any cookies and milk, but the sweet smell that filled the kitchen was not to be resisted. I took one and had a nibble. Crisp and buttery.

"Don't worry," said Mrs. Peddle. "They aren't poisoned." Then she laughed again.

I took a swig of milk and polished off the cookie.

"You're a very good baker," I said politely.

"And you're a very well-brought-up girl," she replied, still with an air of finding me very amusing.

"You know," I said. There was no use beating around the bush. "You know about Ruby and me. That we're twins."

"Oh yes, and a great deal besides," she said. "I knew you'd be back. Your Aunt Meg would look at me with just the same expression you do. Like she could see more than she'd ever tell. She was a curious girl too, just like you. Couldn't leave anything alone. She always had to know. For all the good it did her."

I felt a rise of anger inside me and could feel my cheeks turning red.

The witch laughed. "Temper, temper," she said. "You'll be stomping out of here in a minute like the other one, and no wiser about any of those questions that you're bursting with."

I took a deep breath. Then I had another drink of milk.

"Mrs. Peddle—" I began

"You can call me Nan while you're at it, girl. You knows I'm your Nan."

"Okay, Nan," I said. "You said you could tell me what I need to know. About my . . . my mother. And everything else, you said. I need to know."

"I daresay you do," said the witch. "I daresay you want to know why you were lied to all your life. About who your mother is and who your father is and who your sister is and what your names are—"

"Names?" I asked. "What names?"

"By rights you're Ruth Elizabeth Finn and the other one is Ruby Ann Finn. You're both Finns, through and through, and cursed from the day you first drew breath."

Her angry words rang out in the gloomy kitchen and I felt cold all over. But I spoke up. I wasn't going to let her see she was scaring me.

"Okay. We're cursed. I get that. Like our mothers. But why? I don't understand why."

"Ha!" said Mrs. Peddle, glaring at me. "So you know about the curse, do you? But what do you know?"

"Just that the twins always seem to die young, at the same time. Back through all the Finns, back to Fiona and Fenella, the ones found in the root cellar, and their mother, Catriona and her sister Caitlin."

"Oh, it goes farther back than that," said Mrs. Peddle. "Suffice it to say that once upon a time two girls did a very bad thing, and their daughters and granddaughters and all their line have been paying for it ever since."

"What did they do?"

The witch shook her head. "Never mind what they did. It's enough for you to know that you are cursed. And your mother was cursed. And she brought that curse into my family, to my son, and I'll never forgive her for that. Her and her sister. Meg."

"How?" I asked her.

"They bewitched him when he was nothing but a boy. He followed them everywhere, and it did me no good to tell him not to play with them. I saw them for what they were. Wicked, wicked girls."

"They weren't wicked!" I protested.

"They were Finns, and they were cursed. Molly set her sights on George and wouldn't rest till she had him. And Meg helped her, every step of the way. Always plotting and planning something, that girl was. Oh, I knew no good would come of it. And once George took up with Molly, he wouldn't hear anything against either of them. He even told me—" Her eyes grew bigger, as if she still couldn't believe what he'd said to her. "He told me when he was sixteen that if I said one more word against them he'd leave and never come back! With his father dead and me on my own! So then I had to be quiet. But I never stopped watching them, because I knew what would happen, sooner or later. She'd break his heart." She made a strange sound, like she was trying to strangle a sob. "And so she did, the day she died. Her and her sneaky sister."

She sniffed and made a fierce little swipe at her eyes with a lace handkerchief she produced from her apron pocket.

Then she focused her reddened eyes on me, sharp as flint.

"Those two girls were cursed," she spat. "Just like you and the other one. Nothing good ever came from the Finns. And nothing ever will."

CHAPTER THIRTY-SIX

THE BEGINNING

I wanted to get out of there. The witch was glaring at me, hatred coming off her in waves. Like she was a stove, and all her anger against the Finns was the heat. I couldn't breathe. I stood up.

And then it happened again. Her dark kitchen melted away and I was back in that shadowy room with everything on fire, and the man's body lying on the floor, his eyes staring. In the crackle of the flames I could hear that horrible, strangled voice again, hissing, "By fire! By fire! By fire!"

But this time I wasn't alone. There were two young women beside me, each carrying a small child.

"There you lie, Robert Barrett," said one, in a thick Irish accent. "And may God forgive you for what you did to my sister."

"Come, Eva," said the other. "We need to be gone."

Then everything winked into blackness and I found myself lying on the floor, looking up into the witch's face.

She had me by the shoulders and was giving me a shake.

"Ruth," she said. "Ruth, come back."

I tried to sit up, but a wave of dizziness knocked me down again.

"Just lie there a minute," she said. "I'll get you some water."

She didn't sound like the furious, nasty old woman who'd been railing against Meg and Molly. She sounded old and worried and ordinary.

She knelt down on the floor beside me and offered me a glass of water.

"Can you sit up now?" she said.

I sat up cautiously, and although I was still dizzy, I didn't fall back. My back felt bruised from where I'd fallen on it. I drank some water. Then the witch took my arm and helped me to a chair. I took a deep breath. My head still felt light and strange.

The witch sat down beside me, watching. I felt her eyes were drilling into me, searching for something.

Finally she spoke. "Where did you go?" she asked, as if she knew the answer already.

"Go? Umm . . . What do you mean?"

"Don't trifle with me, girl. You and I know very well what just happened. You had a vision. You were somewhere else. Where?"

I swallowed.

"I . . . umm . . . I'm not sure. But I've been there before. A room that was burning. A man on the floor."

She shook her head. "Ireland," she said softly. "Way back. At the beginning."

"The beginning?" I asked. "The beginning of what?"

"The curse," she answered. She sounded very tired. "I've seen it myself. And your mother saw it." She slumped, like all the fight had gone out of her.

"Every generation," she said. "Every generation there's a Finn who has the Sight. And every generation there's a Barrett who has it. And we're all cursed together."

"Barrett's the name of the man on the floor," I said. "The dead man."

"Oh yes," she said. "Robert Barrett. My great-great-great-great-uncle. His brother Sean Barrett was the first Barrett to come to Newfoundland, back in the 1830s. A long time ago." She sighed.

"And the curse?" I asked. "It goes back to that time?"

"Yes," she said softly. She shook her head again.

I drew closer to her. "Won't you help me?" I asked. "Won't you help me break the curse? Please tell me what happened."

She straightened up and glared at me.

"Now why would I be doing that?" she said. "When the

Finns have been the source of all the bad things that've ever happened to the Barretts? Why would I help you?"

"Because you're my grandmother," I said, and as the words came out of my mouth, I realized they were true. This thin, angry woman was the only grandmother I'd ever had. Not a very nice one, as grannies go. But all I had. I reached out my hand and put it on her wrinkled one. She didn't pull away.

"There's no time when a Barrett ever helped a Finn and it turned out for the best," she said gruffly. "Look at George. Brought him nothing but pain and torment."

"He's got Ruby. He loves her. That's not torment."

She snorted. "That one. A wild rapscallion not fit for any-thing. And if you'd seen him when Molly died." Her voice trembled. "He was heartbroken, snapped in two. He couldn't cope with the child and he left her with Doll to bring up. As if she could care for a child, she never had one of her own—"

I hadn't heard this before. "Ruby was left with Aunt Doll?"

"Until he married that Wendy, when the child was five," said the witch. "Then he brought her into town to live with them again." She lowered her voice, so I had to strain to hear it. "He wouldn't leave her with his own mother, as he should have. He didn't trust me with her."

Her voice broke and a tear rolled down her cheek. She brushed it away angrily.

"I put it all back to Molly," she said fiercely. "She didn't want her child growing up with me. She must have made him promise that would never happen, because otherwise George would have brought her here. With me. Where she belonged."

She stood up and started clearing away the cookies and milk.

"So no, I won't be helping you, Ruth Finn. I won't be helping anybody."

I watched her. She moved about the kitchen quickly, whisking dishes and cookies away till it was spotless again. Something about the way she worked reminded me of Aunt Doll in her kitchen. Nothing out of place. Everything accounted for and tidied away.

I roused myself from the hypnotic daze I had been sinking into and said, "Can you at least tell me what happened with Molly and Meg? How did they keep it secret about Ruth and me? That we were twins?"

She hung the dishcloth on a rack over the stove and came and sat down across the table from me. Her mouth tightened and she shook her head. "All right. I'll tell you. But don't blame me if you don't like what I say." She paused, and her eyes looked faraway, into the past.

"They were always crafty, those two. Always whispering in corners. They wanted to go up to Toronto to go to nursing school, because apparently the one in St. John's wasn't good enough for them. And George was against it, because he couldn't bear to be without Molly, but he had a good job with the power company and he wouldn't leave it. And then, if you please, Molly broke up with him! Told him she wasn't ready to settle down. He was devastated, and she and Meg went off to Toronto. I thought my prayers had been answered, but then after a while, back she comes with a baby, says that George is the father, and they get married. And meanwhile, Meg has a baby herself up in Ontario, and then a year later she's married the father up there. Or what we thought was the father," she added darkly. "And no one's the wiser. Except for me."

She leaned toward me, her dark eyes boring into mine. "Because I have the Sight, my dear, just as you have, and I can see things that others don't. And when I heard that Meg had a baby too, at the same time, I knew that they were twins and the curse would continue. Poor George didn't have a clue. And I never said anything. What's the good? But I knew. And then when Meg and Molly both dropped dead on the same day, I knew it was the curse, and the two babies would carry it on, the way it's been carried on for a hundred and fifty years. And there's nothing you can do about it. Nothing." She looked me, with grim satisfaction in the set of her jaw.

"But my mother—Meg—told me we could break the curse," I said without thinking.

Her eyes sharpened. "What? What do you mean she told you?" She reached out her bony, wrinkled hand and gripped mine. It felt like a claw.

"I saw her," I said. "She's come to me. She told me Ruby and I could break the curse."

"You saw her spirit?" asked the witch, squeezing my hand harder and peering into my eyes. "You saw her ghost?"

"Yes. At first I thought I was dreaming, but—"

The witch smiled. That same hard, mean smile I'd seen before. "No, it was her spirit. She's back. Come to make my life a misery again, like she did when she was alive." She let me go then and stood up. "No, you'll get no help from me, Ruth Finn. Get out of my house now. I've had enough of you."

CHAPTER THIRTY-SEVEN

THE LIE

The rain was still falling. If you could call it falling. More like sitting motionless in the air, brushing against my face and hair like a damp curtain.

I looked up the hill, but there was no sign of Ruby. I turned along the road and started walking back toward Aunt Doll's house. I was full of what I'd seen and what the witch had said, and I felt a heaviness in the air, like everything in the world was weighing down on me.

"Ruth!"

I looked up. Ruby was running toward me.

"Ruth, what happened? I was just about to come in and rescue you." She was laughing, red-faced from the cold. Then she saw my face and stopped.

"What happened? What did she do to you?"

I shook my head. "I'll tell you, but let's go somewhere warm first."

Ruby took my hand. "You're colder than I am. Come on!" and she started running toward home, pulling me along behind her.

I didn't feel like running, but it did warm me up, and after five minutes I was out of breath, begging her to slow down.

When we got into the house, Aunt Doll waylaid us for lunch, and then we couldn't talk until the dishes were washed and the floor was swept. Finally we escaped to our room.

"Doesn't she ever stop?" I asked Ruby. "The house is so clean, there's not a speck anywhere, and still we have to sweep the floor."

Ruby shook her head. "Wendy's just as bad. The house has got to be sparkling, all the time. And Wynken, Blynken and Nod are some dirty. I have to sweep every night after supper, and do dishes, and the boys don't have to do a thing."

"That's not fair," I said.

She shrugged. "No. It's not. There's women's work and there's men's work, and in the house is women's work. I'd rather do men's work, cutting wood and mowing grass and shoveling snow, and helping Eldred fix things, but I always have to do the women's work first."

"My dad's always telling me girls are just as good as boys," I said. "He says I can do whatever I want when I grow up."

"Yeah, but who does the dishes in your house?" asked Ruby. "Your dad or Awful Gwen?"

"Dad, actually. If she cooks. Which she usually does because he's not very good at it. And I always have to help."

"Well, maybe that works up in Ontario, but it doesn't work here. The boys never have to help with dishes, or make beds or anything. But anyway, tell me about the witch. You looked as white as a ghost when I saw you on the road."

Ruby was sitting on her bed, her knees drawn up to her chin.

"It was awful," I said, plonking myself on my bed and stretching out. The homemade quilt felt warm and comforting beneath me, with its thick, brightly colored squares. Aunt Doll had told me her sister had made it. Daphne. Meg and Molly's mother. My other grandmother. I wish I'd known her. She had to be nicer than the witch.

"Did you find out anything?"

"Oh yeah. Lots." And I told her what had happened. Everything. How the witch was so mean, but then changed after I had the vision. How she seemed tired and old then, but soon went back to being witchy and horrible. How she told me about Molly breaking up with Uncle George, going to Toronto, having twins and leaving me behind with Meg.

"Well, we knew all about that part from the letter," said Ruby when I finished. She was lying on her bed by this time, gazing at the ceiling.

"Yes. And what I really want to know I don't think she can tell me."

"What?"

"Where my dad came into the story. Because I always thought he was my dad. But he must have come along after I was born."

"Doesn't he ever talk about Meg? How they met, stuff like that?"

I shook my head miserably. "No. Never. He doesn't like talking about her, so we never do. But I always believed he was my real dad."

"Maybe he adopted you when he married your mom," said Ruby.

"And when was he going to tell me?"

"Maybe never. Some people don't."

We lay there for a while, not saying anything. I thought about Dad in the airport, the last time I saw him, giving me the wildflower book and not wanting to say good-bye. My heart gave a little twist inside my chest. He *was* my dad, and he always would be. And even though he was married to Gwen now, he still loved me. I knew that. I sniffed.

Ruby looked over at me and sat up. She reached over and squeezed my hand.

"Never mind, Rue," she said, unconsciously using my dad's nickname for me. "It'll be okay. You can ask him when he comes back. Maybe he had a good reason for not telling you."

I managed a small smile. "Maybe."

"Now, tell me about this vision you had," she said.

I smiled a little more. I knew she was changing the subject to try and cheer me up. And it was funny, that she thought that thinking about the curse and all those women in our family dying young would make me happier than thinking about missing my dad and wondering why he had lied to me all these years. And what was even funnier was that, in a way, she was right.

I took a deep breath and tried to put my dad right out of my mind. In Greece, with Gwen. Far, far away. I thought of the witch's kitchen, and how I felt the heat coming off her, and then how I slipped into the vision.

"It was the same as the last time. I was in a kitchen. Everything was on fire and the body of the man was on the floor. But this time there were two women there, with babies."

"Did you hear the whispering?"

"Yes. It was inside the fire, like the flames themselves, a kind of roaring saying 'by fire, by fire,' again and again."

Ruby shivered. "Then what happened?"

"One of the women said, 'There you lie, Robert Barrett, and may God forgive you for what you did to my sister,' and then the other said, 'Come, Eva, we need to be gone.'"

"And Nan said it was from the beginning, when the curse began, in Ireland?"

I nodded my head.

"That horrible old woman," said Ruby. "She knows. She knows! And she won't tell us."

"We just have to find out for ourselves," I said.

"But how?"

"Maybe we'll find out when we go to Slippers Cove," I replied.

"Or maybe you'll have another vision."

I was silent.

"Ruth?"

"I don't want to," I said softly. "It's horrible, Ruby. Everything goes black and I'm dizzy, and I feel like I'm falling and don't know where I am. Then all these awful things start happening. Fires. Dead people lying on the floor. That horrible voice. I don't like it."

The bed creaked as Ruby came and sat down beside me. "It does sound bad."

"I thought the witch would help me. I thought she would help me make them go away."

"They won't go away. Not if you have the Sight," said Ruby. "That's part of it. But maybe you won't have them so much if we break the curse."

"I never had them before I came here," I said.

"Maybe coming here woke it up in you. Maybe it was just asleep all these years, waiting to come out when the time was right."

I looked over at her. She had a dreamy look in her eyes. I had to smile.

"Ruby, you're enjoying this. It's all a big fairy story to you, isn't it?"

She turned to me, grinning. "It is, isn't it? What I always wanted—to be part of a fairy story."

CHAPTER THIRTY-EIGHT

NAMES

"A story?" I said. "Being part of a story would be okay. But not a nightmare."

"Who's having nightmares?" asked Aunt Doll. She had come along the hall without us hearing her and was standing at the door.

"Oh, nobody," said Ruby quickly. "Ruth was just saying that sometimes she has nightmares. But not lately, right, Ruth?"

"No," I said, feeling hot and cold at the same time. I just wasn't a good liar. I needed more practice.

"Well, if you ever have a nightmare here," said Aunt Doll

kindly, "you just come and wake me up. I have them myself sometimes and I know how scary it can be."

"Thanks, Aunt Doll," I said, feeling guilty.

She looked over at the painting of the ship. "I just came up to check on the painting. I forgot to ask you about it this morning." She started over toward it.

"It's fine," said Ruby quickly, jumping across my bed and getting between Doll and the painting. "I fixed it. Just a loose wire."

"Oh. Well, you're that handy," said Aunt Doll, smiling down at her. "Just like my father. He could turn his hand to anything." She looked up at the painting with a frown. "But it is strange, just the same." She sighed, and sat down on my bed.

"Why strange?" asked Ruby.

"It's all nonsense, and I should know better than to repeat it, but they used to say if a picture fell off a wall by its own accord, then someone was going to die."

Ruby and I exchanged looks. We knew that it hadn't fallen by its own accord, but we weren't going to say.

"I'll be getting as bad as Eldred soon, with his fairies and ghosts," said Aunt Doll. "But when I was a little girl, if a picture had fallen off the wall, my mother would be off to the priest to get him to come and bless the house to try to ward off the bad luck." She laughed. "My mother was a great one for the old stories, just like you, Ruby."

"Which one was she?" I asked.

"Which what?" said Aunt Doll.

"Which . . . uh . . . which twin? I mean, wasn't your mother a twin?"

"Well, yes, she was. They run in the family. She and my Aunt Lucy were twins. Both as fair as the two of you." She sighed. "Lily and Lucy. Long gone. They died when I was only nine."

"How come all the twins have names beginning with the same letter?" asked Ruby.

"Oh, who knows? It's certainly been a tradition ever since the first two, the ones they found in the root cellar—Fiona and Fenella. And I think there's something in the cemetery about their mother and her sister, on that old stone that was put up after the flood, about all the people who died in Slippers Cove. Catriona and Caitlin, I think they were. Who knows, maybe it goes all the way back to Ireland. It's an old custom, I believe, giving twins names with the same first letter. But we lost track of the twins in Slippers Cove, all those generations. My father said something about a Finn family Bible, when he was dying, but I've never seen one. He was rambling, not making a lot of sense. But that's where all the names would be, if there was one."

Ruby and I stared at each other, electrified.

"A family Bible?" repeated Ruby. "Would it list all the twins, back to Ireland?"

"Maybe even before," said Aunt Doll. "That's the only record people had in the old days, of the births and deaths and marriages. But if there ever was one, it was probably swept away in the flood." She shook her head, as if she didn't want to think about that, and got to her feet.

"I must get on," she said. "I'm going down the shore to visit Ann Murphy, so I'll be gone a couple of hours. I want you to put the macaroni and cheese in the oven at a quarter past four, Ruby."

"Okay," said Ruby.

Aunt Doll gave her a hard look. "Don't forget!" She turned to me. "You see that she doesn't, Ruth."

"I won't," protested Ruby. "I won't forget."

"That's what you always say and then you get caught up in something and dinner's late."

"That was last year," protested Ruby. "I'm older and wiser."

"*Humph*," said Aunt Doll. "Older maybe."

"When are you going?" said Ruby.

"As soon as I change out of this housedress. You go and pack up some of the muffins I made this morning."

Ruby dashed off and Aunt Doll followed. She turned back to me at the door.

"Remember what I said about the nightmares, Ruth. I'm always here if you need me." And she smiled kindly again and went down the hall.

CHAPTER THIRTY-NINE

THE PAINTING

After Aunt Doll left, I sat looking at the painting and thinking about my nightmare. The ship looked like the one in my dream: three masts, one broken, ragged sails. I got up and went over to look more closely at it. Nobody was visible on the deck, but I could just make out the name written along the side, *Cathleen*.

Ruby bounced back into the room with two plates.

"Aunt Doll said we could try her muffins," she said, handing me one. I put it down on the bed.

"Look at this picture," I said to Ruby. "See the name?"

"What name?" said Ruby, peering at it.

"*Cathleen*. Right there," I said, pointing to the name. It was faint, but clearly visible.

"*Cathleen*? Are you kidding me, Ruth? That's the name of the ship that brought the Finns from Ireland, the one that sank—"

"I know," I said. "This must be a picture of that ship."

"But there isn't any name on the painting," she said. "What are you talking about?"

"Well, I'm not imagining it!" I said, poking at the name. "It's right there. Are you putting me on or what, Ruby?"

"I'm telling you, there's no name there!"

We were both getting riled.

"Wait a minute," said Ruby, her eyes widening. "You can see the name, really?"

"I swear," I replied, crossing my heart.

"Whewww," she said. "That is so freaky, Ruth. You can see it, but I can't. You know what this means, don't you?"

My heart sank. I had a feeling I did.

"It's the Sight," she said solemnly, and then ruined the effect by taking a huge bite out of her muffin.

I looked back at the painting. The name was still there, clear as anything. A little shiver trickled down my back.

"That's the ship they came on," I said slowly. "The Finns. And that's the ship in my dream."

"Only it's not a dream, is it?" said Ruby. "It's a vision. You said you never had the Sight till you came here, but you told me you had that dream ever since you were a little girl."

"Can a vision come in a dream?"

"Why not?" said Ruby, licking her fingers.

I sat down beside her and took a bite out of my muffin. Smothered with butter and jam, it was even better than the one I'd had with my breakfast the day before. Partridgeberries. One more thing to love about Newfoundland.

"What I can't figure out," said Ruby, still staring at the painting, "is why they have a spy hole behind the painting, but there's no hole in the painting to look through."

"Maybe the painting came after," I said slowly. "And the hole was to look into the nursery, not to look out."

"That makes more sense," said Ruby. "If the mother and father were sleeping in here, they could look in on the baby without disturbing it by going around and opening the door."

"But why close the room off like that?"

"Whoever hung this painting," said Ruby, "must have known about the room. And they hung it here to cover up the spy hole."

"Who painted it?" I wondered. I stood up and looked in the right-hand corner, where the artist had signed his name.

"Michael Finn," I said. "Who was he?"

"Search me," said Ruby.

Aunt Doll's voice drifted up from downstairs.

"I'm on my way. Don't forget the mac and cheese!"

"We won't," yelled Ruby.

The front door slammed. We looked at each other.

"Come on," said Ruby. "We gotta look in the nursery again. Maybe the Finn Bible is hidden in there somewhere."

I was reluctant. "Aunt Doll said there *might* have been one, not that there *was* one. And we already looked. There's nothing there."

"Come on!" said Ruby, pulling at my arm. "We gotta look. We might have missed something." I followed her into the closet, through the rack of clothes to the middle.

It was tricky to find the catch, even though we knew it was there. But I finally found it, and the door swung open silently, into blackness.

"We'll need the flashlight," said Ruby, and went back to our bedroom to get it. "It's still working," she said, giving it a little shake, and then shone it through the door. We bent down and went in, wedging the book in the door behind us.

Ruby flashed the light around the room, illuminating the rough wood walls and the bare floorboards. And the trunk.

We went over and knelt down beside it. The red paint was faded and worn away in places.

"I wonder where this trunk came from," said Ruby. "It sure looks old. Maybe it came from Slippers Cove."

"Maybe," I said doubtfully. "But I don't know when. It would have had to be before the flood. Everything was swept away." I opened it. There was still a faint, sweet smell coming from the wildflowers and grass we'd left in the trunk. We'd left the book there too. Carefully I lifted them out and set them on the floor.

Then, with Ruby holding the flashlight, I felt around the bottom of the trunk to see if there was any kind of catch for a secret compartment. We turned it upside down and examined the bottom.

"It's solid," I said. "There's nothing here."

"My mom said something in my letter about this room having secrets," said Ruby. "What do you think she meant?"

I shrugged. "I don't know. But let's search the room. Maybe there's a loose floorboard or another secret panel in the wall."

We went over that little room inch by inch, but we didn't come up with anything except a lot of dust and old spiderwebs.

Ruby sat back on her heels. "It's no use," she said. "The Bible isn't here."

"Where else could it be?" I asked.

"I wonder . . ." said Ruth. "Maybe in Pop's room. There's a bunch of old books and stuff in there . . ."

"Your dad's room?" I was bewildered. "Why would he have it?"

She stared at me and then started to laugh.

"Not Dad, Pop. And not really my Pop, Molly's Pop."

"What?"

"That's what we call our grandfathers here. Pop. Nan and Pop, get it?"

"Well, how was I to know that?" She was still laughing.

"What do you call your grandfather?"

"I don't have one. Or a grandmother. Except the witch. My dad's parents died before he met my mom."

"Oh, right. Sorry," said Ruby. "It's just you look at me like I'm from another planet sometimes."

"You are," I said. "The planet of Newfoundland." This started her off laughing again. "But who was this guy? Aunt Doll's dad?"

"Our great-grandfather. Clarence Duggan. He was from Fossil's Cove, a distant relation to the Buckle Duggans, and he married Lily," said Ruby in her storytelling voice. "When Lily died, he brought up all the kids on his own. Aunt Doll says he was a very religious man and was best friends with the priest. They used to sit in his room and talk about the Bible for hours. But that was later, after all his children moved away except for Daphne, and he kept on living here with Daphne and her family. When Daphne died, Aunt Doll came back from St. John's to look after the kids and Pop. Clarence."

I was getting confused again. "I forget what happened to Daphne's husband? Why couldn't he look after the kids?"

"He died before Daphne did, when Molly and Meg were little. He was a fisherman and he was lost at sea."

"Oh, right. I remember now. Aunt Doll told me. But that's so sad, to lose both their father and their mother. At least we had our fathers."

"Well, sort of," said Ruby with a shrug.

And then I remembered something the witch had told me about Ruby. In all the fuss about the vision and everything else I had completely forgotten.

Ruby hadn't had her father all the time. After her mother had died she'd lived here, with Aunt Doll, until Uncle George had married Wendy and brought Ruby to live in St. John's with them. Why had she never told me that?

CHAPTER FORTY

THE SMARTEST DUGGAN

"Ruby?" I said. "The witch told me something else. I forgot to tell you."

"What?"

Suddenly I found it hard to say.

"About when Molly died. That your dad . . . your dad left you here with Aunt Doll."

"Oh, that," she said, and turned away to pick up the book and dried flowers. "So?"

"She said you didn't live with your dad again till he got married, and then he brought you to St. John's."

"Yup." Ruby put the book and the flowers in the trunk, closed it, and made a big deal about tying the green ribbon into a bow on the catch. "I wish he'd left me here," she mumbled.

"But why didn't he keep you with him after your mother died?" I asked. "Like me and my dad? We got on okay."

Ruby shrugged, as if she didn't care. "It's different here. Women look after kids, mostly, not the men. And he would travel for work and he couldn't be around all the time. He still visited me a lot, whenever he could. I got on okay with Aunt Doll. In fact, I got on fine. I loved it here. I had friends and I was going to start school, but then Dad and Wendy got married and I went to live with them. Pretty soon they had a baby, and then it was just babies all the time and . . . well, Wynken, Blynken and Nod took over." She stood up. "At least I get to come back here in the summers."

"The witch said she wanted to look after you. She was really mad at your dad for leaving you with Aunt Doll instead of her."

Ruby shuddered. "Thank goodness he did. Can you imagine what I would be like if Nan brought me up?"

"Little Witch Number Two," I said.

She laughed and stood up. "Let's go look for the Bible in Pop's room."

As I followed her out of the room into the closet, carefully latching the door behind me, I couldn't help wondering about what she'd said. Or what she hadn't said. It was almost like her dad didn't want her after her mother died. And then when he took her back, she had to share him with Wendy and the babies. I thought of Dad and Awful Gwen. At least I had all that time with him, just him and me, before he got married.

Ruby led me downstairs, through the living room to a door on the back wall beside the woodstove. I'd hardly noticed it before, thinking it was a closet. There was something about this part of the house, with its low ceilings and dark furniture, that distorted my idea of space. Upstairs I never suspected there was a hidden room, and here I thought the living room stretched the length of the house.

Ruby opened the door and I stood behind her on the threshold. The room beyond was wreathed in shadows.

"Why is it so dark?" I whispered.

Ruby crossed the room and yanked open some curtains. The late afternoon light filtered in. A large wooden desk sat directly under the window, looking out into the yard at the back of the house.

Ruby was opening more curtains on the right-hand side of the room, and more light poured in.

"Aunt Doll says the light damages the furniture and paintings," she said, surveying the room.

The walls were nearly hidden by paintings above and bookcases below. Behind them I could see a dark flocked wallpaper. There was an old-fashioned sleigh bed under the other window and an armchair. A crucifix hung over the bed.

"He must have been a great reader," I said, looking at all the books.

"According to Aunt Doll, he was the smartest Duggan ever born. She says he could have gone to university, but he was brought up to be a fisherman like his father before him. He never stopped reading."

I looked at an old kerosene lamp sitting on the desk.

"No electricity?"

"No. When the electricity came to Buckle in the 1950s, Daphne wanted to get it, but Pop didn't trust it. Said it caused fires. There was a big family racket about it, and in the end Daphne got electricity for the other side of the house but none for this side. Clarence wouldn't have it, and he didn't die till a few years ago. Aunt Doll said not only was he the smartest Duggan, he was the stubbornest Duggan. By then I guess Aunt Doll must have got used to not having electricity on this side of the house. She says it saves money, so she never got it."

While Ruby was talking, I was scanning the shelves for the Bible. There were all kinds of books. A lot of them had leather covers, their titles etched in gold lettering on the spines. But he also had a lot of paperbacks, Penguins in green and white, orange and white. I found myself lingering over them, dying to take them off the shelves and flip through them.

Ruby was pulling out the drawers of the desk and rifling through the contents. "How big is a family Bible?" she asked, pulling out one of the narrower drawers.

"I don't know." I ran my fingers along a row of books and then looked at them. "No dust," I said. "Don't you think if Aunt Doll dusts in here she'd notice if the Bible was here?"

Ruby's voice was muffled. She had crawled under the desk. "It would have to be hidden away somewhere."

She emerged, her hair sticking up. "No secret panels under there. That I can find, anyway. What about under the bed?" and she dived over there.

I sat back on my heels and looked up at the paintings. There were seascapes and landscapes and a few portraits of solemn men and women sitting stiffly in wooden chairs. One of the seascapes looked familiar, and I stood up to read the artist's name.

Michael Finn. The painting was of a stormy sea crashing against a high cliff. There was a break halfway along the cliff, and a narrow band of water led into a barely glimpsed opening.

Cliffs outside Slippers Cove was painted along the bottom of the picture.

"Ruby," I called. Something in my voice brought her out from under the bed and to my side in an instant. I pointed to the name of the painting.

"Oh my," she whispered and grabbed my hand, squeezing it hard.

A play of light on the water beyond the entrance to the cove hinted that there was something magical and secret beyond the rocky opening.

Ruby reached out and touched the artist's name.

"Michael Finn," she said. "Who was he?"

"Wait a minute," I said. Something was tickling inside my brain. An idea. The secret cove. What had Eldred said? No one could find it from the land. No one could see it from the sea. But Michael Finn had painted it, teasing us with the promise of something behind the rocks. A secret. Behind the cliffs. Behind the painting? There was something behind the Michael Finn painting in our bedroom: the hidden room.

Was there something behind this Michael Finn painting?

I stretched out my arms and gently lifted the painting away from the wall.

The flocked wallpaper framed the door of a small wooden cupboard, set into the wall.

CHAPTER FORTY-ONE

THE BIBLE

R uby turned to look at me, her eyes wide. "How did you know it was there? Was it . . ." She lowered her voice dramatically. "The Sight?"

"No, Ruby, I just used my brains. Look," and I showed her the painting, which I'd laid carefully on the floor, leaning up against the bookcase. "The painting is of Slippers Cove, hidden behind those cliffs. I thought of the picture upstairs, where the room is hidden behind the picture, and then I thought, well, maybe there's something hidden behind this picture too."

"Wow!" said Ruby. "You *are* smart! I never would have thought of that. I wonder if it was Pop that hung both pictures,

217

and he planned it that way. But why would he want to hide stuff?"

"Shall we open it and find out?"

Ruby reached out to the little cupboard door and then stopped. "You do the honors," she said. "You found it."

I pulled open the door.

A faint, musty smell of old books came drifting out. It was dark inside, and the dim light from the windows did little to illuminate it. I reached my hand in slowly, wishing I'd let Ruby do it. What if there was a rat in there? Or a mouse? I shivered involuntarily.

Ruby noticed and laughed softly and said, "Don't worry, Ruth, nothing's going to bite you," as if she'd read my mind.

It wasn't a very big space, and it was crowded. First I pulled out a large brown envelope. Next came a wooden box, about the size of a small box of chocolates. It had a strange design of interlocking silver lines on the top and the sides. I reached in once more and my hands closed on the soft leather covering of—a book. I pulled it out.

It was a Bible. Not very big. I always thought of family Bibles as being the size of big, fat dictionaries, but this one was about the size of a paperback book, only twice as thick. It was tied with a green ribbon, very much like the one that tied the trunk closed upstairs. The cover was crumbling away and it looked like the ribbon was the only thing holding it together. The gilt along the edges of the pages was worn to a soft, shimmering gold.

Ruby looked at me with shining eyes. "It's got to be the Finn Bible," she whispered. "Got to be." She took it reverently from my hands and we went over to the desk where there was some light still coming in the window.

Carefully she loosened the ribbon, and then the cover did come off. The first two pages were covered in spidery script. We stared at it.

"Is it English?" said Ruby finally. The handwriting was so small and flowery, with elegant tops and tails to the letters, that at first it looked like another language.

"I saw a magnifying glass in one of these drawers," said Ruby, rummaging and then coming up with one. "Clarence must have needed it to read sometimes." She held it over the first few lines of writing.

"That's *Finn*," she said triumphantly, pointing to a word that seemed to keep repeating.

I stared at it. "I think you're right."

"And that's *1795*, I think," she said, her finger on a number.

I squinted. "Yes. Let's get some paper and write it out as we decipher it."

"There's paper in here," she said, diving into another drawer and coming up with paper and a pencil.

We set to work. It took a while, even with the magnifying glass. Different people had written the entries, and some of the handwriting was more difficult to figure out.

It started in 1795, with a Finn who married a Murphy. It listed their children. They had ten, but four of them had died under the age of three. There was a Michael Finn born in 1805, who married a woman named Ann Keegan. They had several children. They all died the same year—1879.

"The year of the flood," said Ruby.

Eva and Eileen Finn were born in 1810. Eileen married Robert Barrett in 1828—

"Robert Barrett," I said. "The dead man on the floor."

They had two children, Moira and Martha, in 1830, and both Eva and Eileen died in 1832.

"That's when the *Cathleen* went down," said Ruby, "1832."

I was staring at the names I'd just written down. "Moira," I whispered.

"What?"

"Moira," I said, pointing to it. Eileen's daughter. "That's what my mother called me the last time I had the shipwreck dream, in the barn. She called me Moira."

Ruby's eyes grew big. "Moira," she said. "Why would she call you Moira? Unless . . . she wasn't your mother, but Eileen. And you weren't you. You were Moira."

The room seemed to grow darker and I felt that familiar dizziness creeping around the edge of my vision.

"Ruth!" said Ruby, sharply, reaching out her hand to me and grabbing my arm tightly. "Ruth!"

CHAPTER FORTY-TWO

SEVEN

I dragged myself out of the spin. Ruby's hand clutching my arm felt like a lifeline, and I focused on that. The dizziness receded.

"Ruth?" Ruby's voice was tense. "Are you okay?"

I took a deep, shuddering breath.

"Yes. I stopped it that time. Because of you, holding on to me. I didn't want to go down into it. I'm sorry, Ruby. Maybe we could have found out more if I'd let it come, but . . . I . . . I just couldn't do it." I felt like I'd failed her.

"It's okay," she said, patting me on the shoulder. "It's okay, Ruth. It's good that you can control it, even a bit."

My breathing was coming back to normal. "Yes."

She smiled at me and then gave me a quick hug.

"Don't worry. We're going to figure it out. I know we are."

"Right," I said, and did my best to smile back at her. "I guess we should get back to these names." I looked at my notes. The name Moira jumped out at me like it was the only one on the page.

"What does it mean, Ruby?" I said softly. "Why did she call me Moira? Am I seeing the past? But why does it feel like it's my mother and me? I don't understand."

We sat there for a moment in silence. Finally Ruby shook her head.

"I don't know what it means, Ruth, except that you're connected to those two, Eileen and her daughter Moira. Something to do with the Sight. Maybe they both had the Sight too, so you can see through their eyes somehow."

I looked back at the growing list of names and dates I had copied out from the Bible. I sighed.

"Maybe. But we can't figure it out now. What we *can* do is get some of this written into our family tree," I said. "We need to get it clear, who everyone was."

Ruby agreed and volunteered to run up and get my sketchbook from the bedroom. While she was gone, I went back to deciphering the spidery, old-fashioned writing.

When Ruby got back with the sketchbook, she sat down and started fitting the new names into our tree, starting with

Michael Finn and his sisters Eva and Eileen, and then Eileen's daughters, Moira and Martha.

Moira had married a man named Patrick Keegan and given birth to twins in 1850, Caitlin and Catriona. Moira and Martha both died on June 28, 1858. Ruby and I looked at each other.

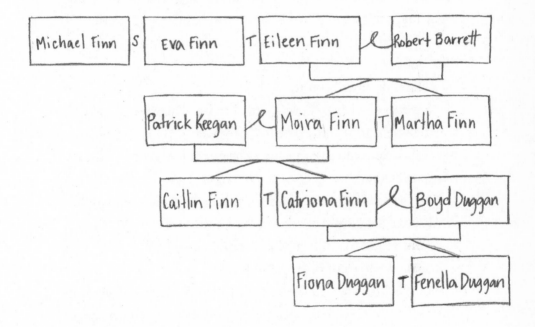

"They died the same day," I said.

"Of course they did," said Ruby.

The handwriting changed. It was easier to read now. Catriona married Boyd Duggan and gave birth to Fenella and Fiona in 1877. All the rest of them died in 1879. In the flood.

It listed off the marriages and children of Fenella and Fiona, including the twins born to Fiona, Lucy and Lily, born in 1900. This is where the information in the Finn Bible tallied with what we'd sketched out before in our family tree.

Lily married Clarence Duggan in 1922 and Doll and Daphne were born in 1926. Lily and Lucy died on May 10, 1935, and Daphne married Bob Duggan in 1945 and gave birth to Meg and Molly in 1946. Bob Duggan died in 1950. Daphne died in 1958.

Ruby did a quick count.

"Seven," she said. "Seven sets of twins who were cursed, if you include Daphne. We'd be . . ." Her voice faltered. "We'd be the eighth generation of twins to be cursed, if we can't find a way to break it."

Our eyes met. "We're going to," I said. "Seven is enough."

"Right," said Ruby. "Seven is a magic number in lots of fairy tales. We've got to make it work for us."

I smiled and went back to the Bible.

Molly's marriage to George Peddle and Meg's to William Windsor were recorded, both in 1967. Ruby was listed as born to Molly on December 10, 1966, and my birthday was listed as born to Meg on December 5. Meg and Molly's deaths were recorded as December 10, 1967.

There was nothing after that. Clarence's death wasn't recorded.

"It must have been Clarence who kept it up to date," said

Ruby. "All the entries since Lily are in the same handwriting."

"I wonder why he kept it hidden away?" I asked.

"Maybe it was here when he married Lily and moved in," said Ruby slowly. "And he discovered it behind the painting. Aunt Doll says this room was always full of paintings and books, even when she was a little girl. Maybe someone else made the secret cupboard behind Michael Finn's painting."

"But why wouldn't he tell someone about it?" I asked. "Why keep it a secret? Aunt Doll said he only spoke about it when he was dying. And why would he keep recording all the births and deaths in it?"

Ruby looked thoughtful. "Maybe for the same reason that Aunt Doll told Eldred not to tell Meg and Molly about the curse. Everyone was trying to keep it secret, thinking that if people didn't know about it, they might not die."

"But Aunt Doll knew about it, and probably Daphne too. It's hard to keep that a secret, with mothers dying all over the place." I was getting upset. "And he kept writing it down. His wife. Her sister. His daughter."

Ruby put out her hand to me. "We're going to get there, Rue. I know we are. We're going to break it."

I shook my head to get rid of the tears and tried to focus on the Bible entries. I couldn't help thinking of Clarence as an old man, sitting in this room recording the deaths of his grand-daughters by lamplight. I shuddered.

"When did he die?" I asked. "Clarence?"

"I'm not sure. I think it was just after I went to live with Dad and Wendy in St. John's. I remember he wasn't here when I came back the next summer."

"How come Aunt Doll never found this little cupboard?" I said. "The way she cleans, wouldn't she have taken down the paintings to dust them?"

"I don't think she likes coming in here much. I think it reminds her too much of her dad. She cleans it, but as quick as she can. She sends me in to dust it while I'm here in the summer. She probably never moved the paintings."

I looked at the list. "Michael Finn was Eva and Eileen's brother. He must have been on that ship with them."

"I guess he and his wife brought up the two little girls after their mother died," said Ruby. "And then he became a painter. I wonder how his paintings got here?"

"There's still this box," I said. "And the envelope."

The box wouldn't open. It didn't seem to have a keyhole.

"We'll have to work on it later. Maybe I can find something in Eldred's workshop that would open it. But meanwhile let's put it all in the secret room so that Aunt Doll doesn't find it—oh no!" she wailed.

"What?"

"What time is it? The mac and cheese was supposed to go in at a quarter past four!"

At that moment there was a far-off bang as the front door closed.

"Ruby! Ruth! I'm home!" called Aunt Doll.

We looked at each other in dismay.

"I'll go," said Ruby. "I'll get her in the kitchen. Put everything back the way it was and take the stuff upstairs once the coast is clear."

"Ruby!" called Aunt Doll again, an edge to her voice. "I don't smell dinner!"

Ruby made a funny face at me and then went out to greet Aunt Doll.

CHAPTER FORTY-THREE

THE FIRE

Aunt Doll was disappointed in me. She gave me a reproachful glance when I came into the kitchen after carefully stowing the Bible, the envelope and the wooden box in the secret room.

"I thought you were going to remind her," she said, hands on hips.

Ruby was setting the table. She gave me a quick look and rolled her eyes.

"I saw that, Ruby Peddle!" said Aunt Doll. "You girls are old enough to take some responsibility. I should be able to count on you to put a casserole in the oven, for goodness' sake.

When I was your age I was doing whole dinners. And baking bread."

"I'm sorry, Aunt Doll," I said. "We just got talking . . . and we forgot."

"*Humph*," she said. "You can make some coleslaw. Ruby, show her how. The macaroni and cheese won't be ready for another half hour at least."

Ruby got cabbage and carrots out of the fridge and handed me a grater. Aunt Doll sat down in her comfy chair with a sigh.

"I'm that tired, from Ann talking my ear off for two hours. That woman has more to say about everything than anyone I ever met."

"How come you were cooking whole dinners when you were our age?" I asked.

"Well, my mother died when my sister and I were nine. My older sisters, Effie and Jane, were grown up and married by the time Daphne and I were twelve, and the boys were no use in the kitchen. So Daphne and I did the cooking. Mostly me, though, because Daphne didn't like cooking and I did."

"What about your dad? Clarence? Did he ever do any cooking?"

Ruby gave a snort of laughter and Aunt Doll smiled. "Men don't cook in Newfoundland, Ruth. No women's liberation here, I'm sorry to say. We leave that up to you on the mainland."

"Told you," said Ruby.

"But you went away to work in St. John's," I said.

"That was during the war," said Aunt Doll. "And a fine time I had, too. I would have stayed, if it hadn't been for my poor sister dying."

"But it's not fair," I said. "You had your career. You had to give it all up just because the men couldn't cook?"

"No. It wasn't just that," said Aunt Doll. "Meg and Molly were twelve, and their brother, Jack, was fourteen. My poor father was gutted and couldn't cope. The girls were running wild even before Daphne died, and they needed a firm hand."

"But you gave up so much," I persisted.

Aunt Doll looked at me with a sad smile. "It's just life, Ruth. It isn't always fair. And I settled in here."

"I'll never give up my career for a man," said Ruby.

"Let's hope you never have to," said Aunt Doll. "But I had to weigh things out. My father had lost my mother years before, and brought up all of us without her, and now he'd lost his daughter." She sighed.

"It seems like a lot of sad things happen to this family," I said.

Aunt Doll looked up at me sharply. "Yes. You could say that. But every family has its sorrows. If you went into the history of every other family in Buckle, you'd find just as many." She stood up. "If you girls can watch the casserole, I'm going to put my head down for a few minutes before supper."

She left.

"She's upset," said Ruby. "Why did you get her going on about all of that old stuff?"

"I just want to find out what happened. I really wanted to ask her about Clarence, what he was like, but I couldn't figure out how to bring him up without letting on we'd been in his room."

"I remember him. I used to go into his room and he'd be sitting at his desk, and he'd stop to talk to me or give me some paper to draw on. He smelled like tobacco. He smoked a pipe, but Aunt Doll always made him smoke it in the other side of the house. I liked him."

"All these people," I said. "Down through the years. Living with the sadness. Losing their wives, their daughters, their mothers. It's not right, Ruby. We have to do something about it."

"I know," she said. "But what?"

❦

By the time dinner was over and the dishes washed, we were both so tired we just went to bed.

"We'll look at the box and the envelope in the morning," said Ruby. "I can't keep my eyes open."

She went to sleep before I did. I lay there, listening to the wind whistling around the corners of the house, thinking about all the people who had lived here. My ancestors. All connected to me by blood. And the curse. As I drifted off to sleep, I started to fall into a dream. I saw seven pairs of twins walking along the Ghost Road, holding hands. Eva and Eileen. Moira and Martha. Caitlin and Catriona. Fenella and Fiona. Lucy and Lily. Daphne and Doll. Molly and Meg. They all looked the same. They all looked like Ruby and me (except for Doll). One after the other, the twins walked slowly up over the hill and disappeared.

I woke to the acrid smell of smoke and the crackling of flames.

"Ruby?" I said, sitting up. A red light filled the room. Ruby was in her bed, not moving. I threw back the covers and put my feet down on the cold floor, but before I could reach out to her, a movement caught my eye by the dresser.

It was my mother. Meg. Her golden hair fell down to her shoulders, and she was wearing a white nightgown, just as when I'd seen her before. She put her finger to her lips as if to say "Shhhh."

"But . . . the fire?" I said. She shook her head and held out her hands to me.

That's when I realized that although I could smell the smoke, there was none in the room. I was dreaming. Or—not dreaming exactly. Having a vision, like before. Ruby was safe. The house wasn't on fire.

Not now, anyway. But sometime in the past?

I walked over to Meg. I had never been this close to her before. She was lit by the red flickering light of flames. She didn't look like a ghost. She looked as solid and real as me.

"The painting," she whispered. I don't know how, but I knew what she wanted me to do. I took the painting down off the wall and looked through the hole.

The nursery was engulfed in smoke and flames. I could just make out two still figures lying on a bed in the middle of the room. I could see they were women, with bright blonde hair. Everything was burning. And in the roaring of the flames, I heard that same dreadful voice screaming, "By fire! By fire! By fire!"

I turned back to Meg.

"No," I said. "Make it stop."

Tears fell down her cheeks.

"I can't," she said. "Only you can. You and Ruby."

I reached out to her, and she moved toward me. I felt her arms encircle me. She held me tight and said, "My sweet Ruth," and at that moment I knew she had done this before, hugged me and said those exact words. I felt something that I'd held locked deep inside me let go and then—

I was standing alone in the dark. The fire, the smoke and my mother were all gone.

CHAPTER FORTY-FOUR

THE DEED OF GIFT

I sank down to the floor, crying. Crying for my mother. All those years without her, all those years longing for her, they all seemed to come together into that one moment of pain, with me kneeling on the floor, rocking and holding my stomach. Everything hurt.

"Ruth?" came Ruby's voice from the darkness. She sounded scared. "Ruth, are you okay?"

I heard her scrambling out of bed and she must have found the flashlight, for a thin line of light came toward me. Then she was kneeling on the floor, her hand on my arm.

"What's wrong? What's happened?"

I couldn't stop crying long enough to tell her. She put her arms around me and held me, and I was reminded of my mother. She was gone, but I had Ruby now. And Aunt Doll. And—strangely, I thought of the witch. My Nan.

Gradually my tears subsided. I dried my eyes on my pajama sleeves.

"Whatever happened?" said Ruby.

I told her.

"The fire," she said, when I had finished. "Who was in the fire?"

I shook my head. "I don't know. But it was twins. And they were grown up."

"Maybe that's why the nursery was closed up," said Ruby slowly. "Because of the fire. It was too horrible to remember, so they blocked it all away. But we should be able to figure it out," she said, getting to her feet. "Come on."

She led the way into the closet, the flashlight a wavering beam of light. I hesitated.

"Come on!" she said, sticking her head back out the door.

"I don't know if I can."

She came out and stood looking at me. She took my hand.

"Ruth, I know. It was awful. But we have to keep going. We have to find out everything and then we have to break it. Everything has been pushed down and forgotten for too long."

I nodded. "I know," I whispered. "But I'm scared."

She gave my hand a squeeze. "Me too. Come on. We can be scared together."

As I bent over to go through the doorway into the hidden room, the smell of burning was strong. Much stronger than the other times I'd been in there, when there had only been a faint trace of it.

"Ruby," I said. She was already on the floor by the trunk, pulling things out. "Ruby, have you ever smelled a burning smell in here?" She looked over at me, her face half-lit by the flashlight she'd placed on the floor. She sniffed.

"Burning? No. Why? Do you?"

"Yes. More now than before."

She shook her head. "The Sight," she said, predictably.

"More like The Smell," I grumbled, and sat down beside her. I couldn't shake the image of those two women in the bed with fire all around them. I took the envelope from her and opened it, extracting a couple of sheets of brittle, yellowed paper covered with a flowery handwriting. Ruby helpfully shone the flashlight on it.

"What is it?"

"It's some kind of letter. From Shelagh Duggan. Who was she?"

"She was Vince Duggan's wife. The one who adopted Fenella and Fiona, the twins who were found in the root cellar."

"Right."

We read it together. At the top it read, "Deed of Gift." It was dated February 20, 1910.

I am writing this deed of gift while of sound mind and body.
On January 1, 1910, my adopted daughters, Fiona Mary Finn
Whalen and Fenella Margaret Finn Brennan died tragically
on account of a chimney fire that burned up the room they
were sleeping in after a New Year's party. Fiona and Fenella
were daughters of my husband's brother, Boyd, and these two
children at age two were the only survivors of the Slippers Cove
Flood of 1879.

Vince and I raised them as if they were our own daughters.
Now that they are gone, Fiona leaves behind two daughters,
Lucy Alice Finn Whalen and Lily Mary Finn Whalen. It is
my wish, and the wish of my husband, that this house is deeded
over to them and their heirs thereafter. Our own children
have their own houses and families, and these two little girls
and their father have moved in with us. The Finns have such a
sad history. Vince and I want to do our part to provide for these
two that are left, and any that may come after. We particularly
want the house to go to the girl children, not the boys, since girls
have a harder time in the world making their way.

This house was left to me by my father, Thomas Walsh,
for the same reason. He wanted me to have something of my
own that was not my husband's, and Vince and I are in perfect
agreement that it should go to Lily and Lucy.

There are those who looked down on Fiona and Fenella
because they were Finns, and from Slippers Cove. There has
been a lot of talk that the family was no good, but it's just talk.

The Finns of Slippers Cove were hardworking people who made a life there for their families and the terrible flood that took them away was not a judgment on them, as some people say, but an Act of God we can none of us understand. They were good people and none of them deserved to lose their lives like that. And Fiona and Fenella were dear daughters to us. We want the Finns to go into the future with something they can call their own. We have discussed this with our other children, and they have all agreed to give up any claim they or their heirs may have on the house, and that it should go to the Finns. We would like them to always keep the name "Finn" to remember who they are and where they came from.

Dated this 20th day of February 1910.

It was signed by Shelagh Mary Duggan and Vince Albert Duggan, and all eight of their children.

"Wow," said Ruby. "That explains a lot. Poor Fiona and Fenella. It must have been them you saw in the fire."

I nodded.

"And that's why this room was all shut off. Shelagh and Vince couldn't bear the memory of it."

I nodded again.

"It's the curse," I whispered. "They died because of the curse. And Shelagh knew that. That's why she left the house to the Finns. She wanted to give them a chance of something, something beyond the curse."

"But it didn't work," said Ruby. "Lily and Lucy still died young, and Daphne."

"And Meg and Molly."

We stared at each other.

"We're next," whispered Ruby.

CHAPTER FORTY-FIVE

OFF WITH THE FAIRIES

Eldred turned the wooden box this way and that.

"What a beauty," he said softly, tracing the lines of the design with the tip of a finger. "Do you know what these are?"

Ruby and I peered at them and shook our heads.

"Celtic knots," he said. "It's an Irish design, goes way back."

"What do they mean?" I asked.

He shrugged. "I'm not sure. But it's a fine puzzle, trying to figure them out."

He spoke slowly, as if he wasn't quite awake yet. We were standing with him at his workbench in the barn, where we'd tracked him down after breakfast.

"Can you open it?" said Ruby.

He turned the box over several more times, inspecting each side carefully. Then he picked up a magnifying glass.

"Look, here's the keyhole," he said, pointing to a slit that was worked into one of the silver knots on the side of the box, almost completely hidden.

"Can you open it?" repeated Ruby.

He found a thin wire and inserted it into the keyhole, twisting it this way and that. Nothing happened.

"I'd hate to damage it," he said. "This is old. And valuable, no doubt. Where did you say you found it?" He spoke absently, and his eyes had that faraway look I'd noticed once or twice before.

We exchanged glances.

"Um . . ." said Ruby. "In Pop's room."

"We think it's connected to the Finns," I said. "And the curse."

I wasn't sure he heard me. He was running his fingers over the silver knots on the box again, looking thoughtful. "Slippers Cove," he said softly. "It all goes back to Slippers Cove. But you know I can't be telling you more. I promised Doll never to tell Meg and Molly. No matter what." He looked more distracted than ever.

Ruby grabbed his arm and gave it a gentle shake.

"Look at us, Eldred. We're not Meg and Molly. I'm Ruby and she's Ruth. You never promised Doll you wouldn't tell *us*!"

241

"Ruth and Ruby, Meg and Molly, Eva and Eileen," he said in a lilting voice. "All you twins look the same. As if you were all the same two girls, born again and again, stuck inside the curse and never to escape." His voice faded away.

"Eldred?" I said.

Ruby put her hand on my arm and shook her head. She stood up and gently took the box from his fingers.

"We'll see you later, Eldred," she said, and we left him there, staring into space.

"What was that about?" I asked once we were clear of the barn.

"He gets like that sometimes," said Ruby. "Aunt Doll says he's off with the fairies. I don't know. He just . . . goes somewhere else."

I shivered. The sun was trying to break through a dense bank of clouds over the ocean, but there was a chill wind blowing in.

"Did you notice he said Eva and Eileen? As if he knew them, just as he knew Meg and Molly? And you and me?" I said.

Ruby nodded. "He knows something more about the old days, that's for sure. It may have been a story his mother told him, one that her mother told her, and her mother before that. His family have all been storytellers since I don't know when. But he won't tell us. Not if he promised."

We went into the house and I pulled Ruby into the living room.

"What he said about all the twins being the same?"

"What about it?"

"I . . . I had a kind of dream last night, or an image or something—"

"A vision?"

"I don't know! It was when I was falling asleep, and there was a line of all the twins, all of them, back to Eva and Eileen, and they were holding hands and walking two by two, along the Ghost Road, up over the hill. And they all looked the same. They looked like you and me. They *were* you and me."

Ruby stared at me. "You think . . . you think . . . we *are* them? Like when your mother called you Moira in the dream about the shipwreck, like you were Moira and Meg was Eileen? We're all really the same people, and it's happening to us over and over again in different lifetimes? Like Eldred said?"

I shook my head. "No," I said slowly. "I don't think we're the same people. But I think they're all inside us, our mothers, our aunts, our grandmothers and great-grandmothers. They're in there, living on in us. And they're carrying the curse with them. So we're carrying it. And we have to fix it. For all of them. Not just us."

CHAPTER FORTY-SIX

THE EAVESDROPPERS

"For all of them," murmured Ruby. "You're right. So they can rest. So they can all rest."

There was a brightening in the room, as if the sun had finally broken through. Ruby walked over to the window and looked out.

"I think it's clearing up," she said. She turned back to me. "Let's go to Slippers Cove today, Rue," she said suddenly. "We may not get this good a day for another week."

I went to the window and looked out. There were still dark clouds over the western hills.

"I don't know," I said, stalling. "It doesn't look that great to me. What if it rains?"

"We'll take raincoats," she replied, coming up beside me. I turned to her.

She smiled. "Ruth, I know you're scared," she said. She'd read my mind again. I wasn't sure how much I liked this twin thing. How would I ever keep a secret from her?

"Yes," I said in a shaky voice. "I'm scared."

She put her arm around my shoulders and gave me a squeeze. "I'll be with you. And I think Meg will be too. And Molly. And all the rest of them. It's come down to us, Ruth. You know we have to do it."

I felt her strength coming into me, and I found comfort in her calm, matter-of-fact way of talking about Meg and Molly and the others as if they were not very far away.

"Yes," I said. "I know."

"Right," said Ruby, grinning. "Let's go, then."

She disappeared into the kitchen to tell Aunt Doll we were going for a long hike, and while they put a lunch together, I went up to our room and fished out my knapsack from inside my suitcase in the closet. I put in a couple of pairs of dry socks and my sketchbook and pencils, and then I sat down on the bed, holding the wooden box in my hands.

The pattern of Celtic knots was intricate and mysterious. The lines kept crossing and crisscrossing, and it was almost impossible to follow one line all the way through. It reminded me of a maze in a coloring book, where you had to run your pencil along to find your way out. The silver pattern was tarnished and black in places. I tried rubbing at a bit of it with my hand-kerchief, and the black gradually disappeared. Now the twisting lines had a soft, silvery sheen. I wondered how old it was. If it came from Ireland, as Eldred said, it must date back to at least 1832, when the Finns came over in the ship. I turned to look at the painting of the ship on the wall.

And then it happened. It was so swift this time, with no warn-ing, just a seamless transition from my present into the past.

Two girls were sitting on the floor beside the dresser, heads bent together. One of them suppressed a giggle and the other one smacked at her shoulder to get her to be quiet.

Molly and Meg, when they were just a couple of years older than Ruby and me. Molly was the giggler and Meg was the smacker. Even though they were identical, it was easy for me to tell them apart. I knew Meg, through and through. Not just because I'd seen her ghost, but because she was my mother. Or at least, she was the mother I remembered and dreamed about, though Molly was my birth mother.

Molly was still trying to stifle her giggles. She looked like she was always laughing, a bit like Ruby, with a lively grin. My mother. They were both my mother.

This was weird. I felt a catch in my throat.

Molly's shoulders were shaking with the giggles and Meg pinched her arm, hard.

"Stop it!" she mouthed. Molly subsided.

Their blonde hair was caught up in two high, identical

ponytails, Molly's tied with a pink ribbon and Meg's with a green. They were wearing baggy jeans with plaid turned-up cuffs and bulky, home-knit sweaters.

They seemed to be listening to something. I could hear a faint murmur of voices from the room below. I got to my feet and tiptoed over, but I needn't have bothered trying to be quiet. They paid no attention to me.

They were bent over an iron grille, some kind of air vent, on the floor between the dresser and the closet door. Evidently it went straight through to the room below, because the voices were clearer now.

A woman was speaking in a high, angry tone. A voice that was familiar, if only I could place it.

"You can pray all you like, Clarence Duggan, but God punishes sinners and all the Finns have to live with the sins of their mothers. And you can keep those girls away from my George or you'll have me to reckon with!"

The witch.

CHAPTER FORTY-SEVEN

GEORGE

Molly began to sputter and Meg pulled her away from the iron grille.

"Honestly, Molly," she said softly as she tugged her sister over to the bed and sat beside her. "You're going to get us into worse trouble if Pop finds out we were eavesdropping up here."

"What are we in trouble for?" protested Molly. "Hanging around with her precious George? Last time I checked it wasn't a crime for a Duggan to be friends with a Peddle."

"You know very well that Mrs. Peddle thinks it is," said Meg. "And especially the Finn twins. You heard her."

"George told me yesterday she was on the warpath about us

spending so much time with him, but I didn't think she'd come and complain to Pop." Molly laughed. "She was some crooked, wasn't she? She was sputtering like a kettle on the boil. I thought she was going to explode."

"She said some awful things about us," said Meg quietly. "And our family. How a woman like that could give birth to someone as sweet as George is more than I'll ever understand."

"Doll says he takes after his father," said Molly. Then she sighed. "George is sweet, isn't he?"

Meg laughed. "And so cute. Admit it, Molly, you have a big crush on him."

"Me? What about you? You get all giggly whenever he's around."

"Do not!" said Meg, giving her a push. Then they both laughed.

"But what about that old Bible Pop took out of the wall?" said Meg. "We gotta get our hands on that, Molly. He said it showed all the Finns going back to Ireland."

"We'll have to wait till the next time he goes to visit Father Doyle and sneak in there," said Molly.

"Yes. I want to see that Bible. There might be something there that would help us."

"I can't get over that old witch coming over here to see Pop to complain about us," said Molly, lying back on the bed and kicking her feet up in the air. "She has her nerve. Aunt Doll told me last week she hasn't ever stepped inside this house because she's a Barrett, and the Barretts have always hated the Finns.

And the Duggans, because they adopted the Finn twins."

"I wonder," said Meg slowly. "I wonder about that. I wonder if the Barretts were involved somehow in the curse? They all came from Ireland around the same time. Maybe the Bible will tell us something. Do you think . . . do you think if we could put an end to that feud we could put an end to the curse?"

Molly shook her head. "How can we put an end to the feud? Mrs. Peddle hates us."

"But George doesn't."

Molly stared at her sister. "What do you mean?"

"Look, if one of us married George, then the two families would be brought together."

Molly gave a hoot of laughter. "Meg, you're awful."

"Why? We both like him. He's a great guy. I'd marry him."

"I would too," said Molly. "But how would we decide who gets him, if we both like him?"

The two girls looked at each other.

"Share?" said Meg, and they dissolved into giggles.

"Mrs. Peddle won't like it much," said Molly.

"No, she certainly won't," said Meg, and then they started laughing again.

"Don't worry, Molly," said Meg when their laughter started to die down. "I've seen the way he looks at you. I know it's you he wants."

"Do you really think he likes me?" said Molly, with an uncertainty in her voice that surprised me.

"Of course he does," said Meg. "He's crazy about you."

Molly laughed. "That would be hard to take, wouldn't it, Meg, if I get a boyfriend before you do? Never mind, there's always Joe Dunphy. You can have him."

"Ha!" said Meg, grabbing a pillow and walloping her sister over the head with it. "Fat chance!"

I heard a clatter of footsteps coming up the stairs and along the hall. Ruby burst into the room.

"Ruth?" she said.

I looked back at the bed. They were gone.

"Aunt Doll's making us a lunch and—" Ruby broke off when she saw my face. "What's wrong?"

I couldn't speak for a moment. I went and sat down on the bed where Meg and Molly had been lying a minute before. I shook my head.

"Was it bad?" said Ruby, coming and sitting beside me. "Like the fire?"

"No," I said. "Not scary."

"Then what?" said Ruby.

My eyes were swimming with tears.

"I saw them," I said. "Meg and Molly. Right here. Talking about the witch and the Bible and Uncle George. They were so . . . so alive." And then I started to cry.

Ruby put her arms around me and gave me a hug. I couldn't stop crying. I felt bereft. I wanted Meg and Molly back— laughing, alive. All their efforts to break the curse had failed.

They'd joined the two families, but it wasn't enough. They'd separated Ruby and me, but that wasn't enough either. The curse had caught up with them, the way it would catch up with Ruby and me, and our children. There didn't seem to be a way out.

"Tell me," said Ruby, handing me a crumpled handkerchief. "Tell me what happened."

After I blew my nose, I felt a little better.

"It's just so hard, Ruby," I said. "They were just as real as you are. They were right here. I'm afraid soon I won't be able to tell the difference between what's in the present and what's in the past."

"Just tell me," said Ruby.

And I did.

When I had finished, Ruby looked almost as sad as I felt.

"They thought they could break the curse by marrying Dad?" she said, shaking her head. "By stopping the feud? I guess it didn't work so good. Seems like the feud is alive and well. Look, Ruth," she said, getting to her feet with a big sigh, "we can only do our best. And we need to get to Slippers Cove. It's a long walk." She started rummaging in the chest of drawers. "We better take some extra sweaters," she said, tossing me one of hers, a thick blue one. "Just in case." She pulled her knapsack out from under her bed and stuffed another sweater into it. Then she hauled out a couple of turtlenecks and threw me one.

"Put it in your knapsack," she said. "It won't hurt to be prepared. The weather can change so fast."

I dried my eyes and finished packing. Ruby was right. I couldn't lose hope now.

When we got downstairs, Aunt Doll doled out the food between us and then started clucking about the possibility of rain. Ruby made a strong stand.

"If we wait for the weather to be perfect, we'll never go," she said. "This is Newfoundland, after all. And Ruth wants to collect some flowers for her dad."

I nodded, trying to look innocent. It couldn't have been very convincing, because Aunt Doll said, "Oh, get on with you. I know you're up to something. Just be sensible and stay safe and don't go near the edge of cliffs or play on the rocks near the ocean."

Ruby rolled her eyes. "I know all that, Aunt Doll. And we're not up to something. We just want a good long hike."

I nodded again. Aunt Doll looked doubtful. "Make sure you're back before dark," she said, and then settled into her chair with her pink newspapers. "At least I'll get some peace and quiet," she said, with a contented sigh.

Ruby turned her back on Aunt Doll and winked at me. Then we set off.

CHAPTER FORTY-EIGHT

CHOCOLATE BROWNIES

By the time we got outside and started down the road, the sun had disappeared and the wind was bitter. We had sweaters and jackets on, with raincoats in our knapsacks, along with what seemed like a huge amount of food, including crusts of bread in our pockets to keep us safe from the fairies.

As we walked, the sun went in and out behind the clouds. When it was out, I was too hot and tied my jacket around my waist. A few minutes later the sky would darken and the wind would cut through my sweater, and I'd put my jacket on again.

Ruby led the way, up the hill into the next valley, then along the road to the top of the hill where I'd met Eldred a few days earlier. It seemed like weeks ago. We stopped for a while on the top of the hill, catching our breath and having a drink. Aunt Doll had given us each a thermos of water and a bottle of lemonade. We investigated the lunch.

"It's too early to eat yet," said Ruth, not very convincingly. "She made chicken sandwiches," she said, pulling out a packet of wax paper, "and she's put in brownies and partridgeberry muffins—" She looked up at me with a grin.

"Okay, give me a muffin," I said, and we sat and devoured a couple. The sun was shining on the far hill, where the Ghost Road climbed up over the rise.

Ruby followed my gaze. "You can see it?"

"Yup," I replied, pointing. She stared, but shook her head. "Nothing," she said.

The path we had been following veered off to the right, to the Fairy Path where Eldred had been heading, and then curved up through the valley, half-shadowed by trees. I turned back to the Ghost Road.

"You see those two tall trees, there on the left side of the hill?" I said to Ruby.

"Yes."

"We should head for them. The road goes up beside them."

She started down the hill, trying to pick out the easiest way. It was slow going. We couldn't really see where we were stepping, because of the juniper and Virginian rose that grew low to the ground. They formed a kind of cushiony mat, but every time

I took a step I wasn't sure how far my foot would go down. There was a profusion of wild flowers, most of which I recognized—white yarrow, bright-pink bog laurel, yellow potentilla—and a few I didn't. But I didn't want to take the time to pick any specimens. We had to keep moving. We had a long way to go.

Slowly we made our way across the valley. It was wider than it looked from the hill. It was hard to get perspective, because it was mostly rock and low bushes, with a few stunted trees scattered around. On the left, the ocean stretched off into the distance, a deep navy blue studded with whitecaps. The sun stayed out, and soon we were down to our T-shirts.

As we got closer, the Ghost Road grew more defined. It looked like a silvery ribbon, twisting up over the hill. A stony road. Every so often Ruby would stop and shield her eyes from the sun, trying to see it. Then she'd shake her head and go on.

At the bottom of the valley the ground got marshy, and although we tried to pick our way around the wet spots, we sank in above our ankles in a few places, and soon our shoes and socks were soaked.

"Never mind," I said to Ruby. "I brought some dry socks and we can change into them later on."

"Good thinking, Twin," she said.

As we started to climb up the opposite hill, I began noticing signs of a faint path. The walking got easier.

"Ruby, can you see that we're on a kind of road now?" I asked. She looked down at the ground.

"Sort of," she said. "But I still don't see anything up ahead."

We kept climbing. Finally we reached the tall trees I'd pointed out to Ruby from the top of the hill where I had met Eldred. They weren't tall by Ontario standards—only about fifteen feet. But they stood out on the mostly treeless hill. The Ghost Road was clear now, to me, anyway: a rough track, sprinkled with stones, that led up and over the hill.

We stood and looked back. Now I could make out a faint track behind us, going down the hill and across the valley, where we had come from. It was like the shadow of a road. I tried to point it out to Ruby, but she still couldn't see it. We turned and I led her up to the crest of the hill.

A series of meadows opened up below us, dipping down toward the ocean and then climbing into the distance. The Ghost Road twisted along, steadily drawing closer to the water.

"Do you see it?" I asked Ruby. She squinted against the sun, which was sparkling off the water now.

"Nope," she said. Then she flopped down on the grass and opened her knapsack.

"Definitely lunchtime," she said, and hauled out a packet of sandwiches.

I joined her and we ate in silence, the sun warming our faces. It was very peaceful, sitting there on the hill, with the world spread out beneath us. It was almost as if we two were alone in the world. There was not a house or another person in sight. The hills and the meadows and the sea stretched on and on, into the distance.

"Funny no one's ever found it, all these years," I said. "I mean, at the beginning, the road must have still been visible and they could have got there easily. And then once it faded away, you'd think they could still find it, just by walking along in the right general direction."

"Eldred told me no one wanted to go. People thought it was haunted by the spirits of all the people who died there in the flood."

I shivered. "Just what I need. More ghosts."

Ruby looked thoughtfully out over the ocean. The sun was just disappearing behind a bank of clouds. Now that we were sitting still, the breeze was a little cool. I shifted uncomfortably on the rocks.

"Don't you think we should get going, Ruby? We've only been gone about two hours and we still have a long way to go. And it might rain . . ."

She turned abruptly away from the darkening sky and started rummaging around in her knapsack. "In a minute. There's one more thing we need to eat to give us some energy," she said. She found what she was looking for and hauled it out, grinning at me.

"Chocolate brownies."

CHAPTER FORTY-NINE

THE SHIP

W e walked for another hour or so. The sun emerged from behind the clouds for a while, and it grew warmer. Although grasses and low bushes had grown over the Ghost Road in places, it was still easy enough for me to follow. A seagull screamed overhead. I looked up. The bird swooped out over the ocean, then hovered in a wind current. I looked beyond it, where something was slowly moving across the water.

A fishing boat? I'd seen a few near Buckle over the last few days, but today the sea seemed pretty rough for a boat to be out. I shaded my eyes and squinted into the distance.

A sailboat? White shapes ballooned out from tall masts. A tall ship? I caught my breath. Ruby had told me that she'd seen a tall ship in St. John's once, a replica of an old schooner, and people paid to go sailing on it. But why would a tall ship be here on this remote part of the coast?

Suddenly the dark clouds that had been hovering in the west were quickly filling the sky, and the wind had picked up, and it was starting to rain.

I looked back to the ship. It was rocketing up and down on a wild sea, and suddenly it seemed a lot closer, and I could hear people screaming—and a hissing kind of shriek, rising and falling in the wind. "By water," it howled. "By water!"

"Ruth," said Ruby, shaking my arm. "Ruth!"

I turned and she was there beside me, solid and real and safe. The sky was just cloudy, not dark, and there was no sign of the sailing ship.

"*Cathleen*," I said. "I thought I saw it—in the storm. Just for a minute."

Ruby shaded her eyes and scanned the ocean. "There's nothing out there," she said.

"We better keep going," I said, and turned back to the road. I felt a sick sense of apprehension, like I was going to the dentist and getting closer and closer with every step. I didn't want to see any more shipwrecks, or visions, or ghosts, but I knew without a doubt that I was walking right into them.

We went on. The terrain was getting rougher, and the road

wound a path through rocky outcrops and dipped closer to the edge of the cliffs. They towered a couple of hundred feet above the water, and seagulls and gannets swept along and dived for the surface. Huge waves crashed and swirled against the jagged coastline. There was no sign of any break in the cliffs ahead.

"It would be hard to get a boat in anywhere along here," said Ruby.

"Maybe that's why Slippers Cove is hard to find from the water," I said, remembering the painting in Clarence's study. "You can't get in close enough to see the gap in the cliffs."

"I suppose," said Ruby. We walked along in silence for a while.

Even with the shadow of my latest vision clouding my thoughts, and my worry about what lay ahead, I felt my spirits lifting. There was something in the wild pounding of the sea below us, the calling of the seabirds and the blustering sky above us that filled me with joy. It was so beautiful and lonely and vast. I was part of it, the way I'd never been part of any-where else I'd ever been. I belonged here.

I stopped and gazed out at the ocean. "It's so beautiful," I said softly.

"I know," said Ruby. "It's the best." She sighed. "Hey, are you hungry? I think there might be some brownies left."

We stopped and dug in the knapsacks again. We polished off the brownies sitting against a rock with the sea spread beneath us and the warm sun on our faces.

"I've been all over the world with my dad," I said. "And been to all kinds of beautiful places. But this is different. I feel it in my bones. Like I'm part of it."

Ruby nodded. "I know. That's exactly how I feel. The rest of my life, outside here, feels like a shadow. Or a black-and-white movie. But when I'm in Buckle, it's in color."

I watched a gannet stop in midair and then drop like a stone into the water in an effortless dive. I thought of my room in Toronto, and school, and Dad and Gwen. It all seemed gray and unhappy compared with sitting on this cliff beside Ruby, with miles and miles of emptiness all around us.

"I don't know how I'll be able to go back," I said.

"Well," said Ruby, getting to her feet, "we can't think about that now. Today we have to find Slippers Cove."

"You're very practical, aren't you?" I said, smiling up at her. Her hair was blowing every which way in the sea breeze and her eyes sparkled.

She reached out a hand to me and pulled me to my feet. "Come on, Ruth," she said. "It can't be too much farther."

CHAPTER FIFTY

LADY SLIPPERS

After about another fifteen minutes of walking, the Ghost Road curved inland away from the sea, and soon we were walking downhill through an area thick with trees. The sky darkened and the trees crowded up on either side of the road, so we couldn't see very far ahead. In some places small trees had sprung up in the middle of the road, and we had to step around them.

My eyes were on the ground ahead of me when something caught my eye off to the left. I looked up and saw a splash of yellow in the gloom. I stopped.

"What?" said Ruby, who was right behind me.

"Look," I said, pointing. "Yellow lady slippers."

There was a patch of them growing together just under the trees beside the road. Hanging from slender green stems, they seemed to be glowing from within like small magic lanterns.

"They're so pretty," said Ruby. "I've never seen them before."

"*Cypripedium*," I said automatically, "meaning 'Aphrodite's sandal.' Lady's slipper, get it? It's a kind of orchid," I said.

Ruby went closer and stared at it. "They do look like little shoes," she said. "Fairy shoes." She started back down the road.

"Just hang on a minute," I called. Then I waded through the tall grass and carefully picked a couple of the stems with the nodding flowers and folded them into my notebook.

Ruby was up ahead, watching me, a funny look on her face.

"Well, we did tell Aunt Doll we were going to look for wildflowers," I said, apologetically, as I caught up with her. "They're a little rare and I might not get a chance to find another one."

"That's okay, Twin," she said. "I get it. You're a flower collector. But now can we go and break this curse? We must be nearly there."

I gave her a little shove. She laughed.

About five minutes later she stopped suddenly.

"More fairy shoes," she said, pointing into the woods at another patch of glowing flowers. This time they were dark purple.

"Wow," I said. "This must be the perfect growing conditions for them. I know they like woods and wet patches, and—oh!"

"Slippers Cove!" We both said. And then "Jinx!" And we laughed.

"I never thought about why it was called Slippers Cove," I said. "I just assumed it was something to do with slippers, like you wear on your feet. Not the flower."

"Me neither," said Ruby. "But it makes sense, doesn't it?"

"I just need to get a couple of samples," I said, stepping off the road and into the woods. "Won't be a minute." I bent down to pick a flower, taking care not to touch the leaves, when something moving gently in the shadows beyond the lady slippers caught my eye.

It was another clutch of wildflowers, growing closer to the ground. Each stem had two delicate mauvy-pink flowers nodding in the breeze.

"Twinflowers," I whispered, and then raised my voice. "Ruby, come!"

"What, what?" she said in an excited voice, galloping up behind me and looking from left to right, as if she expected to see a crowd of ghosts coming out from behind the trees.

"Twinflowers!" I said, pointing to them.

"Oh," she said, disappointed. "What are twinflowers?"

"They were the other dried flower in the trunk, with the lady slippers," I explained, tucking the purple lady slippers into my sketchbook and stepping over to the patch of twinflowers.

Ruby came with me and squatted down to look at them while I picked a couple.

"They're so pretty," she said, touching one of the nodding flowers.

"Yes," I said, and our eyes met.

"They were here," I said. "Or at least Molly was. Someone picked them and the lady slippers and dried them and put them in the trunk."

"Where they've been all this time," said Ruby. "Come on, let's keep going."

We went back to the road and kept walking. Over the next ten minutes, the road led steadily downhill through the woods, and we saw several more patches of *Cypripedium*—yellow, pink and purple. I'd always loved orchids and I hadn't seen many lady slippers in my travels with Dad. These were lovely, a touch of color in a landscape that was growing darker by the minute.

I felt a sprinkle of raindrops on my face.

"Uh-oh," said Ruby, and we stopped to haul our raincoats out from the bottom of our knapsacks.

Just in time. It started raining in earnest. Water dripped from the trees and small puddles formed on the road. We kept slogging on, but the stones were slippery underfoot and the road uneven as it wound down a steeper hill.

It was hard to see anything now because the rain was falling in a thick curtain around us. A fast-running brook appeared on the right, and then suddenly we were out in the open again, and a fierce wind off the ocean stopped us in our tracks. Cliffs loomed up around a small, sheltered harbor. The rain driving into my face felt like hundreds of tiny needles and I couldn't breathe in the wind, which seemed determined to knock me off my feet. The ground was steep and slippery, and I started to slide.

I could hear Ruby yelling something, and then she grabbed my hand and pulled me off to the left, into the shelter of a funny-shaped little hill that seemed to pop up from the ground. There were flat rocks piled up around the side, and then the next thing I knew, she was wrenching open a wooden door in the hill and hauling me down a tunnel into the dark.

CHAPTER FIFTY-ONE

THE ROOT CELLAR

It smelled of damp rock, but it was dry and I could no longer feel the wind, although I could hear it roaring outside like a freight train.

"What is this?" I asked, once I got my breath back. My words sounded muffled in the thick darkness.

Ruby had let go of my hand and I could hear her rummaging through her knapsack.

"Aha!" she cried in triumph and with a click, there was light.

"Is it . . . a cave?" I whispered, looking at the stone walls around us.

Ruby's laugh was loud and normal, and it made me feel a little better. "No, silly, it's a root cellar. *The* root cellar, I'd guess." She turned the flashlight around the space.

"But it looked like a hill," I said. "You brought me inside a hill." The root cellars I'd seen in Buckle looked like little sheds.

"Some of the old cellars have grass growing all over them," said Ruby. "Look at the ceiling!"

The roof was made of flat rock, each piece overlapping the one beneath it, till it gradually formed a peak at the top.

"Like a cathedral," Ruby breathed. "Just like in the story. I've never seen one like this before. All the root cellars I've been in have ceilings made with wood, not flat rock." She shone the light on the perfectly formed triangular arch of the roof.

"Wow," I said. "I wonder how they made it?"

"Eldred would know," she replied, and turned the light over the packed earth floor and into the corners. "Look, it's perfectly dry. Hey, the back of it is actually part of the hill."

The back wall was solid rock.

"So . . . so you think this is where the twins were found?" I said. "Fiona and Fenella?"

"Yes," said Ruby. "It's gotta be. It's up on the side of the hill, away from the stream, so it wasn't washed away with all the houses below."

I eased my knapsack off my shoulders and took off my wet raincoat. "Maybe we can dry out a bit here and wait for the rain to stop," I said, and sat down to undo my shoes and peel off my soaking socks. The floor of the cellar was hard-packed earth, but quite dry.

Ruby sat down beside me and started undoing her shoes. I found some dry socks in my knapsack and handed her a pair. I could just make out her grin in the faint light.

"You think of everything, don't you, Twin?" she said.

We spread our socks out in a corner to dry. Ruth flicked the flashlight around the corners of the cellar. It was quite empty.

"Imagine those two little girls being here all by themselves in the storm," she said. "Poor kids."

"And for two days," I said. "Isn't that how long it took to find them?"

"That's what Eldred said."

Ruby turned off the flashlight to save the batteries and we sat in the dark, listening to the storm outside. I pictured the little girls, hardly more than babies, huddled together, all alone, not understanding what was happening, hour after hour.

"The wind is getting worse," said Ruby after a while.

She was right. The humming was building into a howl.

I shivered. "It almost sounds like screaming, doesn't it?"

"The Old Hollies," said Ruby. "Eldred told me about them. He says that when the wind begins to scream, it's the death cries of all the poor people who've died in shipwrecks over the years in Conception Bay."

I listened. It did sound like people wailing.

"And the people who died in floods," I murmured, thinking

of the Finns and the others who had died here when the brook overflowed and washed them out to sea.

Ruby stood up abruptly. "I'm going to see how bad the rain is." I saw her flashlight zigzagging over the stone walls as she walked through the tunnel to the entrance. She opened the door and a fierce gust of wind blew in.

"It's getting really dark," she called back to me. "It can't be that late, but the rain is just bucketing down."

She came back.

"I hate to say this, Rue, but I think we're stuck here for the night. It looks like a bad storm. And Aunt Doll is going to kill us, that's for sure."

My heart sank. I didn't like it here.

"Don't you think it might let up enough for us to get home later?"

"It doesn't look like it's stopping any time soon. And we'd never find our way home in the dark."

I shivered. "Aunt Doll's going to be worried."

Ruby sighed. "I know. But there's nothing we can do. We might as well make the best of it." She knelt down and started hauling stuff out of her knapsack.

"Here," she said, tossing me a turtleneck sweater. "Put that on under your big sweater." She did the same and then started looking through what was left of lunch.

"Half a chicken sandwich, one muffin and an apple," she said. "And some water. What have you got?"

I had a whole sandwich and a muffin and an apple.

"We can save the muffins and apples for breakfast," said Ruby.

We settled into a corner with our backs against the cool stone and slowly ate the sandwiches. Now that we were out of the wind, and dry, I wasn't cold anymore. But the ground was hard. I wasn't sure I'd be able to fall asleep, with the wind howling outside and the rain beating against the rocks.

"How do you think they ended up here?" I asked.

"Who? The little girls?" asked Ruby.

"Yes. I mean, there was a storm, like today, with wind and rain. Somebody must have brought them up here to keep them safe. But why would they leave them by themselves? And why wouldn't they save themselves if they knew a flood was coming?"

"I don't know," said Ruby. She crumpled up the wax paper from the sandwiches and stuffed it into the knapsack. "It was always a mystery. But they were saved, somehow, and that's why we're sitting here today, Rue, in the dark, and going to get in the worst trouble you can think of when we get back."

I laughed. "What will she do to us, do you think?"

Ruby groaned. "Cleaning duty. Probably for a week. She'll make us scrub the barn, or Buckle Beach, or some impossible thing."

I laughed again. "You know, Ruby, there must be some good luck in our family as well as this curse. It can't all be hopeless.

You and I found each other, and that's a good thing, right?"

"Right," she said, and gave a huge yawn. She snuggled down beside me and leaned her head against my shoulder. "A very good thing," she said sleepily.

"And Fiona and Fenella were saved," I said, catching her yawn. "Or we wouldn't be here. We'd be someone else."

"If we were anybody," murmured Ruby.

"I'm just saying, there's something good working for our family as well as something bad, and maybe it will be okay. Maybe we'll break the curse and live to be little old ladies with white hair and lots of grandchildren and big purses full of sweets and crumpled tissues."

"I hope so," said Ruby.

I was tired too. The fresh air, the exercise, the chicken sandwiches. My eyes closed.

CHAPTER FIFTY-TWO

THE ANGEL

I drifted in and out of sleep. At some point I curled into a ball to be more comfortable, with my head on my knapsack for a pillow and Ruby close beside me.

The storm raged on, and I was aware of it even as I slept. The wind roared and the rain swooshed down. The cellar felt solid around us, which was some comfort, but I began to feel uneasy in my sleep, as if we were encased in a tomb made of stone, floating between the present and the past. I felt the distant presence of all the twins that came before us, stretching out their arms to me, pulling me back into their reality and away from mine. I shook myself awake and reached out to Ruby, clutching the rough wool of her sweater. I could hear her soft breathing. She was warm and real. I fell into a deep sleep.

A long time later I woke up. Or at least, I thought I woke up. A yellow glow illuminated the entrance to the root cellar. Someone was coming in, carrying a lantern.

In the faint light that filtered up over her face, I could see it was a young woman with fair hair, who looked a bit like my mother in the photograph beside my bed. She was wearing a long skirt and had a small child by the hand. Behind her came her twin, leading another small child.

"Now just sit down here in the corner on these quilts with Fiona," said the first woman, as they settled the children in one corner, spreading quilts on the floor. There were wooden crates of potatoes and carrots piled up against the walls of the root cellar. "Your Aunt Caitlin and I have to go back for more food, but you'll be quite safe here." Her accent had a distinct lilt to it, much more Irish than the accents I'd heard in Buckle.

The women's clothes and hair were wet, but they must have been carrying the children wrapped in quilts because the little girls looked quite dry. I could hear the rain rattling against the rocks outside and the wind screaming.

"Don't go, Mama," said one of the little girls, reaching out her arms to her mother.

"Now, don't start, Fiona," said the first woman. "You and Fenella need to be brave girls in the storm and we'll be back before you know it." She bent and gave each of the children a swift hug and kiss.

Caitlin put down a sack she had been carrying. "Catriona, maybe I should stay," she said to her sister.

"No, I need you to help me get more food and blankets up here. And we need to persuade the others to leave."

"Peter thinks they can reroute the brook if they just keep digging—"

"No," said Catriona firmly. "He can't. We've got to get them to leave. Now."

The two women took the lantern with them and ducked their heads as they entered the tunnel that led to the door.

"Mama," cried the twins, and Catriona turned back to them.

"You'll be safe," she said, but there was a tremor in her voice. Then she looked directly at me and said, "Ruth. Look after my dear ones." And in that moment, as clear as anything, I could see it was my mother, Meg, looking out of Catriona's eyes at me.

I caught my breath, and then she turned and left us in the darkness.

The twins were whimpering. I crawled over to them and spoke softly.

"Fiona, Fenella. It's okay. You're going to be okay." I reached out to them and I could feel their little hands grasping mine. They huddled in to me, one on each side, and I encircled them with my arms and bent my head down. Their hair smelled sweet.

"Are you an angel?" came an unsteady voice from under one of my arms.

"No," I said. "Just a friend."

As we sat there in the dark, with the storm raging outside, I slowly became aware of another sound, coming from somewhere inside the cellar—a soft hissing whisper. The girls heard it too, and stiffened beside me.

"What's that?" asked one, terror in her voice.

I tried to calm them but the whispering just grew louder, and soon I could make out the words, in that familiar cracked voice hissing, "By water! By water! By water!" It grew louder and louder, until he was shouting, and as it grew, the storm outside seemed to rise to a crescendo, and then everything began to shake and a roaring filled the air. It went on and on, like a subway train when it first comes thundering into the station. I held the girls tight. Somehow the horrendous noise made the darkness deeper.

Finally it stopped. A deep, ominous silence followed. I knew what it meant. All the people, all the houses—everything had been swept away in the flood.

"I want my mama," said one of the twins, starting to cry.

CHAPTER FIFTY-THREE

TRAPPED

"R uth?" said Ruby in a sleepy voice. "Are you okay?"

I opened my eyes. The wavering light from the flashlight was in my eyes. I turned my head away from it and sat up.

The wind was still howling round the cellar. If anything it sounded louder than before.

"Ruth?" said Ruby again.

"I'm okay," I said, rubbing my eyes. My head hurt.

"You were crying out in your sleep. Did you have a bad dream?"

"I . . . um . . . I'm not sure. I guess it was a dream. I was back in the flood, Ruby, with Fiona and Fenella when their mother left them here."

Ruby switched off the light and sat back against the wall.

"What happened?"

I felt an emptiness around me, where the little girls had been tucked under my arms. It had all been so real. I almost felt like if I turned on the flashlight I would find them still there, clinging to each other and calling for their mother, with boxes of vegetables piled high to the ceiling. I tried to pull myself together into the present, but the feeling of emptiness kept growing inside me, until a huge well of loneliness spread out from the root cellar and filled all of Slippers Cove, out there in the rain.

"They're all gone," I said softly.

"Tell me," said Ruby, squeezing my hand.

I did. When I had finished she said, "So that's how they came to be here, all by themselves. And there wasn't time for the rest of them to get away."

"And Catriona could see it coming," I said. "She had the Sight. I could tell by looking at her. Meg has the same look, kind of a shadow behind her eyes, like she sees farther into things than other people."

"But you say it was Meg at the end, telling you to look after the twins?"

I nodded. "Yes, I'm sure of it."

"Weird. I don't understand. How could she be there? She wasn't born yet."

"I don't know. I just feel like we're all connected, like we're all the same people and it's happening over and over again."

"But what about the little girls? Do you think they really saw you in this root cellar, a hundred years ago?"

"I don't know. But I'd like to think there was someone here with them. Maybe the spirits of their grandmothers or their great-grandmothers keeping them safe, looking out for them."

"Poor little things," said Ruby.

We sat in silence for a moment. She slipped her hand into mine.

"We're all motherless twins, aren't we?" said Ruby softly.

"Yes," I said. And then something rose in me, a wave of fierce determination. "It's going to stop. It's going to stop now, Ruby. We have to stop it. Our kids are not going to grow up without their mothers."

And then suddenly the noise of the storm changed, and a wild roaring filled the air. For a minute I thought I was back in the flood with the little girls, but Ruby grabbed my hand.

"What's that?" she cried.

The wind was howling like a hundred wolves and then the root cellar began to shake, and a rumbling began, deep in the earth below us. Just like in my dream.

Ruby's fingers dug into mine till they hurt. "What's happening, Ruth?"

An earthquake, I thought. I had been in a mild one with my dad in New Zealand and it had felt something like this.

A couple of rocks crashed down from the ceiling of the root cellar, just missing Ruby and me. We clung together. I'd never been this scared before in my life. I thought we were going to die.

And then it got worse.

The whispering began, swelling up from the corners of the cellar, swirling around us, a hissing sound like a swarm of snakes was circling us, hemming us in. It got louder and louder and the voice rose into a shriek. Now I could make out the words.

"By fire! By water! By sudden death!" And then a wall of noise filled the air, and I could hear rocks rolling and thumping against the root cellar as they careened down the hill.

"Ruth!" screamed Ruby as more rocks fell from the ceiling. We clung together and the whispering grew more hysterical and then the rocks and rain and wind were hammering the root cellar from outside and the voice was screeching inside and there was a tremendous crash and it seemed like rocks were falling all around us and something smacked into my head and I fell headlong into a black endless hole.

When I came to, I was lying in the dark with a splitting headache, and there was something heavy on top of me. I heaved myself up and a few rocks that had fallen on me fell away.

I could feel Ruby lying beside me, still.

"Ruby? Ruby?"

She didn't answer. I felt along her arm to her shoulder, and then her face, and it was wet. Blood? Frantically I felt around for the flashlight, and finally my hands closed around it. I switched it on.

Bright red blood glistened on Ruby's face. A rock must have hit her in the head. She was pale, but when I leaned over her I could hear her breath, soft and fluttery.

"Ruby," I said, shaking her gently. She made no sound.

I took a deep breath and tried to remember what I'd learned in the St. John Ambulance course I'd taken last winter. Head wounds bleed a lot. Sometimes people went into shock and you had to keep them warm. I found the knapsacks and took out the extra sweaters and tucked them around her. Then I used a little of the water on a paper napkin to wash the blood away.

She had a gash on her forehead, but it wasn't bleeding anymore. Surely that was a good sign?

The light from the flashlight was growing dimmer. Outside I could still hear the rain driving down and the wind howling. I turned the light to see what damage had been done to the root cellar.

My heart nearly stopped.

There was a huge pile of rocks blocking the entranceway. It looked like the whole tunnel had collapsed. We couldn't get out.

We were trapped. I felt a wild urge to scream and get up

and run, but there was no one to hear me and nowhere to go. Our world had shrunk to this small dark room in the center of a storm, and no one knew where we were. No one would be coming to get us.

So maybe this is it, I thought. This is how the curse ends. Ruby and I die and that's the end of the Finns.

CHAPTER FIFTY-FOUR

THE LONELIEST PLACE

I stumbled back to Ruby and lay down beside her and put my arm around her. She was still breathing softly, as if she were asleep.

I began to cry. I didn't want to die there in the dark, with my father so far away. And Gwen. I even felt bad about Gwen. They would get the news on some Greek island and have to come back here for the funeral. And Dad would be so upset. And Gwen would be too, because she did care about me, I knew she did, even though I was so mean about her. I wished I could take it all back, wished I had never called her Awful Gwen. I just didn't want her to take my father away from me. And now he was going to be away from me forever because I was going to die here with Ruby. I'd never get a chance to ask him about adopting me, and he'd never meet Ruby or Doll and Eldred . . .

I cried for a long time, there in the dark, with the winds still moaning outside and the rain drumming against the rocks. I don't think I've ever felt that lonely. My only comfort was that Ruby was with me, and I could feel her warm body beside mine, and her gentle breathing.

Finally I wore myself out and couldn't cry anymore. I think I even might have gone to sleep for a while, but something woke me up with a start.

It was a sound. Just a small, shuffling kind of sound, from very close by. As if something was there in the root cellar with us. Something like . . . a rat? I sat up quickly, my heart in my throat.

It came again. A scuffling sound. And then, unbelievably, a soft laugh.

Rats don't laugh.

"Who's there?" I said, my voice quavering.

Silence.

Then the sound again, only this time it was a kind of swishing, slowly growing louder, and then I recognized it.

The whispering. It had started so softly, like a mouse in a wall, but now it was moving through the air like a swarm of little flies around my head, with a teasing and a buzzing. I even raised my hand to try to brush it away.

The laugh came again, startling me. And then the roaring began again, filling my ears. I covered them and cowered over Ruby, trying to shield her if the roof started falling in again.

I closed my eyes and wondered how much it would hurt when a stone fell on my head and killed me. The roaring was so loud that I felt like I was inside the sound, that I was the sound, that it would break me in two. Then I felt myself sliding down into a deeper darkness where there was nothing but me and the horrible sound.

CHAPTER FIFTY-FIVE

THE FRYING PAN

Gradually the roaring changed. It diminished till it was just the sound of a man, bellowing with rage.

I was in the dark little room with the fire in the hearth again, and the man whom I had last seen lying dead on the floor was standing upright, staggering from side to side and shouting at a woman as he struck her. Children were screaming somewhere close by, and the woman fell to her knees and held her hands up, trying to ward off the blows that came raining down on her head.

Then the door burst open, and the young woman I'd seen before in this room came storming into the room, yelling, "Leave my sister alone, Robert! Stop it!"

But he wouldn't stop.

The other woman picked up a cast-iron frying pan from the table and hit the man over the head with it. He swayed for a moment and then fell to the floor. The woman bent over her sister, helping her to her feet. She had blood all over her face and she looked stunned.

"Eileen, Eileen, what's he done to you this time?" said the woman. Someone was still screaming, and I realized it was two little girls, about two years old, huddled together on a daybed in the corner, terrified.

The woman left her sister and went to the children. "There," she said. "It's all right now." She brought one to Eileen and held the other herself. "There," she said softly. "Don't cry now, your mother's fine."

"Eva," gasped Eileen, "look to Robert. I think you've killed him."

The man lay motionless on the floor.

"I hope I have," said Eva. "He would have killed you sooner or later."

The man on the floor stirred and clutched at his head, moaning. Blood was pouring down his face. He opened his eyes and fixed them on the two women.

"You've been the death of me, Eva Finn," he said. "You and your sister." Then he coughed and nearly choked.

Eva handed the child to her sister and then poured some water into a cup from a jug and brought it over to him. She bent down to help him drink it but he pushed her away and the water spilled on the floor.

"You've killed me," he said in a raspy voice, and his black eyes stared out at her, filled with hate. "You've killed me and I curse you! I curse you, Eva Finn. I curse you and your sister both. I curse your children. I curse your unborn children. I curse the ground you walk on. Wherever you go, you'll never get away from me. My curse will follow you. You may have killed me, but you'll never live to see your children grow. You'll die first. The two of you. On the same day, at the same time, you'll fall down dead. And the same with your children. As long as there are twin girls in your family, they'll die young on the same day at the same time. Their children's children will die young. You'll pay for murdering me. And your children will pay. And their children will pay. And you'll pay till the end of time." Somehow he struggled to his feet, blood pouring down his face, and took a step toward the two women. He lifted his arm and pointed it at them.

"They'll all die," he said. He was trying to shout, but his voice was a hoarse croak, his face contorted with hate: "By fire. By water. By sudden death."

It was the voice I'd heard whispering over and over again. In the cemetery. On board the ship. In the fire. In the root cellar.

"By fire!" he repeated, taking another step toward them. "By water!" and he took another step. "By sudden death!"

And then he choked, rage filling his throat, and he put both his hands to his head and staggered backward, and fell. With one more horrible cough, the choking stopped and he lay still, his eyes staring up.

I was stunned, his words echoing through my body like my own heartbeat. Like they were part of me, born with me, knit into my flesh and bones. The curse.

CHAPTER FIFTY-SIX

POSSESSION

"Holy Mary," said Eileen in a shaky voice, crossing herself, her face white. "He's dead, Eva."

"Yes. And I can't say I'm even a little sorry." Eva spat out the words, but she was as white as her sister and her hands were shaking.

"But you heard him, Eva. He's cursed us."

"Never mind that now. We have to get out of here. Michael is sailing to Newfoundland from Waterford tomorrow on the morning tide. We'll go with him."

"But they'll come after us," said Eileen. "When they find Robert's body."

"They won't find it," said Eva grimly. "Pack some things, quickly. Then we'll burn the place down, and him with it."

The little girls had stopped screaming, but they clung to their mother, plainly terrified. Eileen brought them to the daybed and started digging through an old dresser, pulling out clothes. She was crying softly and muttering to herself. Eva was pouring the contents of a bottle of whisky over the floor.

Then suddenly Eileen stopped what she was doing and her voice rose in a wail of despair.

"I can't do it," she said. "You heard what he said, Eva! We're cursed. And my babies are cursed. And their children are cursed. It's going to haunt us down the years, as Robert said. It's going to follow our children and their children and we'll never be free of it. We'll never be free of him."

Eva strode over to her, seized her by the shoulders and gave her a shake. "Eileen Finn!" she said. "You listen to me. It's all nonsense, curses and such. We mustn't believe in it. We mustn't give him any more power over us."

But Eileen just shook her head. "It's done," she said. "We've killed him and his blood is on our hands. He's cursed us and it will never end."

Seeing their mother crying, the two little girls began screaming again. I closed my eyes, and the screaming stopped. When I opened them I was back in the dark root cellar, lying on the hard ground with Ruby beside me.

She was still breathing softly.

I felt suddenly tired, so tired that all I wanted to do was go to sleep. Or die. The damp air around us seemed to vibrate with the horror of what I'd just seen. Outside the wind had picked up again, and I could hear it wailing mournfully, as if it was crying for all the Finns down the years who had been cursed by the dying Robert Barrett.

I sat up and felt around for the flashlight. I found it in the corner and turned it on. It still gave out a wavering yellow beam of light. I examined Ruby's head. The bleeding had stopped and the blood had crusted over the wound on her forehead. She felt warm, but not hot.

I gave her a gentle shake. She muttered something but didn't wake up.

"Oh, Ruby," I whispered. "Come back."

But she slept on.

I got up and looked around at the damage again. Most of the ceiling was intact, but just above us there was a gap where the rocks had shaken loose and fallen on us. And the pile of rubble still blocked the tunnel. I went over and knelt down and started to move the rocks, one by one. Maybe I could clear enough space for us to get out. "Yes, in a year or two," I muttered to myself. But I kept moving them. It felt better to do *something*.

I thought about what I'd seen in that dark kitchen in Ireland. The source of the curse. Eva had killed Robert Barrett to save Eileen's life, and he'd cursed them. They'd burned down the house and fled to Newfoundland with their brother Michael Finn. But the curse had gone with them, and the *Cathleen* had gone down, killing both of them.

I shivered. What kind of man curses his own children? And his children's children? Robert Barrett was evil, through and through. His violence and his hatred had lived on in the curse over all these generations, one hundred and fifty years. It had killed my mother and her sister, and now it was going to kill Ruby and me. I gave a choking kind of sob and started pulling harder at the rocks, prying them loose from the pile of rubble and throwing them to the side.

There was a faint noise behind me.

"Ruby?" I said, picking up the flashlight and turning it on.

She was sitting up, her eyes wide open.

"Ruby!" I said, taking a step toward her. "Thank God you're okay."

She didn't respond. She didn't seem to see me. I felt a clutch of fear at my heart. The head injury must be worse than I thought, affecting her sight and her hearing.

I took another step. "Ruby!" I said, louder this time.

She began to murmur something. At first it was so quiet I couldn't make out what she was saying. But as it grew louder my legs turned to jelly and my hand with the flashlight in it started to shake.

It wasn't Ruby's voice. It was deeper, a rasping kind of croak.

"By fire," she whispered. "By water. By sudden death."

Her face twisted and it wasn't Ruby anymore. It was as if Robert Barrett was inside her, using her face and her body as if she were a puppet.

"I curse you," she said loudly in Robert's choking, angry voice. "You and your children forever."

Blood began pouring down her face, making her look just like Robert did when he stood cursing his wife and her sister. She raised her arm and pointed it at me. There was a mad light in her eyes and a hideous grin twisted her mouth.

"I curse you," she shrieked. "I curse you. By fire! By water! By sudden death!"

I felt weak with fear, like I was going to fall down. I was shaking all over.

"No," I called out. My voice sounded thin and weak. "No!" I tried again.

She laughed, a horrible, crackling laugh, then got to her feet and started toward me, her arm still outstretched, her eyes like two red flames.

"By fire," she began again.

"Shut up!" I screamed, backing up against the wall as she got closer and closer.

"By water!" she roared.

"Stop it!" I shouted.

"By sudden death!" she said, reaching for me.

There was nowhere to go.

CHAPTER FIFTY-SEVEN

BRING IT INTO THE LIGHT

I grabbed Ruby by the shoulders. Robert Barrett might be possessing her, but she still had Ruby's body and she was no bigger than I was. I held her off and looked into her face.

"Ruby, come back! Ruby!"

I had dropped the flashlight, and in the dim arc of light that came from it, I could see her eyes. Only they were Robert's eyes, filled with hate.

"I curse you," she whispered in that cruel, cracked voice. "And you," she said, looking behind me, "and you, and you!"

I dropped my hands and spun around. The blocked entranceway to the root cellar was nowhere to be seen and a crowd of people stood there, silent. A pale yellow light illuminated them. They were all there: Eva, with a frying pan in her hand and murder in her eyes; Eileen, her face bloodied and bruised; Catriona and Caitlin in their wet clothes; Meg and Molly in their long white nightgowns; other faces, all young women, all blonde. Seven generations of Finns. All cursed. The same twins I had been seeing in my dreams, walking up over the hill.

And they were all staring silently at Ruby. Only it wasn't Ruby. It was Robert, held inside her, contorting her face with rage.

"I curse you!" she suddenly screamed. "All of you. And I curse your children's children till the end of time!"

There was a gentle stirring behind me, and I turned to see Meg and Molly coming forward. Meg held a candlestick aloft and I realized that it was the source of light that illuminated the others. Her golden hair was shining in the warm yellow light and she was smiling at me the way she had when she first appeared in my bedroom. There was a collective sigh like a gentle breeze behind me, as if all the twins had let go their breath at the same time.

Ruby who was Robert took a step back into the shadows, as if to escape the light, but Meg moved forward and held the candle high. Molly stood beside her.

"Ruby," said Molly, in such a loving voice that it almost broke my heart. "Come back. Come back to me."

A spasm passed across Ruby's face, and for just a moment

she looked like herself again. But then Robert was there again, his eyes burning with hatred.

"I curse you!" she shrieked. "You'll never be free!"

Meg held up the candle, and for a moment, it seemed as if waves of golden light were rolling out from the pure yellow flame, engulfing all of us.

"Let her go, Robert. Just let her go."

There was a hiss like the sound a fiery torch would make as it plunged into a lake. And then Robert was gone, just like that, and Ruby was standing there blinking in the light.

"Mom?" she said, squinting at Molly. And Molly stepped forward and enveloped her in a tight hug.

Meg turned to me, with that beautiful smile and said, "Bring it into the light, Ruth. Bring it into the light." And then the light from the candle grew stronger and stronger until there was nothing but pure golden light everywhere.

It was too bright. I closed my eyes. Everything started to spin and I felt dizzy, and then it was as if I was light as a feather and I was floating slowly to earth. Hard-packed, cold earth. The spinning stopped.

"Ruth?" came Ruby's sleepy voice from beside me. I had my arm around her and it was very dark.

"I'm here," I said. "Are you okay?"

"My head hurts," she said. "And I had the strangest dream."

I sat up and felt around for the flashlight, but all I could find was my knapsack. I pulled out the thermos of water.

There wasn't much left, but I helped Ruby sit up and drink a little. It felt weird to be doing all this by feel, in the pitch-black darkness.

"What happened?" asked Ruby, lying down again. Her voice sounded a little weak, but not too bad.

I didn't know where to start.

"There was an earthquake or something and part of the roof fell in and hit you on the head," I said.

"Oh. I guess that's why I have a headache," she said.

I laughed. I couldn't help it.

"What's so funny?" said Ruby.

It was too hard to explain. "Let's just say that a headache is the least of your problems, Ruby. I thought you were dying there for a while. And we're trapped in here and can't get out. And it turned out that Eva killed Robert Barrett and that's why he put the curse on us, and then he took over your body and—"

"Wait just a minute!" said Ruby, and her voice sounded almost back to normal. "You're going too fast for me. Start from the beginning. You said we're trapped?"

I felt close to tears. "Yes. The tunnel to the door fell in and I don't see how we can get out. I started to move the rocks, but then all the twins came and—" I gulped. "I'm so glad you're okay, Ruby." And then I was crying and she was hugging me, and for a while we were both crying.

When we calmed down a bit she said, "I had the strangest dream, Ruth. I know I should be scared about being trapped in

299

here, but I have this warm feeling inside, and I think we're going to get out of here. Somehow, we're going to be all right."

"What was your dream?"

"Well, it was all mixed up with what happened. I remember the earthquake and the shaking, and then something hurt my head. Then everything was very dark and I was kind of drifting, but I could feel you beside me so I didn't feel too bad, except my head hurt. I felt too tired to move or speak or really wake up properly, and so I kept drifting in and out. Then I started to get really scared and I don't know why, really, because I was still drifting, but it was like that feeling when you're asleep and you know you're going to throw up, and you feel so awful and you're scared to wake up?"

"Yes. I know that feeling."

"Well, it felt like that for a long time, and I was just so scared, like something horrible was about to happen. But I wasn't awake. And then there was a little golden flame in the darkness, and I thought of the candle and the flame, and Eldred . . ."

Ruby paused.

"Then what happened, Ruby?" I asked.

When she started speaking again, her voice was full of wonder.

"My mother was there, Ruth. My mother! She was calling me and telling me to come back to her, and I opened my eyes and she was there, with that beautiful smile I have in my memory, and she held out her arms to me and hugged me and

I was so happy, Ruth. I finally had my mother back, just for a moment."

We started crying again. Then laughing, because we were crying again.

"Honestly," Ruby said. "I haven't cried this much since Wynken tore the heads off my dolls when I was eight. But the thing is, she made me feel safe, Ruth. And even though it was just a dream, I feel like we're going to be okay. It was like she was promising me that."

I was too tired to worry anymore. I hoped that Ruby was right. I closed my eyes and fell instantly asleep.

CHAPTER FIFTY-EIGHT

RESCUE

Someone was calling us, over and over again.

"Ruth! Ruby! Ruth! Ruby!"

I opened my eyes. The root cellar was no longer completely dark. I could see Ruby lying beside me. I turned my head. A sliver of light was coming from the blocked tunnel, at the top, where I'd started to pull the rocks away in the middle of the night.

And someone was on the other side, calling us: a woman with a hoarse voice, as if she'd been calling us for a long time.

"Ruth! Ruby! Are you in there?"

I struggled to my feet.

"We're here!" I yelled. "We're okay!"

By now Ruby was at my side.

"Nan?" she called out, as if she didn't believe it.

"Thank the Lord," said Nan, for it was definitely her, and then she called out to someone else.

"George! Doll! They're here. They're alive."

And then other people were calling out and talking all at once, and Aunt Doll's voice rose above them all.

"I'm glad you're alive because I'm going to skin the two of you as soon as I can get my hands on you!"

Ruby and I looked at each other and began to laugh.

"Ruby," called out her dad. "You need to start moving the rocks on your side and we'll do it from out here and we'll meet in the middle. Mother, Doll, there isn't room for all of us. Let me and Eldred do it."

There were some complaints, and then the women's voices faded away and I could hear rocks being thrown aside.

"You all right, Ruby?" came Eldred's quiet voice.

"Yes!" she said.

"And Ruth?"

"I'm fine, Eldred," I replied.

Then we set to and pulled down as many rocks as we could. When the hole was big enough, Doll came back and insisted that the men hand in some water and a bag of muffins for us.

"They need to drink. And eat," she said. "They'll be dehydrated and half-starved by now."

That first drink of water was as sweet as anything I've ever tasted. And the muffins were just as good. Doll was still scolding, but her voice drifted away and we could hear them moving rocks again.

Finally the gap was big enough that we could see Eldred and Uncle George, their faces covered with dirt.

"Let me look at them," called Aunt Doll, who came in brandishing a flashlight.

We looked even worse than they did. Ruby's face was streaked with grime and dried blood and I'm sure mine was just as dirty.

Aunt Doll gave a sharp intake of breath. "Well," she said, "you're both a sight. If it wasn't for Mildred, we'd never have found you." She turned away, her voice breaking.

I looked at Ruby. "Mildred?" I mouthed.

"Nan," she said.

And then Eldred and Uncle George went back to pulling away the rocks.

It took another half an hour to make a gap big enough for us to squeeze through.

Ruby and I handed our knapsacks through and then climbed over. Ruby went first, and by the time I got to the other side, Uncle George was hugging her so hard she finally started laughing and broke away, saying she couldn't breathe.

Then he turned to me and before I knew it I was enveloped in a bear hug.

It was the strangest feeling. I was being hugged for the first time by my birth father.

"Ruth," he said. "Thank God you're safe," and then he pulled back and looked at me.

I could feel this big emotion coming from him in waves. With tears in his eyes, he enfolded me in another hug.

He knew. I don't know how he knew, but he knew. I pulled back and looked up into his face with a tentative smile.

"You two scared me to death," he said. Then he led us outside and there were hugs and tears from Aunt Doll, and hugs and grins from Eldred, and then to my surprise, a bony hug from Nan. She smelled of salt air and wool. As she held me, she caught her breath a couple of times and I realized she was crying. I pulled back and looked up into her face, whose harsh lines were shattered by her tears.

"I thought I'd lost you," was all she could say.

"No," I said. "You found us." And I hugged her again. And for just a moment, I felt a knot inside me untangle and let go. Meg and Molly were dead. My mother would never hold me like this. But Nan was alive. And Ruby was alive. And Aunt Doll and Uncle George were alive. And my dad and Gwen. And they loved me. And I loved them.

CHAPTER FIFTY-NINE

REST IN PEACE

Even before her tears were dry, Aunt Doll started scolding us.

"You never should have come here; you should have known better; nothing good ever came from going to Slippers Cove! And Eldred, you've done nothing but encourage them in all their nonsense."

Eldred looked a little sheepish, but winked at me when Aunt Doll turned to Ruby.

"I blame you more than Ruth because you should have known better, and she's from Ontario, so she doesn't know anything—" At this, Uncle George began to laugh.

"Come on, Doll," he said. "Let's get them home safe first, and then we can lecture them the rest of the day."

She scowled at him.

"But how did you find us so fast?" said Ruby. "And what are you doing here, Dad?"

"I called him last night when you two didn't come home," put in Aunt Doll. "He drove half the night in the rain to get here. Eldred said you might have come looking for Slippers Cove, but we didn't know how to find you, and that's when Mildred arrived at the door, saying you were in Slippers Cove and we had to go by boat because there'd been a landslide. I thought she was mad, but Eldred convinced me to listen to her. So we called Ed Dunphy and he agreed to take us out in his boat at dawn. And Mildred led us right here. Ed couldn't see the opening in the cliffs. None of us could, but Mildred kept insisting we go forward and suddenly there it was, the way in. And well, here we are."

I looked at Nan. She had regained most of her usual dour expression, but now it was mixed with an air of self-satisfaction.

"I could see it," she said. "That's all. I could see it."

"But how did you climb up here over the landslide?" I asked.

"Well, it's the oddest thing," said Aunt Doll, "but you'll have to see for yourself."

They moved aside so we could see down into Slippers Cove.

"It's uncanny," said Aunt Doll. "The whole thing is uncanny."

The landslide had swept down the hill, carrying rocks, trees and earth with it. But it had veered off to the left below the root cellar, blocked by a huge boulder. On the right, the footpath down to the harbor was completely clear of debris. Behind us the path and the hillside were gone, leaving nothing but a sheer mass of rubble, impossible to climb. But the way down to the water was open.

"Almost as if the landslide knew what it was doing," said Eldred in a dreamy voice. "Leaving us a path clear to climb up and find you."

The sun was sparkling on the calm water. A fishing boat floated sedately in the middle of the harbor, and a rowboat was pulled up on a little rocky beach.

"So it was a landslide, not an earthquake?" I asked.

"Earthquake? What earthquake?" said Aunt Doll. "Isn't a landslide good enough for you?"

"It's just that the earth kept shaking underneath us and I thought—"

"It must have been the vibrations from all the rocks falling down the hillside," said Uncle George. "Let's get you home," he said, throwing one arm around Ruby's shoulder. "And Doll can cook us all a proper breakfast."

"More than they deserve," said Aunt Doll, but I could tell she wasn't really mad anymore.

"Wait a minute," I said. "Ruby and I have to do something first."

Nan gave us a sharp look, but Aunt Doll just shrugged her shoulders. "Be quick."

The grown-ups turned away. Eldred pointed out something to them up the hill and they stood for a moment, looking at the landslide and talking.

I bent down and started fishing through my knapsack. Ruby stood watching me.

I found my sketchbook and pulled out some of the flower specimens I had picked in the woods. I stood up and drew Ruby back into the entrance of the root cellar.

"We may never be back to Slippers Cove," I said quietly. "I want to leave something in memory of Caitlin and Catriona and Michael, and all the rest of them who died here."

Ruby nodded.

I knelt down and laid two yellow lady slippers and one delicate pink twinflower across the threshold.

"Rest in peace," I said. And we stood there in silence, for just a moment, thinking about them.

"We'll never forget you," said Ruby.

CHAPTER SIXTY

GOING HOME

E d Dunphy was waiting for us in his fishing boat. He was about Uncle George's age, with a wide, weather-beaten face and blue eyes. Ruby threw herself into his arms in a big hug. He grinned and looked embarrassed, giving me a shy nod.

"Thank you for rescuing us," she said.

"Oh, it wasn't me," he answered. "Thank your Nan. She led me here like she'd been here a hundred times before."

"I've never been here," said Nan stiffly.

"Well, I've sailed past here many times and never knew about that opening. You'll see, it's as narrow as can be, but the water's deep, and it was nothing to slip in once I knew it was there. This'll be the talk of Buckle for many a day, Mrs. Peddle, you'll see. They'll be calling you a witch!" And he laughed.

Ruby and I looked at each other and it was all we could do not to burst out laughing. I could see Uncle George and Aunt Doll exchanging glances too, trying unsuccessfully not to smile.

"They already call me a witch," said Nan. "I've got the Sight, that's all. Nothing to be ashamed of. I see things other people don't." She squared her shoulders and moved toward the wheel. "Will you be needing me to get you out of here, Ed Dunphy, or do you think you can manage that by yourself?"

He grinned, and started the boat.

Ruby and I looked back as the boat headed toward the narrow opening. The cliffs reared up on all three sides of the harbor, and the root cellar stood high and lonely off to one side. The rubble from the landslide lay in a tumble down the hill. The sky arced above, a brilliant blue.

Ruby slipped her hand into mine.

"It's the saddest place in the world," said Aunt Doll, who had come to stand beside us. "Like a tomb. All those poor people, gone."

"But it's beautiful, just the same," said Ruby.

The boat was chugging toward the opening between the cliffs, and it was so narrow we could almost stretch out our hands and touch the rock on either side.

"It's very deep here," said Aunt Doll. "I've never seen anything like this. A real hidden harbor."

The boat passed through, and we looked way up to the stretch of blue sky high above, where a number of gannets swooped and settled on an outcropping of rock.

"They must have nests up there," said Ruby, shading her eyes to see. "That might be how we could find it again, by following the gannets."

"I don't think you'll be wanting to come back," said Aunt Doll.

I was silent, looking at Ruby.

"Maybe someday," she said.

"Not if I can help it," said Aunt Doll grimly. "Now let me look at that cut on your head, Ruby Peddle."

Aunt Doll moistened a handkerchief and wiped away the blood on Ruby's forehead. A bluish bump had come up.

"You'll live," she said after she cleaned the wound. "The cut's not too bad. I don't think you need stitches. What do you say, Mildred?"

Nan took a look. "That will close up nicely by itself, I'd say. Just put a cold compress on it for now."

Aunt Doll wet the handkerchief again and Ruby dutifully held it to her forehead.

The trip home took a couple of hours. It was a glorious ride for me. It was my first time out in a boat on the Newfoundland coast, and the view was breathtaking. High cliffs on one side, punctuated by little coves here and there, with meadows stretching back into the barrens. Open water on the other side, going on forever, blue-gray, with little waves dancing away from the boat. It was still fairly calm, but the wind had picked up a bit. Seagulls followed us, shrieking.

Aunt Doll brought out blankets to wrap around us, and a couple of thermoses of hot tea and some sandwiches. So we ended up having a picnic on the boat.

Uncle George spent most of the time talking to Ed, while Eldred and Nan sat together, not talking much. Aunt Doll, exhausted by a sleepless night and all her worry, ended up going down into the cabin and lying down. Ruby and I sat huddled together under our blankets, lulled by the waves and the fresh air into a kind of dream-like state.

When we got to Buckle, a little crowd of people was at the wharf to greet us. They fussed over Ruby and me and congratulated the grown-ups on finding us safe.

Doll flushed. "You can't keep a secret in Buckle," she said.

Ruby and I looked at each other, thinking how wrong she was. There were too many secrets in Buckle. Way too many.

Suddenly I remembered my last vision, with Meg telling me to "bring it into the light." I wondered if that was what she meant. Bring all the secrets into the light.

Nan took hold of my shoulder with a bony grip and bent down to speak to me so that no one else would hear.

"You and Ruby come and see me later. I need to tell you something. Bring the wooden box. The one with the silver knots on it."

I looked at her in surprise.

"You know about the box?"

"Yes. Just bring it." Then she turned away and started toward her house. A couple of women went after her, wanting to hear the story.

We wound our way home. Suddenly I felt too tired to take another step. A few people accompanied us, talking all the way to Uncle George and Aunt Doll, trying to get the story out of them. I swayed, and Uncle George reached out an arm to steady me.

"We need to get these children to bed," he said to the neighbors. "We'll tell you all about it later."

Then they fell away and we finally made it home. It occurred to me that Eldred must have slipped away at the wharf, because I hadn't seen him once we got on dry land again.

Ruby and I went upstairs and were about to crawl into bed in our clothes when Aunt Doll bustled in and made us change into pajamas.

"You're that damp," she said. "You'll be lucky if you don't catch your deaths." When we were changed, she tucked us both into our beds and kissed us. "Don't ever do that again," she said. "I've aged ten years." Then she gathered up our dirty clothes and left the room.

As soon as Aunt Doll closed the door, I felt everything drop away, like I was slowly floating down on a current of wind, like the gannets above the cliffs in Slippers Cove, and I fell instantly, deliciously, to sleep.

CHAPTER SIXTY-ONE

CINNAMON BUNS

When we woke up, it was lunchtime, but Aunt Doll insisted on cooking us a full breakfast.

"I promised George," she said, and he grinned as she heaped fried eggs, home fries, bacon and mountains of toast onto our plates.

"Now," said Aunt Doll, after we'd cleaned our plates and washed it all down with several cups of strong tea creamy with condensed milk, "I'll say no more about last night. You know you were foolish, and I trust you never to do it again. Eldred's filled your heads with all kinds of nonsense and I want to hear no more of it, do you understand?"

"But—" protested Ruby.

"Okay," I interrupted, giving Ruby a quick kick under the table. "You're right, Aunt Doll. We just got carried away."

"Very good," she said, standing up and starting to clear the plates.

Uncle George watched her for a moment, then turned to us.

"I'm going to stay for the weekend," he said. "I've called Wendy and she was so relieved to hear that you were okay, Ruby. She and the boys send their love."

Ruby opened her mouth, and I gave her another kick under the table.

"Oh, uh. That's nice," she said.

I stood up and started helping Aunt Doll.

"No, you never mind about these," she said. "I'll do them. You two go on upstairs and do something nice and quiet that can't get you into any more trouble. Read a book. Or have another nap."

We nodded our heads obediently and went out.

I held a whispered conference with Ruby in the hall.

"Why did you have to kick me?" said Ruby, rubbing her leg. "That hurt!"

"I wanted to get out of there, and I didn't want to get into anything with them. We need to go to Nan's. She wants to tell us something. And she said to bring the box."

"What?" said Ruby. "How does she know about that?"

"How does she know about anything?" I said. "Let's go get it."

We listened to Uncle George and Aunt Doll talking for a moment, to make sure they were going to stay in the kitchen, then went upstairs, into the closet and opened the secret door.

The room was stuffy. It seemed a little more ordinary than it had before, perhaps because we'd been through so much since the last time we were here. It just looked like a dusty, forgotten place. The red trunk sat against the wall, where it had stood for—how many years had it been there? Fifty? One hundred?

Ruby crossed over to it and undid the green ribbon. She opened it and pulled out the little wooden box with the silver knots on the lid.

We shut up the secret room again, went quietly down the stairs, grabbed our jackets and went out into the fresh air. Ruby persuaded me to leave a note in our room, saying we had gone for a walk, just in case Aunt Doll checked on us.

"She'll say no if we ask her, but at least this way she can't get too cross."

I wasn't so sure about that, but I did as Ruby asked.

It was warmer than it had been since I arrived, and a soft breeze was blowing down from the hills. There was that delicious smell of wild grass and salt water.

As we passed different houses, people would come out and wave at us and ask us if we were okay and ask what had happened. It was all we could do to be polite and get away from them all without going into long explanations.

We finally made it to the witch's house and knocked. This time I wasn't so apprehensive as we waited for her to answer the door.

The door swung open into the dark hallway, and there she stood, looking as severe and forbidding as always. A tantalizing smell of fresh bread and cinnamon wafted out into the street.

"Mmmmmm," said Ruby. "What have you made for us, Nan?"

"Cinnamon buns," she said. "Not that you deserve them, running off like that and worrying us all to death."

Ruby gave a little skip over the threshold and went in. I followed, and soon we were in the kitchen, where a plate of buns and two glasses of milk stood ready for us.

We sat down and ate a couple, which was quite an accomplishment, considering the breakfast we had just put away. The witch watched us silently.

"There now," she said, as we pushed our chairs back and groaned. "Maybe that will go some way to making up for a long hungry night in that godforsaken place."

"How did you find us, Nan?" I asked. "How did you know where we were?"

She sniffed. "I told you. It was the Sight."

"Did you have a vision?" asked Ruby, her eyes big.

"Stuff and nonsense," said Nan with a noise that sounded very much like a snort.

"Please tell us," I said, putting my hand over her gnarled

fingers and smiling at her. I was catching on to her. She liked to be thought of as a miserable old witch but she wasn't really. At least—not completely.

"Oh very well," she said. "You'll be pestering the life out of me if I don't. Well, your Aunt Doll phoned me about seven to ask if I'd seen the two of you that afternoon, or if I knew where you'd gone, because you were late coming home. I didn't have any idea, so I told her to let me know when you got in. An hour later she called back and said that you were still missing, and George was on his way to help look for you. I went over to sit with her. When he got there, it was late, so he insisted I go to bed and get some sleep and they put me in Clarence's study on his old bed.

"I couldn't sleep; I was that worried about the two of you. And there was the storm, and I thought I heard the Old Hollies screaming in the wind—"

"We heard them too, in Slippers Cove, didn't we, Rue?" put in Ruby.

"Well, I was lying there, tossing and turning, when I heard someone crying. It wasn't the wind, just someone crying as if their heart would break. I sat up to listen, and then it came to me like a dream, the way it does. I saw you, Ruth, lying in a dark place with your arm around Ruby, who had her eyes closed and had blood on her face."

She stopped. She looked at Ruby. "I was afraid you were dead," she said softly.

Ruby's mouth dropped open and she just stared at her. "You were worried about me?" she said in a squeak. "Me?"

"Yes, of course I was," snapped Nan. "And it was Ruth I had heard crying. There wasn't much light, but I could see you were in a place made of stone. And then it was gone, and I was sitting in the dark in Clarence's study and there was no light to switch on because that man was too bullheaded and stubborn to put—" She broke off and took a deep breath.

"Anyway, there I was with no light. I got out of bed and found some matches by the kerosene lamp and lit it. The first thing I saw was that painting on the wall, one I'd had reason to take note of years before, a picture of high cliffs and stormy seas, with a narrow entrance to a harbor. Slippers Cove. And then I knew."

"Knew we were in Slippers Cove?" said Ruby, her eyes big.

"Yes. As sure as you're sitting at my kitchen table today, I knew that's where you were last night. So I went out and found Doll and George still awake in the kitchen, and told George to get Ed Dunphy and his boat lined up for first light because I knew where you were. At first they didn't believe me, but I soon had them persuaded," she said grimly. "Both of them have reason to know I have the Sight, and it's not to be taken lightly. Then I went back to bed and got what sleep I could before it was time to get up and go find you."

"Wow," said Ruby. "You're almost as good as Ruth."

Nan glared at her. "Enough of that," she said. "Ruth, did you bring the box with the silver knots?"

CHAPTER SIXTY-TWO

THE KEY

I pulled it out of my knapsack and placed it on the table. The sunlight coming in the window reflected off the silver, making it gleam. We all sat looking at it for a moment.

"How did you—?" I began, but the witch put up her hand to stop me.

"I need to tell you this my own way," she said. "It's difficult." She was silent for a moment.

"I was brought up to hate the Finns," she began. "My mother and her mother before her and her mother before her had passed it down through the generations. The Finns had done the Barretts wrong, back in Ireland. A deep wrong. Something that never could be fixed. We were never to have anything to do with the Finns, because they had dealings with the devil. And the way the story went, it was the twins that were responsible. Twins ran in that family, and they were unnatural, evil."

She was silent again for a moment. "There were whispers about a curse, and it was clear that the twins never seemed to live too long, and it seemed right that they didn't, because they were wicked." She sighed.

"And then when George was a boy, he started playing with Meg and Molly. I did everything I could to keep them apart, but all it did was drive George away from me. I knew what was going on but I couldn't stop it. His father just laughed at me and told me I was foolish. There was no one left of my family to remember the stories about the Finns, just me. It seemed that there was nothing I could do about it. But when they were thirteen, and I could tell that it was starting to be more than just childhood friends between Molly and George, I got even more worried about my boy, and finally I went to Clarence Duggan to have it out with him. Meg and Molly's mother and father were gone by then, and Doll was caring for them, but I knew she wouldn't listen to anything that she thought was superstition, so I went to Clarence.

"He was a thoughtful man. He had more books in his room than I'd ever seen in one place, and rumor had it he'd read them all. I sat there and told him that there was a curse on the Finns, and I wanted to keep George out of it. He listened and then he got up and opened up a little door in the wall, behind that picture of the cliffs at Slippers Cove, and brought out an old book.

"I could see it was a Bible, falling apart with age, with gold lettering on the front. And a wooden box, covered with silver knots. Celtic knots they were, from Ireland. He told me he'd found that Bible and the box in that cupboard after his wife Lily died, and he'd kept it secret all this time. But now he thought I should see it, so I could understand about the curse.

"He opened the Bible and showed me the record of the Finns' family tree. There it was, all written down, how the long line of twins had all died young, tracing back to two in Ireland, Eva and Eileen. And it had Eileen's husband written down as Robert Barrett. His death was recorded as 1832, the year my family and the Finns all came to Slippers Cove from Waterford, Ireland.

"I always knew the curse went back to that time. That was the story in my family. That something had happened to Robert Barrett, so he never came to Newfoundland with his wife and children. They'd come on the boat without him, and that's all that was known. But rumor had it that his wife, Eileen, and her twin sister, Eva Finn, had made away with him, and that's why the Finns were cursed.

"One minute I was sitting there with Clarence, looking at those names in that Bible, all those Finns down through the generations, twins, and how they all died young. The next minute Clarence and his room and his books and paintings had all disappeared, and I was back there. In Ireland. At the beginning.

Robert Barrett lay dead on the floor in a dark old kitchen, with a fire burning all around him. Two women with blonde hair stood over him.

"Just as sudden as it had come, it was gone, and I was back in Clarence's room. He hadn't noticed, but was talking on about the family all that time.

"I was fuming. My great-great-great-great-uncle, Robert was. And the two Finns standing there, watching as he died. I felt a dark anger rise up in me then, against the Finns, and Clarence Duggan, and I felt the weight of my mother and grandmother and great-grandmother going back through the years, back to my great-great-great-great-uncle who was murdered by those women, I had no doubt. And I felt a whispering all around me and I wanted to scream, but Clarence was sitting there quietly, saying we must pray together for it to come to an end, and for the two families to put away their hatred and forgive each other.

"I wanted to hit him. The room was turning red around me, I was so angry. I felt my uncle's blood calling out for revenge. And then I felt something else. I was holding the Bible in my hand, gripping it tight, and there was something hard tucked inside the cover, where it was falling apart. I said something to Clarence to distract him—I don't know what—and then I edged the little hard thing out of the cover and hid it in my hand. Then I handed the Bible back to Clarence and stood up to go. I told him he could pray all he liked, but God punished sinners and the Finns would have to live with the sins of their mothers. Then I left."

Ruby and I sat mesmerized.

"What—what was it?" whispered Ruby.

The witch reached into her apron pocket and drew something out, which she laid on the table beside the wooden box.

A small silver key.

CHAPTER SIXTY-THREE

TWISTED

R uby reached out her hand for the key, but the witch stopped her.

"No. There's something else." She frowned and took a deep breath.

"I overheard Meg and Molly talking a few days after that. I was out hanging laundry and they were waiting for George out behind the shed. They couldn't see me. 'If only we could find the key,' said one of them, Molly I think.

"'It's probably at the bottom of the ocean, in Michael Finn's pocket,' said the other.

"'Do you really think there could be anything in that box that would help?' said Molly.

"'I don't know,' said Meg. 'But unless we find the key, we'll never know.'"

The witch stopped speaking. I could see tears in her eyes.

"I should have given it to them. I know it. I've always known it. But they were taking my boy from me, and winding their spells around him, and I hated them for it. Maybe if I hadn't been so selfish, they would still be alive today." A racking sob burst out of her and she covered her eyes.

Ruby and I just stared at her.

"You had it?" said Ruby finally. "All this time? You could have saved our mothers and you didn't?" She stood up, shaking, and pointed her finger at the old woman. "You are a horrible old witch. You really are."

I stood up and touched her arm.

"No, Ruby. No. We don't know that. We don't know what's in the box. And we can't break the curse unless we stop hating each other. That's what started it."

"No," said Ruby furiously. "What started it is her great-great-great-great-uncle beating his wife and nearly killing her. Eva only killed him to save her sister. It was self-defense. Ruth saw it happening, Nan. It was him, Robert Barrett, who was evil, not the twins. He was hurting her in front of their two little girls, Nan. And then when Eva hit him, he cursed them. He began all the hatred, and the Barretts have kept it alive. You're the evil ones, not the Finns."

The witch just sat there, staring at Ruby. "Is this true?" she said, finally, in a hoarse voice, turning to me.

I nodded. "I saw it, Nan. With the Sight. I saw it all."

The witch shook her head. "I don't believe it. How could it all get twisted like that?"

"Because you're twisted," yelled Ruby, pounding her fist on the table. "You're twisted, and evil and bitter and—" She began to cry, laying her arms on the table and burying her head in them. "My mother," she said. "My mother, Molly. Meg. All of them."

The witch looked like a balloon someone had sucked the air out of. She looked older than I'd ever seen her.

"I'm sorry," she whispered, reaching out to Ruby and laying her hand on her head. "I'm so sorry. You're right."

Ruby kept crying, and tears were rolling down Nan's face. There was nothing I could do for either of them. I looked down at the table, where the silver key sat gleaming in the sunshine coming in the window.

I picked up the key and took up the box. I found the little hidden slot and slipped the key into it.

At first I couldn't turn it. I gave it a wiggle. Something clicked, and a crack showed along one edge of the box. I put my fingernails in the crack and pried it open.

Immediately a smell of sweet grasses and dried flowers filled the room, the same as when we had opened the red trunk. Ruby and the witch lifted their heads and sniffed the air.

"What's that smell?" said Ruby through her tears. "It's so . . . sweet."

The witch was watching me.

Inside the box lay some folded papers, sprinkled with bits of dried grass and dried lady slippers. I pulled them out and carefully unfolded them. There were several sheets of thin paper, covered in spidery handwriting.

I began to read.

"Read it out loud," demanded Ruby. "I want to hear."

"Slippers Cove, July 5, 1858," I began.

Before I could read any further, there was a knock at the door. The witch got up with a heavy sigh and left the room. She was walking slowly, as if each step hurt.

We heard her open the door and speak to someone, but their voices were low and we couldn't make out what they were saying.

Her footsteps came slowly back down the hall, followed by someone with heavier steps. A man.

She came into the kitchen, followed by Eldred.

"I thought you might be here," he said. He looked with concern at Ruby, whose eyes were red from crying. He went and sat on the chair beside her. Then his eyes rested on the plate of cinnamon buns on the table.

"Would you like a cup of tea?" said the witch. "And a bun?"

Eldred nodded with a faint smile, and the witch set about getting him a little plate and fetching another teacup from the cupboard.

Ruby was beside herself with impatience.

"We were just about to read a letter," she said. "It was in the box we couldn't open. Remember, Eldred?" She pushed the box toward him.

"Oh. You got it open, then?" he asked, picking it up and examining it.

"Yes. Nan had the key. All this time," said Ruth with a scowl.

"Fancy that," said Eldred, looking sideways at Nan, who was pouring him a cup of tea.

"And she could have given it to Meg and Molly years ago, and she didn't, just out of spite, because she's a horrible old witch, and I hate her," said Ruby.

"Now, Ruby," said Eldred. "We've all been through a bad time of it this last twenty-four hours, including your Nan, and we'd be better to stay friends, don't you think?"

"Tell her that," said Ruby.

The witch opened her mouth to reply, but Eldred put up his hand.

"I think you said you were going to read that letter?" he said to me. "Who is it from?"

I looked to the last page of the letter.

"Michael Finn," I said.

"Eva and Eileen's brother!" said Ruby. "The one who did the paintings."

All of them were watching me now. I took a deep breath and began to read the letter out loud.

CHAPTER SIXTY-FOUR

MICHAEL FINN'S LETTER

Slippers Cove
Newfoundland

July 5, 1858

I am writing this letter one week after the deaths of my two nieces, Martha and Moira Finn. They both died on the same day, at the same time. They seemed to be taken by some kind of brain fever and died suddenly, without warning. Moira has left behind two children, Catriona and Caitlin Keegan.

My wife Ann and I have brought up Martha and Moira as if they were our own. Their mother was my sister Eileen Barrett, and she died in the shipwreck of **Cathleen,** *in 1832, along with her twin sister, Eva Finn. It seems that tragedy has followed our family from Ireland and afflicts us still.*

There are some people who say the Finns are cursed. I am a man of science myself, and I don't believe in curses. I am an educated man. I was a teacher in Ireland before I emigrated, on that same ship, **Cathleen,** *and I wish to make a record of what happened.*

Eileen's husband, Robert, mistreated her. He was violent. She kept it secret from everyone except her sister Eva. On the night before I was sailing to Newfoundland with my family, on May 10, 1832, Eva went to Eileen and Robert's house and found Robert attacking her sister. Eva hit him over the head with a frying pan.

It seems this was his death blow, but before he died he cursed the sisters and their children and their children's children. Eileen and Eva set the house on fire to cover their crime and left the next morning at dawn with me on the **Cathleen.** *They told me what happened. I knew they both would have hanged if they had stayed, and I didn't blame either of them for what they did. If I had known how Robert was treating Eileen, I might have killed him myself.*

We kept it quiet on board the ship, but then we ran into bad weather off Newfoundland and the ship was blown off course from St. John's into Conception Bay. It was a bad storm, and we feared for our safety. Eileen was upset and said it was Robert's curse that had caused the storm, and she was overheard by some of the other passengers. The ship went aground not far from the little community of Buckle. We did our best to get the women and children to safety, but Eva and Eileen were both lost.

In the next few days there was a lot of talk about a curse and the Finns, and in the end it was made very clear that we weren't welcome there. With our good friends from Ireland, the Keegans, we sailed a few miles up the coast and found this little hidden harbor of Slippers Cove, and we settled here. Unfortunately there were Barretts in Buckle, and eventually rumors reached them from Ireland about Robert's death. No one was ever sure exactly what had happened, but the rumors and the bad feelings about the Finns grew, fed by the Barretts.

Over the years, we've made our lives here. We have some contact with the inhabitants of Buckle, but we mostly keep to ourselves. There have been a couple of weddings joining our families to families there, and the talk about the curse died down a bit.

But now with the death of Martha and Moira, I fear those rumors will begin anew. I have forbidden my family to talk about it, because it is my strong belief that a curse lives only in the minds of those who believe in it, and the misfortunes that come to those who are cursed come because they believe they will come, not because they are preordained.

I do not believe my sisters did wrong. Eva was defending Eileen, and Robert could very well have killed her if Eva had not struck out at him. The shipwreck was caused by the bad weather, not the curse. And now Martha and Moira's deaths, I believe, were because of some weakness in their brains, something they were born with, and not caused by the curse.

The Barretts in Buckle hold a lot of bad feeling for the Finns. They refuse to speak to us and they warn their children against any contact with ours when we visit the town. I also know that there are people here in Slippers Cove, Finns and Keegans, who believe in the curse. Despite everything I can do to persuade them it is all in their minds, they persist in believing in it. I will do my best to keep any knowledge of the curse away from Moira's twin girls, Catriona and Caitlin, but I fear that there are enough people who know about it that they will find out about it as they grow up.

I wanted to lay out the facts in this letter, for those generations that come after, because the rumors about the curse may grow and people may forget what really happened. My sisters Eva and Eileen were good women, and so were Eileen's daughters, Moira and Martha. My deepest wish is that their children and their children's children can live out full lives without this shadow of horror poisoning their lives.

I am giving this letter to my good friend Homer Duggan, of Buckle, whom I would trust with my life. He has always treated me and my family with respect, and I am going to ask him to keep this letter hidden away in my grandfather's silver box and never to read it unless there is some trouble in the future about the curse and people need to know the truth. I will give him the family Bible that records our sad history, and we will start using a new one with the slate wiped clean. I am also giving him two of my paintings he has always admired, along with the old red traveling trunk that came with us from Ireland. I will rest easy, knowing that the Duggans will keep our secret as long as it is necessary.

Michael John Finn

CHAPTER SIXTY-FIVE

THE WHIRLPOOL

"So he didn't believe in the curse," said Ruby.

"No. He says he was a man of science. Like my dad," I said. "Maybe he's right, Ruby."

"Ruth, after everything that's happened, don't tell me now you don't believe in the curse," said Ruby. "You've had the visions. You've seen how they've all died. Moira and Martha— some kind of brain fever he said. Like Meg and Molly."

"But maybe he was right about that. Maybe it was a condition they were born with, that they both had because they were twins. Maybe that's why they died."

"The fire wasn't because Fiona and Fenella were twins. The shipwreck wasn't because Eva and Eileen are twins. They all died because they were cursed. It's just crazy to say there's no such thing when we've seen what it can do. What about the flood in Slippers Cove—that killed Michael too!"

"Hang on, Ruby," said Eldred. "Just hang on. I think Michael had a point. He said that because people believe they are cursed, bad things happen. It's the power of the mind he's talking about."

"But just believing in something can't make it real," persisted Ruby. "I can believe in Santa, but that doesn't mean he comes down the chimney every Christmas Eve."

"Ah, but when you were little," said Eldred, "as far as you were concerned he did come down the chimney, didn't he? In your mind, he was as real as this table we're sitting at."

"Yes, but—"

"Are you saying that there's no such thing as the curse, Eldred Toope?" said the witch.

He shook his head. "No. I'm saying what I think Michael was saying, that the curse is real as long as people believe in it."

"So if we stop believing in it, we won't die?" My voice came out a lot more shaky than I wanted it to.

"We're all going to die," said Eldred. "Sometime. But I think there's a bit more to this curse than that. Like the man said, the

Barretts kept it going. All these years, they hated the Finns, and they helped keep it alive."

"You kept it alive," said Ruby viciously to her Nan. "You did."

Eldred put his hand on her arm. "Not just your Nan," he said. "She was taught by her mother to hate the Finns, and her mother before. But the Finns had their part in it too. All that guilt and shame came down from one generation to another. You can't blame Mildred for all of that, Ruby."

"For my part," said the witch slowly, "I want it all to end. It's cast a long shadow over my life and over my son's life, and I want it to end. I want it to end now and I'm willing to do anything to end it—" She stopped. "But I don't know how," she finished.

I felt waves of sorrow coming from her, and I suddenly could see it as if I were inside her head. All that hatred and fear, ingrained in her when she was a child, that she could never get away from. And then the feeling that she was losing her son, and would never be close to her granddaughters, and all the while the hatred eating her up inside.

"You've been cursed too," I said. "Haven't you, Nan?"

She turned to me and said simply, "Yes, I have. And my mother before me."

"But how do we stop it?" wailed Ruby. "How can we ever make it stop? We can't help it if we believe in it."

There was a silence.

"Well," said Eldred finally. "You must believe that you can break it. If you believe that, you can."

His words hung in the air. They were all looking at me for some reason. The witch had a ravaged look, like all the emotion and the exhaustion of the last day had taken a deadly toll on her. Eldred looked sad and a little withdrawn, as if he were watching a play. Ruby's face was the picture of despair, tears brimming in her eyes again.

"It's no use, Ruthie," she said. "I can't stop believing in it. The curse caught up with all the rest of them. It will catch up with us."

I felt the weight of the curse, and the past, descend slowly into the room, almost as if it was a giant rock being lowered, crushing us. I still held the letter in my hands, its brittle paper connecting us to the past. To the beginning.

And then the whispering began. Very softly at first. A shiver started at the back of my neck and trickled down my spine. I didn't want to hear that horrible voice again. It came from the four corners of the kitchen, rising and falling, circling us.

"Ruth, what's wrong?" said Ruby.

"Can't you hear it?"

She shook her head. But Nan was staring at me, a look of horror in her eyes.

"Hold hands," she said. "Make a circle. Quick!"

Ruby and I grabbed hands, and Nan and Eldred did the same, then we joined across the table.

Eldred closed his eyes.

Ruby stared at me. "What's happening, Ruth? Why is everyone acting so weird?"

"Be quiet!" ordered Nan. The whispering grew louder, until it was swirling around us. I wanted to get out of there, run away from it, but I couldn't move.

Somebody laughed. A man's laugh.

And once again, the words came clearly through the room, spoken by that cracked, hate-filled voice.

"By fire. By water. By sudden death. I curse you! I curse your children. I curse your unborn children. I curse the ground you walk on. I curse you! I curse you!"

The room began to rock and sway. The whispering grew into a swirling kind of wind that wrapped itself around us and drew us into a whirlpool of insistent sound. It pulled us in, deeper and deeper, until it felt like we were drowning.

Then I realized there were more people there: Eva and Eileen on the sloping deck of the ship as it crashed against the rocks; Fiona and Fenella in the nursery, smothered by smoke from the fire; and all the others, all of the twins, caught in this vortex of hatred. Dying. They were all dying. We were all dying. There was no way out.

CHAPTER SIXTY-SIX

THE STORYTELLER

And then the wind and the whispering stopped, and a deep silence fell. Slowly I realized we were no longer spinning. Ruby and Nan were on either side of me, still gripping my hands. Then the darkness seemed to lift, and I could see that we were still sitting around the table, but the kitchen had changed. We were in that dark little cottage in Ireland. Ruby's eyes were closed. A man was sitting opposite us, with the faint glow of fire in the hearth behind him.

And then someone sighed, so loudly I thought it might be the wind. Then a door opened on the right, and someone came in, carrying a flickering candle in a candleholder.

It was Meg. My mother. The way I had seen her that first night in Buckle, dressed in a long white nightgown, her blond hair falling down to her shoulders. She looked over at me and smiled, then put the candle down on the table in front of the man.

The yellow light from the candle flame lit up his face. It was Eldred. He was sitting quite still, with his eyes closed, just the way he had been when I last saw him sitting at Nan's kitchen table.

Behind him, stretched out on the floor, lay the dead body of Robert Barrett.

Meg stood for a moment looking down at Robert's body. Then she turned back to us and stood there silently, watching us.

Nan stiffened.

"Meg," she said, her voice broken and raw, "Meg, I'm sorry. I'm so sorry."

And then my mother smiled at her with so much love that it seemed she was lit up from within, and she was the candle flame, and warmth spread out from her.

"It's over now, Mildred. Don't worry about it anymore," she said. Then she turned to me.

"You and Ruby need to tell a new story," she said. "Eldred will help."

She walked over and laid a gentle hand on Ruby's head.

"I love you both," she said. "I always will." And then she turned and stood over the body of Robert Barrett, looking down on him once more.

"Rest in peace," she said, and dropped something that floated in the air over him for a moment, then drifted slowly to rest on his chest. It was a flower. A yellow lady slipper, on a long green stem.

I was watching the flower as it fell, and when I looked back at Meg, she was gone.

Eldred opened his eyes. He had that dreamy, not-quite-there look. He turned around and looked at the man on the floor behind him. Then he began to speak in a calm, quiet voice, just as if he was telling Ruby and me a story in the barn.

"Robert Barrett had a murderous rage that hurt everyone around him, but hurt himself the worst of all. It killed him. But it was so big and so ugly and so powerful, this rage and this hatred, that it lived on after his death, in the people who knew him. Through fear and hatred it was kept alive through seven generations of Finns and Barretts, until they decided together to put an end to it. The two families joined together in love, and there was no more room for hate, and Robert Barrett and his curse faded away in the bright sunshine and had no more power over any of them."

As he spoke, in that slightly singsong, storytelling voice, the dark little cottage kitchen, the body on the floor, the fire on the hearth—all of them faded away. And by the end of it we were back in Nan's kitchen, sitting at the table, with Nan and Ruby and me still holding hands. Eldred sat with a half-smile on his face and a dreamy expression in his eyes, half-focused on the plate of cinnamon buns and the teacups on the table.

Ruby opened her eyes. She was smiling.

"That was a good story, Eldred," she said. Then she looked at Nan and me. "What happened? Why do you look so weird? Did I miss something?"

Nan and Eldred and I just sat there, looking at each other.

"That's the end of it," said Eldred slowly. "You can count on that."

Nan pulled a handkerchief out of her sleeve and blew her nose. Then she reached out to lay a hand on the teapot.

"Tea's cold," she said. "I'll put the kettle on and make another pot."

CHAPTER SIXTY-SEVEN

SUNSHINE

Over a hot cup of tea, I told Ruby what had happened. Then we left Eldred and Nan together and headed home, taking a tin of cinnamon buns for Aunt Doll and Uncle George. The sun was shining, and there was a warm, gentle breeze blowing down from the hills, bringing all kinds of sweet growing smells. Buckle looked a lot more cheerful in the sunshine. The deep blue sea stretched out until it met the bright blue sky at the horizon, with no clouds in sight.

We walked for a while in silence. I felt washed out inside, tired and happy.

"So, do you really think it's over?" said Ruby finally, looking at me sideways.

I sighed. "Yes. I really do. Don't you?"

"Yes, I guess so. I mean, it feels like it's over, doesn't it, deep inside?"

I knew exactly what she meant.

"Yes. But there's still something we need to do," I said.

"Tell Aunt Doll," we said at the same time.

"Jinx!" I said, and we laughed.

"And Uncle George," I went on.

"And your dad," said Ruby.

"Yes. We need to bring it into the light, all of it. Like Meg said."

"Even the secret room?" said Ruby wistfully.

"I think so. It won't be secret anymore, but maybe we can get the round window opened up and could bring the light in and use it for . . . I don't know. A playroom?"

"We're too big for a playroom," said Ruby. "What about a study? We could get bookshelves and bring up a lot of books from downstairs, and a couple of comfortable chairs . . ."

"And maybe put a desk by the window, where I could draw my flowers," I added.

"Yes," said Ruby. "Aunt Doll will be so surprised when we tell her about it."

"Do you think so?" I said. "I think Aunt Doll knows a lot more than she lets on. I think she tries to keep it all in a secret compartment in her head, like the secret room, and not think about it, but now she's going to have to open it all up to the light." We walked a little farther. The sun sparkled off the water.

"What about your father?" said Ruby. "How are you going to tell him?"

I sighed. "I think I should ask Aunt Doll to get him and Gwen to come here on their way home, at the end of the summer. I think we should tell him in person. There's a lot I don't understand. When he married my mother, he must have adopted me. I don't think he ever knew who my real father was. But why did he never tell me? He's always made such a big deal about how I took after him, with my interest in flowers and science and—"

"I guess he wanted to persuade himself as much as you that he was your real father. He must really love you a lot," said Ruby.

"Yes. I know he does, really. But I felt like he was replacing me with Gwen, like there wasn't room for me anymore."

"I know. It's the same with my dad and Wendy and the boys. It's like there's only this little space left for me."

"And now you'll have to share him with me," I said.

She laughed and gave me a push. "I think I can handle that. Boy, is he going to be surprised when we tell him. Meg and Molly sure pulled the wool over his eyes."

"Actually, Ruby, I think he knows already."

"What do you mean, he knows?"

"He knows about us being twins. About me being his daughter. I could feel it, when they found us in the root cellar. He must have guessed when he first met me in the kitchen at Aunt Doll's. He acted pretty weird. As soon as he saw us together, he knew that we were twins. Like Eldred did. Aunt Doll must have known too, except she didn't want to know, so she blocked it out."

"I think anyone seeing us side by side would know right away that we were twins, not cousins," said Ruby.

"You didn't."

"Neither did you!"

"Well, maybe not right away, but I had my suspicions."

"You never did!" said Ruby, giving me another little push, and we both laughed.

We were nearly home. The gray clapboard on the old house gleamed with silver in the afternoon light.

Ruby took my hand and swung it back and forth.

"Twins," she said, grinning at me. "And we've got the whole summer ahead of us."

The sun shone, the waves lapped against the rocks, and far out in the harbor, the gannets dived deep into the ocean.

THE END

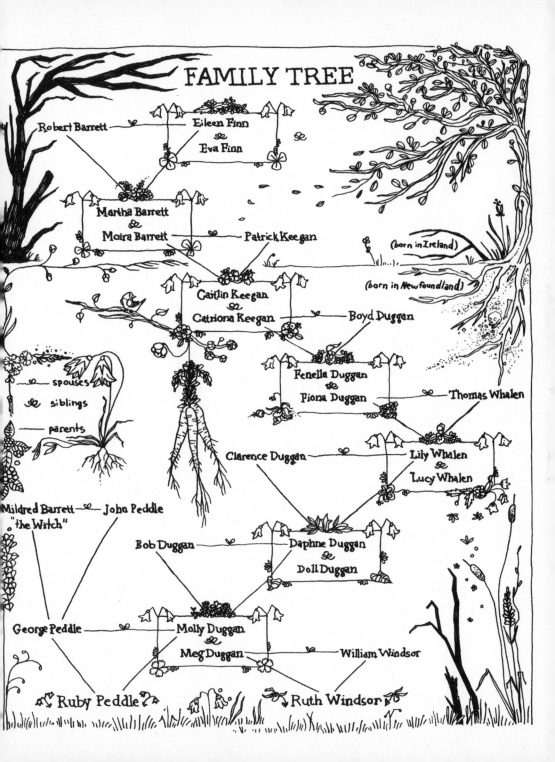

ACKNOWLEDGMENTS

I wrote most of *The Ghost Road* during a long, hard winter at my home in Newfoundland. As I explored the story and kept the fire going, battered by storm after storm, the spirits of my female Irish ancestors drifted across the Atlantic. They came to haunt me, much the same way as Ruth was haunted by seven generations of twins. My mother Evelyn, her mother Daisy, her mother Anne, her mother Margaret and all the rest stood behind me, a long line of strong women fading into the past, trailing their struggles and their triumphs. It was very fitting that my daughter Zoe, representing the next generation, was such a help to me while I was writing. Working out the plot had me flummoxed more than once! Zoe spent a few days talking over the story with me and helping me find my way through the maze. Her ghost lore is far more extensive than my own, and she gave me some excellent suggestions for the scary parts.

I cherish the friendship of the Three Ruths; so much so that I named Ruth Windsor after them. When I started writing *The Ghost Road,* I knew three women named Ruth, all of them over ninety: Ruth Darby, Ruth Resnick and Ruth Redelmeier. Three strong Ruths, who wore their years and their experience like badges of honor. Ruth Darby died while I was still writing this book, but I felt her presence with me as I wrote about her namesake. She was a woman who loved books, Newfoundland and afternoon tea, as I do, and her encouragement and support has meant a lot to me over the years.

My late stepmother, Margaret Baily, was another woman who inspired me with her strength and determination, and I was always grateful for her cheerful appreciation of my books.

My neighbors, Boyd and Marie Whalen, have been an ongoing source of local history and expressions, as well as many entertaining cups of tea on cold afternoons. Tony Power, a storyteller, is a living, breathing link with old-time Newfoundland and he casts a spell on me every time I listen to one of his stories. Once he took me on an enchanted walk along the Fairy Path in Branch, and I have used that walk and the stories he told me in the chapter where Eldred talks about the Fairy Path in Buckle. I had advice about genealogy from my sister, Cate

Cotter, and my twin, Laurie Coulter. In the early stages of the book, Robin Cleland gave me some perspective on the story that helped me dive in.

Grants from the Canada Council for the Arts* and ArtsNL (Newfoundland and Labrador Arts Council) gave me the time I needed to write *The Ghost Road*. If not for them, the book would not be written. I am so grateful to live in a country and a province where the arts are supported.

I want to thank the dedicated team at Tundra Books and Penguin Random House Canada: Sam Swenson, Tara Walker, Lynne Missen, Sylvia Chan, Vikki VanSickle, Terri Nimmo, Sam Davotta and Peter Phillips. I appreciate all your efforts to make my words clear and my books beautiful, and the many things you do to deliver them into the hands of readers. I know how hard you all work at this! A particular thank you to Sam Swenson, my editor, for her perceptive editing. She can always put her finger on what needs doing, and has an excellent understanding of the importance of butter on muffins.

---

* I acknowledge the support of the Canada Council for the Arts, which last year invested $153 million to bring the arts to Canadians throughout the country.

I am delighted with Jensine Eckwall's artwork for the cover of *The Ghost Road*. She has designed three of my book covers, and every time I see her new work I'm dazzled by it. This time, she used the Newfoundland wildflowers from the book along with the Irish shamrock to weave her magic. Many of the flowers Ruth identified on her walks can be found on the cover: twinflowers, lady slippers, Labrador Tea, harebells, creeping buttercups, potentilla, violas, wild roses, wild geranium and crackerberry.

Finally, I want to thank my father, Graham Cotter. He has been enthusiastic about this book from the beginning, reading all the drafts and cheering me on my way with his humor and his unique outlook on the world of family secrets, ghosts and shifting realities.